BE MY LITTLE BABY

Stephanie R. Caffrey

Warning: Not intended for persons under the age of 18. May contain coarse language and mature content that may disturb some readers. Reader discretion advised.

Cover Art Design by: Kelly Moran/Rowan Prose Publishing
Photo Credit: Adobe Images
First Edition
ISBN: 978-1-961967-37-3
Rowan Prose Publishing, LLC
www.RowanProsePublishing.com

Published in the United States of America

GET THE FIRST BOOK NOW!

For Matthew, the hero of my love story.

Acknowledgements

Mistaken Identity was supposed to be a standalone novel, however, a year or so after turning it into my agent, I couldn't let James go. I loved him too much. And so, the story of *Be My Little Baby* came to me.

Thank you to the late Dawn Dowdle for encouraging me to write this sequel and agreeing that the story wasn't finished.

Thank you to Kelly and Shelly at Rowan Prose Publishing. It has been so wonderful working with you on this series, and I know that my books are in great hands.

As always, thank you to Louise for being an amazing Brit Picker. My characters would be so much less British without you, and London would be so inaccurate without your keen eyes.

To Sydney, Laura, and Ally – Thank you for being amazing readers and pointing out all my huge plot holes and pieces of the story that simply didn't work. This book wouldn't be half as good as it is now without your help.

To Arthur, who wrote alongside me during November as I worked on this book. Thanks for being an amazing son and writing partner. I love our writing sessions together.

Beatrice for being such a tolerant toddler during the time this was written and doing her best to entertain herself while I was trying to write with friends in various restaurants.

Sharon, Jamie, and Sarah for being my ride or dies. Can't wait for our next writing retreat and everything that comes with it. I couldn't do any of this without you all by my side.

My parents and sisters for always encouraging me in continuing with my writing.

And finally, to my husband, Matthew. You have always been so supportive of this dream of mine, and none of this could be achieved without you. Thank you, and I love you.

CHAPTER 1

JAMES

"I am hearing what you're saying, Mrs. Williams, but I am going to tell you one more time, we don't really do this sort of work." James Moore ran his hand through his red hair and rolled his eyes. This was the third time this week Mrs. Williams had called their office, so this was the third time he would have to turn down her business.

"But Muffy has been missing for a week. I want to find my Muffy."

"Mrs. Williams?" James' partner, Patrick, mouthed at him from the desk opposite his in the small office.

James nodded.

Patrick rolled his eyes and motioned for James to hand the phone over to him. Which he gladly did.

"Mrs. Williams, is poor Muffy still missing? Did you check at the RSPCA?"

While Patrick took care of Mrs. Williams and the Case of the Missing Tabby Cat, James turned to the computer with their shared document to go over what other cases they had still open at the moment.

A year and a half ago, he, along with Patrick and his fiancée Evelyn, helped take down a notorious crime family in London. Since that time, their meager little private investigator agency that barely scraped by had exploded because of the publicity of the case. Not only were they earning enough to live off of comfortably, they could move their business out of their flat and into its own space, which made the work life balance a little easier.

Well, easier for Patrick. James had nothing else really taking up his time. While Patrick and Evelyn had moved into a new flat together, stating they needed a fresh start in their own space, James had moved in with Joseph McCleary, a police officer, to help pay the rent and to make the flat feel not so empty. The two had gotten along ever since Joe had helped with the case the year before. Living together was pretty easy as they kept the same schedule: neither was ever really home.

James kept busy with work. He loved the thrill of the chase and the satisfaction of solving a case brought him. Nothing could beat how he felt while he worked. He pulled double the cases Patrick did, mostly because Patrick actually separated work from the rest of his life.

Patrick hung up the phone and sighed. "Well, I think I just promised Mrs. Williams one of us would go over and help her find Muffy."

"Patrick!"

"I'm sorry! I apparently have a really hard time saying no to little old ladies. And easy money. I have a honeymoon to pay for soon."

"So, does that mean you're going over to take Mrs. Williams to the RSPCA?"

"Fuck. I guess it does." He stood from his desk and grabbed his coat as he moved toward the door. "I'm going to head over there now and get this over with. And then I'm going to head home from there. Watch the time. Don't stay here too late. It's a Friday night. Go home, grab Joe, and hit a pub."

"You have big plans for your Friday night?"

"Oh yes, Evelyn and I have the exciting plans of putting together a seating plan and making sure we have all our vendors in order."

James pulled a face. "Oh yes. Very exciting."

"Have you written your speech yet?"

"Not yet. But it will get written."

"The wedding is in two weeks, mate. I'm just going to tell Evelyn you have everything done. Let her cross something off her bloody list."

"Works for me. Now, you enjoy the RSPCA, and I promise I will leave the office before it gets too late, and I will not work the entire weekend."

"And you will go to the pub and pick up a bird."

"And I will go home and watch a movie."

Patrick shook his head. "As long as it's not here, I honestly don't care what you do. You're working too hard, James. We're allowed to let some of these cases go. We don't have to work every single one that falls into our lap."

"Logically I know this. However, we don't know how much longer this Fitzgerald Bump is going to last. I want to milk it for all it's worth, and build up my savings for when it all falls flat again."

"It's been nearly a year and a half. I think it's safe to say, any bump from the Fitzgeralds has run its course. This is more than likely our new normal based on our reputation and word of mouth. We'll be fine."

"Yes, well, I'm going to keep on keeping on, so to speak. You're the only one uncomfortable with my workload."

"Not the only one, Evelyn worries about you, too."

"Well, Evie is a gentle soul who worries about everyone. Tell her to stop worrying about me and focus on your wedding. She can worry about me after you return from your honeymoon."

"I will pass that along. And now that my job of telling you to work less is done, I have a date with an old lady and an animal shelter."

"Good luck, mate."

"Ta." Patrick gave him a mock salute before exiting the office.

James shook his head and turned back to the computer. They started using a shared spreadsheet in order to keep track of cases and their status. Besides their open cases, they had an overflowing email inbox with potential cases. Patrick was probably right. Any bump from the publicity of taking down Mickey Fitzgerald and the subsequent trial had probably already worn off. Their overflowing email and the need to juggle half a dozen cases at a time was because they were fucking good at their job and word was finally getting around London. They were *the* team to go to if you needed to employ the services of a private investigator.

After finishing up some notes about a cheating spouse case they were working on, he shut down his computer and began packing up for the day. He looked at the clock. Nearly six. A very reasonable time to sign off and go home. As he put his laptop in his backpack, he wondered if maybe Patrick was right. Maybe he should go out to the pub. It had been a while since he tried to pull a bird. If anything, it would be nice to at least chat up someone new.

He pulled out his phone and texted Joe. He wasn't sure what his work schedule was this week. Sometimes he worked days, and sometimes he was on nights. He couldn't remember which he was on currently. As soon as he finished composing the text, but before he could hit send, there was a knock on the door.

He frowned. No one really ever came to their office. While it was exciting, they had an office separate from their flat, the office was quite small. Barely enough room for their two desks and an extra chair for when Evie would come and visit when she had time. They did most of their business via telephone or would meet off site. Knocking on their door was not normal.

He finished packing his bag and moved around his desk to go answer the door. He opened it to find a young woman, probably around his age, late twenties, early thirties, standing there, hand poised to knock again. She had her black curly hair pulled back into a ponytail, but it still ran down to the middle of her back. Thick rimmed cat-eyeglasses framed her brown eyes, the purple a bold contrast to her copper skin. When she saw he opened the door, her face broke out into a smile, however it didn't reach her eyes.

"Can I help you?"

"Yes, is this Miller and Moore Investigations?"

"It is. I'm James Moore." He offered his hand, and she took it. Her smaller hand easily engulfed within his.

"Tessa Lopez," she replied.

"What can I do for you, Ms. Lopez? I have to admit, we don't get very many clients knocking on our door."

"Well, I had emailed you two days ago about my case, but I have yet to hear anything from you, so I thought I would try my hand at coming down in person. My case is rather urgent."

"Our email is pretty backlogged at the moment, so I apologize. We would have gotten to your email in the next day or so. If your case is urgent, wouldn't you be better served to go to the police about it?"

"Well, that's the problem now, isn't it? I went to the police, but they told me they can't do anything until a crime is committed. When I asked them if my case would fall under harassment, they asked me if I knew who the harasser was. When I told them I didn't, they told me they couldn't do anything. Since then, things have escalated a bit, and I've gotten worried about my safety. My friend told me about you and your partner, and so here I am."

James frowned. "I was about to leave for the night, but now you have me both intrigued about your case and worried about your safety. Please come in."

He stepped out of the way, letting her into the office. As she passed, he caught a whiff of coconut and vanilla. She moved to sit in Evie's chair as James shut the door and went back to his desk. Rather than pull out his laptop again, he found a legal pad and a pen pulling both in front of him. He opened the pen and poised it, ready to write everything she said. He nodded to her to show he was ready.

"Well, a couple of weeks ago, I started getting letters to my place of business. Like actual letters. I almost never get letters to my shop. People mostly communicate to me through email, my website or review sites, so I was already thinking it a little odd."

"What's your business?"

"I own a bake shop, here over on Redchurch Street. It's called Cake Me Home Tonight."

"You own Cake Me Home Tonight? You make the best Victoria Sponge."

She blushed as her eyes strayed down at her hands. "Thank you."

"You're welcome. Anyway, you were telling me about the letters?"

"Yes, they started off innocently enough, praising me for something I had baked. Asking me if I would make something specific to have in the shop the next day. Things like that. Then they got more personal. Asking me if I had a boyfriend. Asking me what my favorite position to fuck is. Things like that. It was when they turned in this direction I went to the police. But because whoever is sending these letters is doing it anonymously, and they have never come in contact with me, the police say they can't really do anything. They called it a prank."

"And you don't recognize the handwriting on the letters? Could it be someone you already know?"

Ms. Lopez shook her head. "They're all typed. And I think they're all hand delivered through my letterbox, none of the envelopes have been addressed. Just blank on the front."

"Hand delivered? That makes things a little easier. I'll put in a request to get the CCTV footage from in front of your shop.

If the letters were hand delivered, we'll be able to see who did it."

"Really? That simple?"

"Hypothetically. I mean, any number of things could occur. We'll get a really clear picture of the bloke's face, case closed. Or it will be a grainy image and we won't be able to tell who it is, but it will be a lead. Now, you mentioned something earlier about how the harassment has escalated, which is what brought you here in the first place?"

"Yes. Hold on, let me show you." Ms. Lopez pulled her handbag, which had been slung across her chest hanging at her hip, into her lap. She opened the flap and pulled out an envelope. It was a little larger than a standard envelope, but not A4 sized. She set the envelope on the desk and pushed it across to him.

He picked it up and opened the flap. There was a folded sheet of A4 paper next to a glossy photograph. He unfolded the paper and frowned when he read it. "That color looks good on you." Then he looked at the photograph and his hands formed into fists, almost crushing the picture between them.

"Do you live above your shop?"

She nodded. "I do."

The picture was a spy shot, taken from the street up through what appeared to be Ms. Lopez's bedroom window. Framed perfectly in the window, between the crack of her curtains, was Ms. Lopez, shirtless, and poised with her hands behind her back, taking off her emerald green bra. Completely oblivious to the cameraman below.

CHAPTER 2

TESSA

Tessa could feel her face warm as she watched Detective Moore look at the picture she gave him. To be honest, she had left out the more risqué ones. She couldn't bear watching a stranger look at her bare chest. It was already incredibly embarrassing to have to come in here. She should be able to handle a few letters. She got worse in reviews around the internet. People felt bold enough to say many horrific things while hidden behind the anonymity of a screen. However, there seemed to be something a bit more sinister about these letters. Whether it was the content, the frequency they arrived or the manner in which they were delivered, she couldn't decide. She knew something was off way before she got the surveillance pictures two days ago. She simply couldn't put her finger on what.

She pulled her bottom lip between her teeth and shifted her gaze down to the photographs in the detective's hands. She drew her eyebrows. He was gripping the photograph tightly. The pictures were quite upsetting to her, but she didn't think they would upset other people.

"So, you have a stalker."

"I have a stalker."

"Stalking is a crime in the UK, but I don't think I need to tell you that."

"Like I said, I have gone to the police, and they've shrugged it off. Told me it's probably a prank. That I should be flattered."

"Here's the thing. It is after six on a Friday night. I can't do much until after the weekend. Have any of the letters been threatening?"

She shook her head. "No. No actual threats."

"Good. On Monday morning, I will put in the request to get the CCTV footage from outside your shop. Once we get the footage, I can go through and see if I can find anything that feels suspicious. On Monday I would like you to bring in everything he's sent you. I'm assuming you kept everything."

"I did. I am at the shop from 3:30 am until a little after midday baking. I will bring you everything in the afternoon on Monday if that is okay with you?"

He wrote notes on his legal pad. "Are you in the shop at 3:30 every morning?"

"Every morning except Sunday when the shop is closed."

"Are the letters already delivered in your letterbox when you arrive? Or do they appear later on in the morning?"

"They are already there when I arrive."

"And the shop closes around midday?"

"No, I leave around midday. The shop closes at five each night. I have a manager and a girl who helps run the shop. They're usually there alone between midday and five. Tonight, I stayed and closed because my manager is on holiday."

"So, sometime between the shop closing at five and you arriving at three-thirty, our mysterious author is delivering letters in your post."

"Yes, that seems right."

Detective Moore set his pen down and looked at her. His green eyes locked with hers. "Since the letters are being delivered to your place of business and not your home and they are not of a threatening nature, while it's concerning, I'm not overly worried. Go about your weekend as normal. If anything changes before Monday, please give me a ring, and I will come sort it out. Your stalker seems to be acting the role of a secret admirer at the moment. If you start getting letters that are more threatening, call me." He slid his card across the desk to her. She picked it up and slid it into the pocket of her jeans.

"Thank you. I know you're busy, so I appreciate you taking the time, on a Friday night, no less, to meet with me. And I appreciate you moving quickly on this."

"Most of our cases right now deal with cheating spouses or money laundering, which are cases that, while important, don't quite have the urgency attached to them as 'man who sends letters to woman and takes her picture unknowingly.'"

"You keep referring to my stalker as male. Do women tend to not do this whole stalking business?"

"Oh, I'm sorry. How heteronormative of me. I just assumed. Well, yes. Women do, do the stalking thing. When I get the

CCTV, I can expand my search to men and women exhibiting suspicious behavior."

She tried to hide her smile as his face grew red, accentuating the freckles that peppered his nose. Not for the first time since she entered his office, she noticed how attractive the red-headed detective was. His shaggy rusty hair covered his ears and swooped across his forehead, while his beard was light enough it was almost impossible to see. He was taller than her, which she noticed from when he answered the door, and she had to look up to meet his gaze. Even though he came off a little nerdy, he was definitely out of her league. And now he thought she wasn't into men because of the way she worded her question. She had meant it to be playful. Instead, she seemed to be offended.

"I'm into men," she all but blurted out. She closed her eyes and let out a silent groan.

"What?"

"I'm simply putting it out there. I'm into men, so would it likely be a male?"

"Likely. But like you pointed out, it could be a woman. Someone who has fallen in love with you through the bakery and knows your preferences and maybe feels jilted. And for the record, it doesn't matter to me, men, women, both, whoever you prefer, we're not discriminatory around here."

She opened her eyes and met his gaze. He was smirking at her, like he knew her gaff completely embarrassed her. "I'm glad to know I'm doing business with such a forward-thinking group." She moved to get up. This seemed as good a time as any to excuse herself before she embarrassed herself any further. But then something he said hit her. "Do you think my stalker has come to my shop regularly? As like a customer?"

"It's likely. I honestly wouldn't be surprised if they came in at least once a week. They might even be one of your regulars."

Tessa closed her eyes and mentally sorted through everyone who came in regularly. There were so many loyal customers. People came to her when they were hosting parties, when they needed treats for the office, or craving a sweet treat. For the past five years Cake Me Home Tonight had grown in reputation for having affordable cakes and pastries that didn't skimp on the taste or the looks. She had poured her heart and soul into that bakery, and was thrilled the first day they ever sold out of goods because of having so many customers. Word of mouth built her a loyal customer base, and some blogger posted about her shop on a travel website and now tourists come out of their way to visit her. To get a slice of her famous Victoria Sponge.

She tried to pick out one person who stood out to her. Someone who would look a little creepy. Someone who screamed, 'I'm a creepy stalker,' but no one stood out.

"Would it help if I made a list of my regulars? At least those whose names I know?"

"It very well could. If you got me a list, I could try to cross reference them with the CCTV footage, see if any of them are poking about in the night."

"Brilliant. I'll work on my list on Sunday. Is there anything else you need? It's nearing the middle of the night for me and I'm completely knackered. I'm going to head home and get some rest before my alarm reminds me it's time to head back to the kitchen for baking.

"Oh yes, please feel free to leave. I'm going to work on typing up my notes and uploading them into a shared folder for my partner to look at. First thing Monday morning, I will put in my request for that footage. It will take a couple of days to come in, but I would love for you to bring in the list of names and all the letters. And if you think of anything over the weekend that you think might help, no matter how small it may seem, jot it down on a notepad and bring those in as well. My partner will be in the office Monday afternoon and two heads are better than one, and we'll go over the case."

"Thank you." She stood from her chair and made her way to the door. "Thank you so much. I can't even thank you for everything you've already done. Knowing you're taking me seriously and going to work on figuring out who this is, I think I may actually sleep tonight."

"I'm glad I could do that, at least. Please keep my number close. If things escalate over the weekend, call me. If the stalker makes contact physically, call the police. My flat mate is a police officer here in Tower Hamlets, his name is Joseph McCleary. If you need to call, ask for him."

"McCleary. Got it."

"Have a good weekend, and I will see you on Monday."

"See you on Monday."

Tessa left the office and made her way down the stairs of the building to the street. She wasn't lying when she told him talking to him had eased her mind. The idea of her having a stalker still freaked her out but having Detective Moore tell her just receiving a few photographs and letters that did nothing to outright threaten her was nothing too worrisome helped take a weight off her shoulders. She could breathe slightly easier.

She walked down the sidewalk toward her home. She was glad the notorious detectives who took down an entire crime family lived in her borough. She hated the Tube. She enjoyed walking through the neighborhood.

She pulled her coat around her tighter as she walked. The wind had picked up and, combined with the mid-October temperature drop, she was regretting her choice of the lighter coat. As she neared the street with her shop, she could feel her pulse quicken. The nights were already longer, so the sun was disappearing over the horizon, streetlamps were lit, and the world was full of shadows. She never enjoyed being out after dark, but with the whole stalker business, she especially disliked being out.

She picked up her pace and breathed a sigh of relief when she could see the shop. Almost there.

As she walked down her familiar street, she looked across the street where whoever was taking pictures of her through her window had to be staked out. Right now, the street was filled with cars. It was Friday night and there were shops and restaurants that stayed open much later than hers. People bustled about, ducking in and out of storefronts and up and down the sidewalk. It was impossible for her to pick out anyone familiar. Anyone who could be watching her. Waiting for her to go upstairs and change. A shiver ran down her spine that had nothing to do with the cold.

Finally, she was at her shop. She pulled out her keys, letting herself in. As she shut the door, she glanced at the post basket and breathed a sigh of relief to see it was empty. Whoever delivered her daily letters obviously hadn't been there yet. Maybe they were busy. It was a Friday. They could be out on the town. On a date. With someone else forgetting all about her. She could only hope.

She locked the door and moved through the shop to the back stairs. Ascending them, she was exhausted. She didn't realize how much this whole situation was taking out of her. Unlocking the door to her flat. She smiled at the silence of the flat. It was a pleasant contrast to the chaotic bustle of her shop.

She walked into the kitchen, flicking on the kettle to make some tea. After devouring a small bag of crisps, also known as dinner, she prepared herself for bed. As she walked into her bedroom, she checked and double checked her curtains. A routine she started two nights ago after receiving those photos. Not one crack. No one would see into her sanctuary tonight. No one.

CHAPTER 3

JAMES

The cursor blinked on the screen of the computer as if mocking him. Blink. Blink. Blink. Nothing. Nothing. Nothing. James had been sitting at his computer for the better part of the hour, and he had checked his email, checked his social media, read the news headlines, but had yet to write one word of his best man speech. He didn't understand why he was having such a hard time putting words on paper. Patrick was his best friend, and after living with her for a year, Evie was as well. But why couldn't he find it in him to put anything down? Evie told him last night at dinner to just say something short and sweet. To stop putting so much pressure on himself. Told him to make it funny. Throw in some pop culture references.

But that was the problem. He didn't want to make jokes about their friendship. They meant everything to him. He wasn't close to anyone like he was to them. And how did you convey everything he felt about them into a brief speech? He sighed and ran his hands down his face. To this day, he still could see their battered bodies in their hospital beds after they were rescued from the Fitzgerald lair. The images seared on his brain. The relief when he learned they would be okay was probably the strongest feeling he had ever felt.

Being able to convey that all in one brief speech? Impossible. Maybe he would simply have to write a speech for the masses and a separate letter for Patrick and Evie to read later. He perked up. That was exactly what he would do. First, he would write the speech for the crowd and get it over with. Get Evie off his back. Then, once the wedding was over and they were on holiday, he would work on the longer letter and deliver it to them when they got home.

Brilliant idea, James. Well done, chap, he thought to himself as he prepared himself to type. As soon as he pressed down the first keys, mercifully filling the blank page he had been staring at for what felt like forever, his phone buzzed, showing an incoming text. He sighed. It was probably Evie asking him about his progress. Not even twenty-four hours since he left her flat after dinner and a movie night, a Saturday night tradition, they continued even after they moved out of their shared flat, and she had to check in on his progress.

He picked up his phone and did a double take when he noticed it was not from Evie but from an unknown number. He frowned and opened the message.

UNKNOWN: Hi this is Tessa. The woman with a stalker. Wanted to remind you before you went in tomorrow morning I live above my shop. CCTV footage from one location only.

James smiled. Tessa. Ms. Lopez. His new client. Even though his weekend had been filled with helping Patrick finish his list for the wedding and movie night, Ms. Lopez had never been far from his mind. He worried things would escalate over the weekend. If the person was truly stalking her, would they have seen her go into his office and decide now was the time to act? Her being on his mind had absolutely nothing to do with how beautiful she looked even after working a long day in the bakery, or how when she smiled, her entire face seemed to light up...

He shook his head, banishing those thoughts from his mind, and answered Ms. Lopez.

JAMES: Thank you for reminding me. My memory isn't as bad as you're making it out. I had remembered. I'm not that old.

He sent the message and then immediately wrote another.

JAMES: Quiet weekend?

He set his phone aside and turned back to his document, working on his speech. His phone buzzed before he could write more than three words.

TESSA: Complete opposite. My manager is still on holiday, so I worked a full day at the shop yesterday. And today we opened the shop for a special event. I'm completely knackered.

He smiled.

JAMES: I didn't realise your shop did special events. When do you sleep?

TESSA: Right now. It seems sleep comes when I can no longer hold my eyes open while I watch the telly after work. Special events are a recent development. May need to rethink. We hosted a six-year old's fairy party today. Never. Again.

JAMES: Oh, come on, it can't have been that bad.

TESSA: Detective Moore, I have sprinkles in places there should not be sprinkles.

James blushed at the image of sprinkles in inappropriate places.

JAMES: James. Call me James.

TESSA: Tessa

James smiled down at his phone. Tessa. He didn't know why it thrilled him to be on a first name basis with her. She was a client. And one he had only met once. He shouldn't be this involved with her already.

JAMES: Any escalation this weekend with our mutual friend?

TESSA: No. In fact, I have received nothing from them this weekend at all. Is that a good thing? Has he given up?

JAMES: There's no way of knowing. Even if we're entering a lull, it will still be good to figure out who this person is.

TESSA: I agree. My manager will be back from their holiday tomorrow. I will bring everything I have tomorrow around one. Will that work for you?

JAMES: It will.

TESSA: Well, I better sign off. My eyes are struggling to re-main open. See you tomorrow?

JAMES: Sleep well, Tessa. See you tomorrow.

James set his phone aside and laughed a little. He wondered if all of their conversations would go that smoothly?

"You've got quite the goofy grin on your face? Meet a bird this weekend, Jimmy?"

James nearly leapt out of his skin before whipping around to see his roommate, Joe, leaning against the kitchen counter, arms folded across his chest. A big grin spread across his face.

"Fucking hell, Joe. When the hell did you get in?"

"About a minute ago. You were completely absorbed in whatever you were doing on your phone to notice. Did you meet someone? Because if you did, good for you."

"No. I was only messaging with a client."

"Bullshit. You don't look all moony eyed at your phone when you're simply chatting with a client. This is something more."

"I promise you, it's only a client. She came in as we were closing on Friday. Stalker. We were arranging our meeting tomorrow afternoon."

Joe shook his head as he stood up from the counter and began unbuttoning his uniform shirt. "Sure, keep telling yourself that. I give it a week before you're no longer just client and detective and you've got her bent over your desk. Mark my words."

"Fuck off. You know we don't date our clients. We keep things completely professional."

Now Joe truly laughed. "Sure, you do. I think I'm in a wedding in a couple of weeks that completely contradicts that statement."

"That's different."

"How? Evie was a client, wasn't she? And then Patrick went and fell in love with her. And now they're getting married. Please explain to me how it's different. I'm waiting."

James opened his mouth to tell him *exactly* how it was different, but faltered. It really wasn't different, was it? Evie may have fallen into their lives by accident, but before she and Patrick fell in love, she was a client. A nonpaying client, but still technically a client.

"Fine. It's not different. But I am not Patrick. Tessa is a client, and nothing more. Now, where were you all weekend?"

"Oh, no. We're not changing the subject. I want to talk more about how you're apparently on a first name basis with this client."

"Were you working all weekend, or did you meet someone? I don't think I've seen you around the flat all weekend."

"Both. I worked over night on Friday, but went to Clint's flat when I got off. I was there the rest of the weekend."

"Clint, eh? That's two weekends in a row with him. Things getting a little serious for you two?"

"Nah. Well, at least on my end. He may be getting a little more attached than I am. I will probably have to end things between us soon. Which is a shame, since he lives so much closer to the station than I do."

"Is that why you're dating him? You don't have to go as far to get home?"

"My primary goal in life is to not have to ride in some weirdo's Uber at four in the morning. You know this. And how did we get on the subject of my complete disaster of a love life? We were talking about you following in Patrick's footsteps and falling in love with someone who has come to you to protect them."

James shook his head. "You're reaching and you know it. Hey, I have a question for you. If someone came into the precinct with letters that had been delivered to them that were stalkery but not threatening, what would you do?"

Joe walked over to the couch and flopped down on it. "Well, if the letters were not threatening, we wouldn't be able to do much of anything, unfortunately. Stalking is a crime, so I would probably take the person's information and ask to read a letter or two, maybe make a report to create a paper trail. But beyond that, I wouldn't be able to do anything."

"It's fucking insane, mate. We're still short staffed after getting rid of all the corrupt bastards. And they still can't get us on a consistent schedule. Bloody exhausting. Cheers mate."

Joe got off the couch and walked to the back to the back of the flat to where his room and the bathroom were.

After he left, James turned back to his computer and tried to work on his speech. But he couldn't get a cute girl with purple glasses out of his mind, causing him to be distracted the rest of the night.

CHAPTER 4

TESSA

"Guess who's back! Which means it's time for you to get the hell out of this kitchen and out of this shop."

Tessa smiled as she finished drying the bowls she was holding. Freddie, her best friend, business partner, and manager of her shop, was home. "I'm finishing up in here, and then I plan on leaving. I've got to meet that detective I was telling you about."

Freddie let himself into the kitchen wearing a frown. He looked as meticulously put together as he had every day since they met in Year 2. Always wearing grey pants, even when he wasn't in school uniform, a button-down shirt with a jumper pulled over and his dark brown hair styled just right, he was the yin to her yang. Logical where she was emotional. Organized to her disarray. When she talked about opening Cake Me Home Tonight, he took care of lining up the business side of things, explaining to her how everything worked, showing her how he had organized everything, while she worried about the baking side of things. Their twenty years of friendship were the most precious thing to her. He was the sibling she always craved.

"I'm so glad you went to the detective."

"I'm glad you found their information for me. I never would have thought to go to them without your nudge. So, thank you."

"You're welcome. It makes me uneasy you are receiving these letters in the first place. But when you called me and told me he was taking pictures of you without knowing? That was the last straw. You mentioned something about CCTV footage in your texts?"

"Yes, he was putting in a request this morning to get the footage from our street. He's hoping it will be a lead."

"Are you going to view the footage now?"

"No, I'm going over there to bring him all the letters and photographs I've received."

"Good. Maybe he can make sense of them. I can't believe the fucking police refused to do anything."

"Yes, you and me both."

She set the bowl on the shelf and used the rag to wipe down the counters.

"How did the birthday party go yesterday?" Freddie asked with a little apprehension. It was his idea to open up to special events. And prior to this weekend, it was mostly old ladies who wanted to come in with their friends and decorate cakes and gossip over tea. This was the first child's birthday party, and when he realized it had been booked for his weekend away, he offered to cancel his holiday. She had turned him down.

"How do you imagine it went?"

"Little girls high on sugar, swinging from the rafters while screaming, 'More cake, Mummy! More cake!'"

Tessa laughed, taking off her apron and hanging it on the hook near her baking station. "You're not too far off. It was chaos. So many tears. I had the wrong color icing, even though it was exactly what they had requested, and the birthday girl was inconsolable and the mum kept acting like I was deliberately ruining her princess's special day. By the end of the party, I felt I needed a strong drink, and you know I don't drink."

Freddie winced. "I'm so sorry. I promise, no more little girl birthdays. Only old ladies and tea from now on."

"It's fine. We can do another one, but maybe those are a two-person operation party, yeah?"

"Done. I will double and triple check my calendar before we book another to make sure I am in town."

"How was your holiday?"

"Exactly what I needed. I could relax and read a book, and I took in the new art installation at The Louvre."

"And you could get she who will not be named off of your mind?"

"We can name her. It doesn't hurt as much anymore. Maybe it's a good thing Alice broke our engagement two weeks before the wedding. I rather enjoyed going on our honeymoon alone. Lots of time for self-reflection."

"I'm glad. I'm still sorry it worked out the way it did. I'm almost glad I never finished writing my best man speech. I was always stuck on something nice to say about Alice."

"You two never got on. I should have seen the writing on the wall. If someone can't get along with my sister, they're not worth marrying. That is the lesson I've learned from this whole endeavor."

"I'm just glad she called it off before I made the massive cake she wanted."

"Honestly, missing out on the cake is my one regret from this total fiasco. I was really looking forward to it. The vanilla sponge with the mango? Probably my favorite thing you've ever made."

"What would you say if I make one up for our Sunday brunch this weekend? But a miniature version of it?"

"I would say I love you and I don't know what I would do without you. I'll make veggie omelets to balance out the cake. Make us feel less guilty."

"Deal. Now, I must run. I told him I would be there at one. I'll be cutting it close." She grabbed her coat off the hook next to her apron, pulling it on. Then she grabbed her messenger bag, slinging it across her chest until it rested against her hip.

"Yes, good luck. I hope he's able to catch this bastard. Are you sure you don't want to come stay at mine for a while, just until he's caught?"

"I'm sure. I will not let this prick chase me from my home."

"I love that about you. Not letting some creepy nutter get you down. Now go. I have cake to sell."

Tessa gave Freddie a quick hug and dashed through the back door. If she left through the front, she was sure to stop and talk to whatever customers were currently in the shop, and she didn't have time to stop and talk to Mrs. Haberdash about her grandchildren.

She moved down the street and shivered. The sun was out, but the temperature did not reflect the vision of the beautiful day. The breeze cut through her light coat. She really needed to pull out the thicker one and give up the hope of warmer weather sticking around just a tad longer. She should fully give herself over to the inevitability of winter. At least the sun was out. It could have been rainy.

Luckily, the walk to the detective agency didn't take long. She opened the door to the building and sighed as her glasses fogged up. Easily the most annoying thing as the weather grew colder. Once she could see again, she walked to the office and knocked on the door. She glanced down at her watch. Right on time. Her shoulders relaxed. It was a point of pride for her to be on time everywhere she went.

"Come in."

She turned the knob and pushed the door open. As she stepped into the small office, she was a little taken aback. She had assumed she was going to be meeting with James. She'd forgotten he had told her his partner was going to be there. She didn't know why her stomach dropped in disappointment at the thought she wouldn't be alone with James, but it did.

"Hello."

"Tessa, this is my partner, Patrick Miller. He's going to be working on the case as well."

"Nice to meet you, Ms. Lopez. I'm sorry to hear about your situation, but we're going to work this out."

"Actually, we've already met. I'm making your cake for your wedding. Please call me Tessa."

"That's right! I'm so sorry. I can't believe I didn't remember you. You make the best cakes. Evelyn gets this dreamy look on her face whenever she is on a video chat with her mum and they talk about the cake."

Tessa laughed, "It's alright. You were only at the initial cake testing, and honestly, the cake is the genuine star of the shop. It's understandable you wouldn't remember me."

"We've put in the CCTV request this morning, and they have told me we will get it by the end of the week," James explained, gesturing to the empty seat in front of the desks, bringing them back to the reason they were there.

She moved to the chair and sat down. She pulled her messenger bag around to rest it in her lap. She felt awkward with everyone's eyes on her. "That is good, right? Do you know how far from my shop the camera is situated?"

"We don't. But we know your street has at least two cameras. We requested all the camera footage for the last month. Unless the letters started arriving earlier than that?" James asked.

"No, they started arriving about three weeks ago? Two and a half. I have them all here." She reached into her messenger bag and pulled out the manila envelope she put together the night before with all the letters and photographs and handed it over to James.

James took the envelope and opened it, pulling all the contents out. "Holy shit, did they deliver a letter every day for the last two weeks?"

"Yes, nearly."

He let out a low whistle and handed part of the stack to Patrick. The room was silent except for the rustling of papers, which made Tessa feel even more awkward. Should she go? Was she expected to stay?

"The author of these letters isn't very chatty, is he?" Patrick commented, not looking up from his letters.

"No, he is not."

"These letters only have one or two lines. No punctuation, but otherwise perfect grammar. Which, on the one hand this doesn't give us a lot to work with as far as identifying factors. On the other hand, the style could be something we could easily identify."

James handed Patrick one picture. "Patrick, does it look like they took directly these photos across the street from the flat?"

Patrick took a second and studied the picture. "Could very well be. The angle is pretty direct. We'll scrutinize the pictures and see if we can pinpoint where exactly they took them."

"You'll be able to tell only from the picture?"

"Maybe. We'll also need to go to the shop and confirm. Stand where he probably stood. Things like that," James explained.

"Brilliant."

"If we can work out the angle, then when we look at the CCTV footage, it may be possible for us to identify the photographer. Which could be another way to identify him if we can't get a clear picture off of the front of your building," Patrick explained further.

"What are the odds of us getting a clear picture of the letter writer?"

"I'm going to be very conservative about our odds and say it's about 50/50. We could get really lucky and find the footage and show it to you and you'll be able to tell us exactly who it is, and case closed. Or we could get the footage and it will be clear footage and you'll not recognize them, and that will add a little extra work, because we'll have a clear picture we can ask around with. Bad news would be we don't get a clear picture at all, and we'll be back here where we started," James explained.

Tessa nodded. "Right. I have also included a list of all my regulars who I could identify by name. I don't know how much it will help, but I wanted to give it to you, too."

"This will help, thank you," James turned his gaze to her, and smiled.

Their eyes locked, and Tessa's heart quickened. What was wrong with her? Why was this happening? She was paying him to find her stalker. She wasn't here to find a boyfriend. *Maybe after they solved the case...*she shook her head to clear that thought away.

She wasn't here to find a boyfriend. Full-stop. She was here to get rid of the creep, leaving her brief letters in her post and taking spy shots of her from her bedroom window. Which when she laid it out like that, it seemed rather silly she was hiring them at all. She could save her money and let this whole thing fizzle out. Why did she let Freddie talk her into this?

"Do you have everything you need?" She spoke up, startled at how loud it came out. She was nervous. She needed to go home and get some sleep and wait for James and Patrick to do their jobs.

James looked down at the pile in front of him and then back at her. "I think so. Thank you again for bringing everything in. We'll be in touch later this week, once we have all the CCTV footage."

Tessa stood up and hurried to the door. "Thank you again. I look forward to your call."

James stood from the desk and quickly moved around it, opening the door for her. "Have a good night, Tessa."

As she left the building, all Tessa could think about was how James' hand lingered on her arm as she walked out the door.

CHAPTER 5

JAMES

"She's cute," Patrick commented after the door to the office closed.

"Is she? I hadn't noticed."

James walked back to his desk and picked up the papers and pointedly looked at them.

"Bullshit. You have absolutely noticed. You went all heart eyes the second she walked into this room."

James scoffed. "I did not."

"You did. I didn't think you could have had a goofy look on your face, but as soon as she walked in, you looked all dopey."

"Fuck off."

"I'm sorry, I don't mean to take the mick, but seriously, it's okay if you think she's cute. You're allowed to have a crush. In fact, I encourage it. Have a crush. Have several crushes. For the

43

last several years, you've become quite the workaholic. When we close this case, ask her out for a drink or something. Pretty sure if I tell Evelyn, you have a crush on the cake lady, she'll be completely behind this match. Especially if it means baked goods will start arriving on Saturday nights."

"You're impossible."

"I'm optimistic."

James shook his head and focused on the letters in front of him. "It doesn't matter. We don't date clients."

"The future Mrs. Evelyn Miller would like to disagree with that statement."

"She wasn't really a client. We both know that. We don't date paying clients."

"By the end of the week, we'll have solved her case and then she won't be a paying client. Then you should ask her to be your date for the wedding."

"I thought you and Evelyn finalized the details over the weekend?"

"Well, she's already coming to the reception. We offered her a plate since she has to bring the cake in and set it up. But we could have her sit at your table. You know what?" he pulled out his phone and started texting. "I'm going to have Evelyn put her at your table. We can move someone around."

"Don't bother Evelyn with something like this. She's probably very busy."

"It's afternoon. She doesn't teach in the afternoon. She has office hours. I'm sure she's sitting in her office working on research or wedding plans or something. This is not a bother."

Patrick's phone chirped, signaling an incoming message. "And she has agreed it's a good idea. And she wanted me to tell you to wait until after the wedding to sleep with her, otherwise if things go pear-shaped, she doesn't want the cake lady to fuck up the cake as revenge."

"Nice. Very nice, Patrick. Can we please move on and discuss the case? You know the whole reason she's come into our lives in the first place?"

"Fine, spoil sport. Looking at the letters, I can't really tell if this is someone who knows her really well, or someone who is only casually acquainted with her."

"I agree. When she mentioned she was getting letters daily, I thought this would be someone with a lot of time on their hands, but if all they're doing is writing one sentence on a page and delivering it through a letterbox, they honestly don't need that much time. This person could spend one afternoon making a batch of letters and portion them out to be delivered throughout the week."

"It's the photography that takes some time."

"But not much more. If they know her schedule, they could easily time it to be at her window when she would change and then leave. Print the photos at home and then deliver."

"But if they didn't know her schedule, he or she would have to spend a lot of time on the pavement waiting for her to appear."

James sighed. "It all comes down to whether we think this is someone who knows her really well, or someone who barely knows her."

"Pretty much."

"Statistically, a person who stalks a woman like this is someone who knows her."

"True. Write this down: exes, jilted lovers, unrequited love. We need to ask Tessa if there is anyone who falls into these categories. We need their names so we can scour their social media and get images to compare to the CCTV footage."

"We should also add angry customers, loyal customers who seem a bit too loyal, and business competition."

The door to the office opened and Evelyn walked through. She gave the boys a smile as she shut the door and made her way into the small space. She leaned over and greeted James with a quick peck on the cheek, and then greeted Patrick with a proper kiss before settling into her chair.

"What are you doing here? Aren't you supposed to be keeping those Uni students in line?" Patrick asked.

"No one signed up for my office hours today, and once I got your text about James and our baker, I needed to come down here and get some more information."

James narrowed his eyes. "Why would you need more information?"

"Because it appears you're crushing on my baker, and I need to make sure you won't scare her away. I need her cake, James. It is very important."

"I won't scare your baker away. You'll get your precious cake."

"Good. Because her cake is life."

"You're being ridiculous."

"I am the bride. I'm allowed to be ridiculous. Now, tell me about her case. Is it pretty easy? Someone stealing from the shop?"

Patrick held up one of the tamer pictures. "Someone is stalking the creator of your new favorite food."

Evelyn reached over and grabbed the picture out of his hand. "No! Poor Tessa! Any leads?"

"None yet. We're waiting for footage and we're making lists of suspects," James explained.

"Have you looked into her business partner?" Evie asked.

"She has a business partner?" Patrick leaned forward, resting his elbows on his desk. "Did she tell you she had a business partner?"

James shook his head. "First, I'm hearing of one."

"Oh, so, apparently, she and her best friend from childhood went into business together. He handles the business side of things, and she handles the baking. He was engaged to get married and then poof! Two weeks ago, the fiancée dumps his ass like a week before the wedding."

Patrick looked at her, confusion written all over his face. "How on earth do you even know all of this?"

"I'm an American and I have no boundaries. Anyway, apparently the fiancée never really liked Tessa. She would say all kinds of rude things under her breath. Tessa told me she was pretty sure she was jealous of how close she and the partner are."

"All of this came up during your cake tasting session?" James asked, bewildered.

"No. So, don't judge me, but Cake Me Home Tonight isn't very far from both our flat and the University. It's way too close to the University for my waistline to still fit into my dress in a couple weeks. I've been stopping in on my lunch hour at least once a week since our tasting two months ago, and Tessa and I have been eating together. Or sometimes just having a cuppa and a biscuit and calling it lunch."

"You're friends with our baker?" Patrick was incredulous.

"Yes. I like her." She swiveled and pointed an accusing finger at James. "And if you, fuck things up with her and I can no longer have tea with one of the few girlfriends I have managed to make here I will not be held responsible for my actions."

James held his hands up in surrender. "Oi. Let's not get ahead of ourselves, yeah? I will admit, I find her attractive. The few times we interacted have been pleasant, but I have no intention of trying to start a romantic relationship with her. Not as long as she's a client."

"Ah hah! You admit you have a crush on her and have an interest in asking her out!" Patrick shouted, pointing his finger at him.

"Oh, my God. Are we back in secondary school? Are you going to sing rhyming songs about me and Tessa in a fucking tree?"

"K-I-S-S-I-N-G!" Evie and Patrick sang loudly through laughter.

The three of them dissolved into hysterics after that, and James' chest was warm, and his heart grew full. He loved his friends, and he knew they had to move on to the next stage of their life as they were getting married in a few weeks, which meant they wanted their own space, and a space to grow at that. Even though he knew all of this, and it made sense on a logical level, he missed the days of the three of them crammed in the small flat, shouting and laughing over stupid shit. Saturday nights were nice, and he held them close to his chest, never making other plans on a Saturday night but nothing could compare to a random Wednesday when all of them would be home from work, arguing over dishes and who the better Darrin on *Bewitched* was.

"Are you two done taking the piss? Can we please move on?"

"Yes, yes, sorry." Patrick took a deep breath, and wiped under his eyes. "She has a business partner with a jealous ex. This all seems very promising."

"But are we looking at the partner or the ex? Who looks good for it?"

"That's the thing, isn't it? If we could get this person to make some threats, this would be a lot easier to figure out. Or be a little more aggressive in their interest in her. These are all very bland for stalking notes. So, I think it could be either or neither at this point."

"How long has she been getting letters?" Evie asked, pulling her feet up under her.

"Two weeks daily, except this weekend."

"Her partner was on his honeymoon this weekend, alone. If he was out of town, he couldn't deliver letters."

Patrick clicked his pen and wrote something down on his legal pad. "Business partner is looking fantastic right now."

"Motive?" James asked, leaning back in his chair.

"Unrequited love. His fiancée guessed correctly, he loves her, she only sees him as a friend. He tries to get in her good graces by passing on these flattering letters, testing the waters. They don't go as well as he would like, and so he escalates to taking photos, but not for malicious reasons. He feels they could be a compliment. He does like that color on her. He goes away for the weekend, and obviously can't deliver letters while he's gone," Patrick explained.

"Sounds plausible. But I'm also liking the ex-fiancée for this. She has a motive. And maybe she wants to scare Tessa into wanting to quit or move or something," James pointed out.

"Not as strong a motive, and really doesn't fit in with the timeline. Why would she stop writing letters for a weekend after consistently delivering them every day?"

"I don't know. Maybe you're right. Maybe it is the business partner," James turned to Evie. "What's his name? Maybe we can get a search going on him and see if he has anything suspicious."

"Freddie, but I don't know his last name."

"That should be enough to go on. We can also pull business licenses and get a last name from that." Patrick pulled out a pen so he could take notes. "This is a good lead. Thank you for being a nosey American and becoming friends with our cake lady."

"You're welcome."

James' phone chimed, and he pulled it out. It was a text from Tessa. He frowned. He wasn't expecting to hear from her. Maybe she thought of something and wanted to let him know. He opened up the message, and it was a picture. His heart skipped a beat.

"So, I'm thinking maybe we can scratch Mr. Honeymoon on his own, off our list of suspects."

"Why?"

James turned his phone to show the other occupants of the room. Patrick immediately leaned forward and grabbed the phone out of his hand to get a better look.

"Oh, my God," Evie gasped, bringing her hands to her mouth.

James didn't need the phone in front of him to know what she was reacting to. The image seared itself into his brain. It was a picture of Tessa leaving their office on Friday night, coat wrapped tightly around her body, looking somewhere to the left of the camera. But that wasn't the shocking part. No, the shocking part was someone had taken a red pen and put a large X across her face and scrawled, "YOU'VE MADE A MISTAKE," across the photo.

CHAPTER 6

TESSA

JAMES: Are you safe?

Tessa stared at the message from James for several minutes, debating how to answer. Was she safe? Technically, she was. She was not in any immediate danger. Did she *feel* safe, though? That's where things got fuzzy. She knew logically she should be fine. She was in her flat, Freddie was downstairs, this person had not made themselves physically known. They were still contacting her through letters in her post. However, this felt different. This wasn't someone perched outside her house where they knew she would be. This was someone following her around the city.

Taking pictures of her.

And now they're threatening her. Because she sought help? But was it a threat? 'You've Made a Mistake' wasn't a direct threat against her. It was more of a warning? A warning of what she didn't know, but she was less anxious if she thought of it as a warning and not a threat, so she was going to choose to think of it as a warning. For now.

TESSA: I'm fine.

JAMES: That doesn't answer my question.

TESSA: I'm safe. As far as I know.

JAMES: Evie told us about Freddie and his fiancée. Any chance it's either of them?

Tessa was completely taken by surprise. Freddie and Alice were suspects? She shook her head. Impossible. Freddie was her best friend, and he would never do something like this. Besides, he was out of town on Friday. There was no way he could have followed her to the detective agency. He was in Paris enjoying his honeymoon with himself.

Alice hated her, but why would she go through all of this trouble? Tessa was pretty sure she didn't blame her for the dissolution of her relationship with Freddie. Unless Freddie really downplayed her role in the breakup.

Tessa thought back on every interaction she had with Alice and tried to determine if it was an interaction where they would have been at odds. But nothing seemed out of the ordinary. Most brunches, Alice kept to herself. She rarely came into the shop, citing she was trying to keep her figure, and the two of them spent no time alone together if they could help it. On the rare occasion Alice and she were alone together, Alice would often comment about how she better remember her place. Whatever that meant. It was easier for her to avoid being alone with her.

TESSA: I don't think it could be. Freddie was in Paris for the last week, and honestly, I don't think Alice could be arsed to care this much about me.

JAMES: We should still look at them. Make sure they have strong alibis. It always helps to mark off the people closest and then expand the search from there.

She bit her lip. Of course. She watched enough crime shows to know they always look at those closest to the victim first. But the thought of having to investigate Freddie felt wrong to her. Really wrong.

TESSA: I'm sure it's protocol, but I promise you, Freddie can't be the person doing this. He would never do something like this.

JAMES: Then it will be a quick investigation.

Tessa let out a growl of frustration. Apparently, there was no talking them out of looking into Freddie.

TESSA: You're just going to be wasting your time.

JAMES: I'm just going to call it being thorough and move on.

TESSA: You're very frustrating

JAMES: I'm going to take that as a compliment. Trust me. You'll appreciate us being thorough.

TESSA: The CCTV footage will clear him and prove he was out of town all weekend.

JAMES: Which is when the letters stopped. Fits the timeline.

TESSA: Now you're contradicting yourself. Whoever took the latest picture of me was in town on Friday. He left Thursday night. It can't be him.

JAMES: What are Freddie and Alice's full names?

TESSA: Freddie Kaur and Alice Lewis.

JAMES: Great. Leave the investigating to the professionals.

Tessa glared down at her phone, frowning. And instead of responding to the last message in a way she wanted to, she instead acted like the grown up she was and put her phone in her pocket. She needed to take a break from James. Obviously, they would not agree on the matter, and arguing with him was just going to make things worse. She was paying him to solve the case of who is stalking her. Why would she hinder the investigation? Because deep down somewhere inside of her, she worried about what they might dig up. What if it was Freddie?

She shook her head. "Stop it, Tessa. You're letting this mess with your head," she muttered to herself.

She glanced at the clock. It was only three. The shop was still open, Freddie was down there with Mariel, and she really needed to keep her mind off everything. She slipped on her shoes and walked down the back stairs into the kitchen. Clean, exactly how she left it two hours before. She pushed her way into the shop, and it was bustling. Mondays were not a typically busy day, but now that they were firmly in autumn, her pumpkin flavored items were becoming hard to keep on the shelf. It was a risk, making pumpkin flavored items when they weren't super popular here in the UK. However, she wanted to take a page from the Americans and try something new for the season. Apparently, the risk was paying off.

She did a quick glance into the display case and noticed even with two hours until close; they were running low on most of the items. She would have to make sure she baked more supply tomorrow.

"What are you doing here?" Freddie asked from behind her. "You're supposed to have your feet up and reading a book before finally calling it a night as the sun sets."

"I know, but I was feeling antsy, and I didn't really want to be alone."

"Fuck. Another one? When the hell did it get delivered? I was here ever since you left."

"I found it in the post when I got back. I checked this morning when I opened, and it wasn't there."

"So, you're telling me this fucker delivered the letter in broad daylight, with me and Mariel working five feet away?"

Tessa nodded.

"He's getting bolder, Tess. I don't like this. What was in the letter this time?"

"A photo. Of me leaving the Miller and Moore agency on Friday. With vaguely threatening words scrawled across it."

Freddie brought his hands up to his hair, grabbing it by the fistful before dropping his arms back to his sides. "Did you tell the detectives?"

"I did."

"Great. After I close up shop, I'm going to go grab a few things and I'm going to stay on your couch for a couple of days."

"You are not!"

"I am. I would feel better if I did. They're escalating, Tess. It's getting worse. Now they're following you around town? What the fuck is up with that?"

"I'm an adult, Freddie. I can take care of myself. I don't need you going all toxic masculinity on me. I'll be fine."

Freddie sighed. "Fine. But maybe you should sign up for one of those self-defense classes you've always talked about wanting to take. It might help you feel safer, and it would definitely ease my mind knowing you could drop a man twice your size."

Tessa smiled. This is what she was trying to tell James. There is no way Freddie is the culprit. Why would he be offering to sleep on her couch or suggest she get better at defending herself if he were the one causing the mischief?

To throw you off his scent, the small voice in the back of her head piped up, sounding an awful lot like James. She shook her head to clear it. There would be none of that.

"I'll think about it. The problem is they're all after normal people get off of work and I'm well on my way into the middle of my night."

"I'm sure they have some sessions for people who work the night shift or just stay at home during the day. We'll investigate it. Listen, this conversation isn't over, but it looks like Mariel needs some backup. What the hell did you make that has everyone swarming in here like they're going to miss out if they don't get it?"

"Nothing out of the ordinary. I really leaned into the pumpkin spice craze this year and made pumpkin bars. Those are new."

"Pumpkin bars. I bet that's it." He leaned over and placed a kiss on her forehead. "It's going to be okay, Tess. I promise you. You've hired the best detectives in London. They will find whoever is doing this. I know it."

And they think it's you, she thought as she watched him move back to the counter to help Mariel. She smiled a bit forlornly. How well could you really know a person? She didn't know Freddie and Alice's problems were so bad that she was going to call off the wedding until after the wedding had been called off. The problem was, she was too trusting. She should learn to be more suspicious.

But he was not wrong. Miller and Moore were the best in London. Ever since they took down the Fitzgerald family and cleaned out all the corrupt cops in their borough, they had been all anyone could talk about. Their faces were a mainstay in the tabloids and news during the trial. Back then, she thought they were very attractive men, but thought nothing beyond that. And then she landed the coveted role of making the wedding cake for Patrick Miller and his American fiancée, Evelyn Stevenson, a key witness to the case. It was going to be the biggest wedding of the year. And she was going to make their cake. And then she and Evie became friends. Never in her life did she think she would hire them to solve a case. These things didn't happen to people like her. They happened to more interesting people.

"Good afternoon, Ms. Lopez. You're not usually in the shop at this time of day."

Tessa turned around and smiled when she noticed one of her favorite customers. "Fraser! You're here later than usual. And unless I'm mistaken, it's not Wednesday."

"Yeah, me mum heard about pumpkin bars in the shop from one of her friends, and she sent me out to pick some up before you sold out. Grabbed the last two. These are new, aren't they?"

"Yes, I made them on a whim this morning. Didn't know they would be so popular."

"Ah, well, word is getting around if me mum heard about them."

"Well, I guess I'll have to keep them on for a bit, then. How is your mum?"

"She has her good days and her bad days. She's had a good week so far. She's hoping to make it into the shop on Wednesday for tea. She had me block off a full hour in my schedule that morning. Will you be making pumpkin scones again? I remember those were a favorite of hers last autumn."

"I will be. Tell her I'll save one just for her, so she doesn't have to worry about rushing in here."

Fraser smiled widely, his eyes lighting up. "Oh, that will be wonderful. If she can't make it on Wednesday morning, I'll swing by and pick it up for her after I finish work. Though she is determined to make it. She misses her chats with you."

"I miss her, too. Please send my love to her."

"I will, Ms. Lopez. I best be going. She's going to feel like she's won the lottery when I get home and tell her we scored the last two pumpkin bars. I'll be seeing you."

"Be seeing you Fraser."

Tessa watched as he pushed his way through the crowd and out the front door. Fraser and his mum were some of her first customers, always coming in on Wednesday mornings to have tea and eat scones. She looked forward to seeing them every week. And then his mum grew ill and their visits grew infrequent. Fraser still stopped in once a week to get a treat for his mum, but she didn't get to see him very often because he usually stopped in after work.

She closed her eyes and sighed. Both of their names were on the list she gave to James this afternoon, which meant Patrick and James were looking into them. It made her so angry. Thinking about everyone she loved on the list, she really hoped Patrick and James hit brick walls with everyone on them, and once they got the CCTV footage, she would see a perfect stranger leaving her notes. The idea of someone she cared for stalking her devastated her more than if it were a stranger doing the stalking. She could trust no one again if that were to be the case.

CHAPTER 7

JAMES

"They're here," Patrick spoke up as soon as James walked into the office on Thursday morning.

"A day early, they're getting quicker."

Patrick shot him a look. "I'll forward you the files. We can both go through them and make notes to go over together later."

It had been a long week. After texting her on Monday, concerned about her safety, James hadn't heard from Tessa the rest of the week. Looking back over the texts, he was pretty sure she was annoyed at him. Which was fair. He was a bit of a tosser there at the end. At first, he was okay not hearing from her. She was only a client, after all. But as the week progressed, he tried to think of an excuse to message her, but really couldn't think of any.

With her case paused until they could get the CCTV footage, he had kept busy with the dozens of other cases they were juggling at the moment. They closed three in the last few days.

He pulled out his phone and opened up the text thread with Tessa. He hesitated for a brief minute before typing.

JAMES: CCTV footage arrived

TESSA: (...)

James frowned. He could see her typing as if she were going to respond. But then, nothing. He set his phone aside, opening up his computer. He clicked open the shared files and sighed. It was a lot of footage. A lot. He knew it was going to be a lot, based on the number of days they requested, but seeing it all lined up was daunting.

He clicked open the first file, put in his ear buds, opening up Spotify. He clicked open his 'Back in the CCTV' playlist and settled in for the long haul.

***

James took out his ear buds and rubbed his eyes. He checked the time. They had been at this for three hours and he'd barely made a dent in the footage. His stomach growled. Lunch time. Well, close enough.

He tapped on the desk, getting Patrick's attention. He took out his own ear buds and looked at him quizzically.

"I'm going to get some food. Want something?"

"Where you going?"

"Just the chippy. And I may swing in and get something sweet."

Patrick narrowed his eyes. "Something sweet?"

"She's still not answering my texts, mate. I need to make sure she's okay."

Patrick just nodded. "I would like lunch. And a pumpkin bar. Evelyn had tea with Tessa yesterday and said they were the best she's ever eaten."

James grinned. "Fish, chips and a pumpkin bar. Coming right up."

He stood from his desk and stretched. His back always protested to long periods where he would just sit still. He was getting old. If you could call early thirties old. He grabbed his jacket, and as he was putting it on, he eyed his umbrella. He looked out the small window and frowned. It was autumn, and the sky was grey. Plus, it *was* London. He grabbed the small umbrella, stashing it in his pocket. He opened the door and walked out of the office and out into the world.

It was nippy and windy. He was glad he had upgraded to his heavy coat the day before. There was also a mist in the air. It was the right decision to grab the umbrella.

As he walked down the pavement, his mind turned to the case, as it always did when he was alone. It really bothered him that Tessa wasn't texting back. Evie was the only reason he knew she had received nothing else from the stalker since the photograph on Monday. Which worried him to no end. It was never a good sign when the perpetrator went off script. For weeks, they had been delivering letters daily. And now, nothing? It could mean one of two things: they gave up, they had achieved what they wanted to achieve, or they were building up to something that was much more sinister. He really hoped it was the first one. The first one made their job easy. However, his gut was telling him it was the second. The stalker was gearing up for something big. They were probably watching and reveling in the anxiety that was more than likely building up in Tessa's anticipation for the next move.

He hit up Cake Me Home Tonight first. Nobody wanted cold fish and chips. As he approached the shop, a knot formed in his stomach. He reached up, scratching his beard. He was making a mistake. A big mistake. She obviously didn't want to talk to him, and here he was, forcing himself into her life like some kind of caveman? This was exactly why she stopped talking to him. Unfortunately, it was too late to turn back now. He was at the shop, and he had promised Patrick a pumpkin bar. If he came back without it, he was pretty sure Patrick would kill him. He was surrounded by a group of people who were completely and utterly obsessed with sweets. Every time he and Joe were in the same room, Joe asked him if he was sleeping with Tessa yet and could he get him a discount at the shop. Obsessed.

As he reached out to open the door, the hairs on the back of his neck stood up, and he froze. He dropped his hand and glanced around. The street was bustling. It was the lunch hour, and this was a busy part of the borough. People were ducking in and out of shops up and down the street. He turned around and looked directly across the street with narrowed eyes. He took in everyone, but no one really stood out to him. Everyone seemed to be going about their business as usual.

It was as he turned back toward the shop; he caught a glimpse of him out of the corner of his eye. Dressed in black, with a black beanie pulled down low, sunglasses perched on his face. He was standing in the shadows of the alley between two of the shops across the way. Barely noticeable, but watching. James whipped back around, dashing across the road, dodging traffic. He cursed as a lorry nearly took him out, but he didn't slow his stride. He kept running directly to where the man had been standing. As he approached the alley, he knew he was too late. He hadn't been remotely stealthy. The alley was empty. The man was gone. Instead, laying on the ground where he once stood was a discarded receipt from Cake Me Home Tonight with 'Nice Try' hastily scrawled on the back.

"Fuck!" James shouted into the sky. Many people stopped to look at him, particularly mums and their young children. James smiled sheepishly at them as he quickly snapped a picture of the offending piece of paper before picking it up and shoving it in his pocket.

He made his way safely back to the shop, and this time didn't even hesitate before opening the door and marching inside. The shop was busy, and the girl behind the register seemed overwhelmed. There was also a man about his age manning the baking case, pulling orders for people. That was probably Freddie. And unless he was the fucking Flash, he was not the man standing and watching the shop in the shadows.

He approached the counter.

"What can I get you today?" possibly Freddie asked.

"Two pumpkin bars, please."

"Anything else?" he asked as he boxed up the goods.

"Is Tessa around?"

The man narrowed his eyes. "Who's asking."

James reached into his pocket and pulled out his card, handing it over to him. "James Moore."

The man looked at the card and reached his hand over the case. "Freddie. I'm Tessa's business partner. Follow me. I'll take you back to her."

"I still need to pay for these pumpkin bars."

"They're on the house. Tessa wouldn't want to charge you for them. Come on back."

James shrugged and followed him around the counter. They walked through a doorway with hanging beads and back into the kitchen. His breath caught in his throat as he caught sight of the vision in the kitchen. Tessa was in her element. She was wearing denims, a purple form fitting t-shirt, with an apron over her clothes and had her long curls pulled up into a haphazard bun on the top of her head, with a wide purple headband to keep her hair off her forehead. With flour smeared across her cheek, you could tell she'd adjusted her glasses more than once. She was fucking adorable. And he realized all the teasing Patrick and Evie had put him through was for nothing. He had feelings for her. He was fucked.

"Tessa, Detective Moore is here to see you," Freddie announced.

Tessa startled and turned around. "James."

"Tessa."

"*Ooookay*. I'm going to go back out front. Leave you two to be all awkward together." Freddie didn't wait for a response. He turned and left.

Tessa and James stood there, their shuffling feet the only sound to break the silence.

"You weren't answering my texts."

"I didn't think it was a requirement for you to solve my case."

"It's not. But I was, am, worried about you. Evie told me you haven't received any more letters?"

She shook her head. "No, which is probably worse than if they were still sending me daily letters. The anticipation of waiting for the letter to arrive. Will it be a letter? Another photograph? Something worse? It's the not knowing that's killing me."

"That's part of what gives stalkers the thrill. Keeping their victim on edge. What's troubling me is how they've switched their M.O. suddenly."

"Really?"

"Yeah. When a criminal switches their M.O. it usually leads to an escalation. In order to ensure your safety, you should always be on the lookout and taking note of your surroundings, alright?"

"You really think they're going to escalate things? Further than they have already done?"

James only had to think for a second before deciding he should tell her what he saw when he arrived. "I caught someone lurking in the alley across from your shop. However, when I ran across to catch them, they were already gone, but they left this." He produced the receipt and handed it to Tessa. "Do you recognize the handwriting?"

She shook her head. "Maybe? I don't know. I just—"

He lifted his arm, placing his hand on hers, causing her to move her gaze from the receipt to his. "It's going to be okay."

"Did you get a good look at whoever it was?"

James shook his head. "Not really. He had his face covered. The only thing I can say with certainty is he was male. The good news is, unless your friend, Freddie, has super speed, he can't be our guy, so we can cross him off our list of suspects."

Tessa gave him a tight smile before turning her attention back to the receipt. "This is from today. The person who is stalking me came to my shop *today* to buy sweets, and then stood outside and watched the shop. What was he doing? Waiting for me to leave? Staking the place out?"

"Maybe a little of both? I don't know. If I hadn't been looking for someone suspicious, I would have never seen him. However, now I know what to look for, it'll make scouring all the bloody CCTV footage easier. We can look at the alley and see how often he is skulking there."

Tessa brought her gaze up from the receipt to his face. "Do you think he's been out there often?"

"Can't say, but I'm guessing if we scour all two weeks of footage, we'll find him at least daily. I'm nearly certain he took the spy shots of you in that exact location."

"Oh, my God." She brought her hand up to her neck. "It was scary before, but why is it scarier knowing for certain he's watching me?"

"When we have evidence to back it up, these types of situations become more real."

She shook her head, and brought her hand up to wipe away tears on her cheeks, which only smeared the flour around even more.

James moved closer. He brought his arms up as if to embrace her, but stopped himself short. He didn't know if his comfort would be welcome. "Hey, do you want me to go out and get Freddie? You look like you need someone."

Tessa moved until she stood right next to him, and she didn't stop. She stepped into his space and wrapped her arms around his waist. She laid her head against his chest and started crying.

James' heart raced in surprise, and he only needed a fraction of a second for his brain to catch up to his body. He quickly brought his arms up, wrapping them around her trembling body, holding her tight against him. He ran his hands up and down her back, trying to soothe her.

"It's going to be okay," he whispered. "You're going to be okay."

CHAPTER 8

TESSA

Her shop was being watched.

When James left to return to his office to go through more footage an hour ago, she busied herself cleaning up her kitchen. The only thing going through her mind was James seeing the person who has been stalking her. Saw him. With his own eyes.

The only good news from his visit was that Freddie was now off the hook. He couldn't be her stalker. He was in the shop when James had seen the person hiding in the shadows. That was an enormous relief for her. She now knew she could continue to trust him. She needed a friend right now, and one she could trust.

She finished drying her bowl, set it up on the shelf, and threw the towel she was using into the dirty laundry before taking off her apron and hanging it on the hook. She stood there, frozen.

Her face was heating, tears were welling behind her eyes. She brought her hands up to either side of her face, willing herself not to cry. This was not who she was. She was a strong, independent Latina. When her mother left her and her father when she was ten, she held it together for her father. Three years ago, when her beloved father was diagnosed with stage four cancer, she became her father's strength. If she could make it through those tragedies, she can make it through this. Some arsehole who wanted to be some kind of fucking movie villain would not be the thing that broke her. She wasn't willing to let that happen.

She looked around the kitchen. She built this. This was her accomplishment. Her dedication to her father, the man who taught her how to bake and love being in the kitchen. If someone was trying to scare her off of this dream, it would not work. At least, she thought that was the stalker's goal, wasn't it? To scare her into closing the shop? She couldn't think of any other reason someone would take the trouble to harass her. She had seen some comments and reviews around the internet. There were people who didn't like a Latin woman, the daughter of an immigrant, becoming a successful business owner. As much as people liked to think the world was a less racist place, it really wasn't. And she lived it every day. This stalker was just another one, hiding behind his anonymity in order to be a horrible person. Even though none of the letters had been overtly racist, they were still misogynistic.

She rubbed her temples, feeling her chest tighten. The whole fucked up situation was going to give her an ulcer. She needed to get away. Go somewhere else to clear her head. What she really wanted was to go back to her childhood home and curl up with her dad and cry. Unfortunately, she couldn't do that, but she could do the next best thing.

TESSA: *Heading out to see Dad.*

FREDDIE: *Want me to come?*

TESSA: *No, stay and help Mariel. I'll be fine.*

FREDDIE: *If you're sure.*

TESSA: *I'm sure.*

FREDDIE: *Text if you need anything.*

Tessa grabbed her coat off the hook along with the large black umbrella she had leaned against the wall. She dashed out the back door of the shop and into the alley. She hated the alley; it gave her the creeps. But if the front of her shop was being watched, she would brave the rear to make sure her stalker wouldn't follow her.

As she walked to the Tube station, she constantly looked around her, scrutinizing every person she met on the street. James told her to be aware of her surroundings, and she was hyper aware. Even once she made it to the Underground station and hopped on, she stood holding the bar, constantly looking around for a man dressed all in black following her. If anything, she was more upset about the stalker stealing her sense of safety rather than the act of stalking itself. The anxiety she had whenever she left the flat, the feeling of always being watched, it was worse than anything the stalker had actually done. And she hated it.

She breathed a sigh of relief when she got off at her stop and started walking. Her body and mind became further relaxed as the crowds thinned out, and the buildings began to line only one side of the street.

She let herself in through the wrought-iron fence of the cemetery, quickly making her way along the path she had long ago memorized, letting the overgrown trees and bushes that filled the cemetery become her protection, only stopping when she was in front of the headstone.

Javier Lopez

Her dad.

She knelt on the ground and cleaned the headstone a little before settling in. Today's visit was going to be longer than normal.

"Hi, Dad. I know it's been longer than normal between visits, but I've been really busy with the shop. I never would have guessed autumn to be my busiest season. I always thought summer would be my busiest time with wedding season, but I was wrong. Apparently, my pumpkin bars are so delicious people are traveling from all over the city to get one, and fight over them. I had to special order cans of pumpkin from the States to keep up on production. Yesterday, I watched as Freddie had to break up a fight between two grannies about who would get the last pumpkin bars. I've started making triple what I started and still can't keep up with demand. When I switch from autumn to Christmas, I don't know what will happen. I'm worried the nans will start a riot in the street.

"But that's not the reason I came here today. Well, not the entire reason. I did come here to boast a bit. I mean, come on, grannies are fighting over my pumpkin bars. How wicked is that? No, I came here because there's something wrong, and I don't know what to do. Well, I do know what to do. I hired someone to take care of it, but I don't know what to do. Am I making any sense? I don't think I am."

Tessa took a deep breath and let it out slowly.

She needed to get this off her chest. To tell someone who wasn't Freddie what was happening.

"Someone has been harassing me for the last few weeks. It started off innocently enough. Only a few letters, but…" She took a breath, trying to calm herself.

"He's following me, Dad." Her voice cracked as she tried to hold back her sobs.

"Following me. James, one of the detectives, actually saw him posted outside of my shop just *watching*. I don't know what to do. It makes me never want to leave my flat again. But that's what he wants, isn't it? For me to be too afraid to do anything. But how do I carry on? I don't want him to win. I want to carry on with living, but what if the next time I go out he doesn't simply snap a picture of me? What if he grabs me? Or hurts me? Kills me?

"I wish I knew what to do, how to feel. Freddie has offered me to stay at his, or he would stay at mine, but I don't want to inconvenience him. And having to rely on him defeats the purpose of being independent and solving my own problems.

"If only you were here, to tell me what I should do. I wish I could lay my head on your lap, and you could run your hand along my head, smoothing my hair, like we did when I was younger. You always gave me the best advice. Please, send me a sign about what I need to do next. I need a little nudge."

Her phone dinged, showing she had received a text message. She pulled her phone from her coat pocket and smiled at who it was from. James. She swiped it open, and her grin grew wider.

JAMES: Just checking in to make sure you're okay.

And below it was a GIF of a little ghost giving an air hug with the phrase, 'Ghost hug, you can't feel it, but it's there.'

Smiling, she typed back:

TESSA: I'm doing okay. Any luck on the CCTV footage?

JAMES: None yet. So. Boring. May need more sugar. (Snoring Emoji)

Tessa laughed. This was exactly what she needed. She looked back at her dad's headstone. "Thanks, Da. I best be going, so I can get home before it gets dark. It gets dark so early these days. I love you, and I'll make sure I don't leave so much time between visits."

She stood and before she started heading back to the shop, she sent one more text to James:

TESSA: Do you need me to make a delivery? I don't know what's left at the shop. I just know there are no more pumpkin bars.

JAMES: (Crying emoji) No more pumpkin bars? Why must you be so cruel? Patrick is telling me to say no to a delivery. My stomach is saying yes. Please don't inconvenience yourself. We will soldier on.

TESSA: Don't you think you're being dramatic?

JAMES: I'm always dramatic. It's in my nature. Just ask my mum.

TESSA: That will be the first thing I ask if I ever meet her.

JAMES: I can't wait.

Tessa blushed at that last message. How had they gone from being goofy and flirty to something so serious as meeting the parents so quickly? She tucked her phone back in her pocket and began her walk back to the train. She didn't need to be distracted while she walked. Even though she was certain no one had followed her, it was prudent for her to be aware of her surroundings at all times.

She took the train back to her station. Once she emerged from the station, she was thankful she remembered to grab her umbrella. It had started raining. She put up her umbrella, walking briskly toward her flat. She quickly glanced at her watch and realized it wasn't as late as she thought. The shop would still be open for another half an hour. As she neared the shop, she debated which way she would enter: the front door or the alley?

She thought about her conversation with her dad. Whoever this was, they wanted her scared. They wanted her to hide. Going in and out through the alley would let them win. Under no circumstances would she allow that to happen. She had agency and power in this situation. She would not let some anonymous person dictate how she lived her life. She was fierce. She was woman, hear her roar.

She rolled her shoulders back and strode down the street with her head held high. As the hour was nearing dinnertime, the sidewalks were bustling with people. She looked around, trying to figure out if she could see the man James had seen earlier, but as she looked in the alley across the way from her building, she couldn't see a thing. The crowds were thick this time of night, and it was starting to get dark. If he were wearing all black, like James had said, it would be nearly impossible for her to pick him out of the crowd. He would blend in nicely.

As she went to open the door, she paused. She turned around and stared across the street into the darkening evening. She looked in the general direction she thought her stalker would be. She held her back straight and glared toward the alley, trying to telegraph how not afraid of him she was. Like some sort of leading lady from a thriller film. The one who survived to the end, not the one who died halfway through. After she had given enough of an 'I am not afraid of you' vibe into the abyss, she turned around and let herself into the shop, feeling lighter than she had felt in days.

CHAPTER 9

JAMES

"Bugger. Fuck. Piss," James yelled, throwing his pencil at the computer screen. He and Patrick had been scrolling through the footage for two days now, and he couldn't find his man in black anywhere. They couldn't see anyone approaching the shop. They couldn't find anyone standing across from it. It was like this person didn't exist. Then, just when luck seemed to smile on him, and there was someone all in black approaching the post slot in the shop, it was as if he knew where the cameras were and he kept his back to them. No pictures of his face. And that was the case with every other occurrence of the man on film. The man was an expert at keeping his identity a secret, and it frustrated James to no end.

"Calm down," Patrick chastised from his spot at his desk.

It was Saturday, and they had come into the office to plow through the remaining footage and see if there were any pictures of his face. It was kind of Patrick to do so, especially since his wedding was a week away. Well, it was kind of Evie to let Patrick come with the wedding a week away. With her family due to arrive from the States this morning, and a full day of plans with her sisters and parents, she was happy for Patrick to come to work and help her friend.

Of course, movie night was not on the table for tonight, but James was okay with it. He was going to go have dinner with his mum, who he hadn't seen in a few weeks.

"Don't tell me to calm down."

"I understand being frustrated, but yelling at the computer and tossing things at it won't solve the problem."

"How the fuck does he keep his face hidden in every bleeding shot? Every shot, Patrick."

"He must be familiar with the location of the cameras. Which means he's from around here. Only a local who has lived here would know the exact locations of the cameras to avoid them so easily."

"Which only narrows the suspect pool slightly."

"I think we're going about this all wrong. We need to go back to square one and look at the letters and the pictures again. Maybe have Tessa get her regulars to write a phrase on a paper so we can compare handwriting to the picture and the receipt?"

James perked at that suggestion. "That's brilliant. I wonder if we can have her do a raffle for a sheet of pumpkin bars. We know that would draw in people. Then we can sort through the slips and compare the writing. I knew I kept you around for a reason."

"What it's not for my devilish good looks?"

James shook his head, crumpling a paper and tossing it at Patrick, who easily batted it away. "You ready to get married next weekend?"

"More than. It feels like it's just all for the pomp and circumstance, you know? I already feel like Evelyn and I are married. However, my dad keeps telling me the big do is for the bride, and I will do anything to make Evelyn happy. So big wedding it is."

"You ready for a week with your future in-laws hanging about?"

After everything with the Fitzgeralds, Evie's parents were not too fond of Patrick, and they were not shy about expressing all the reasons. James had been witness to many loud video calls while they lived together. However, Patrick had mentioned the last couple visits had gone really well, but they were short, sweet visits. A full week may prove things may not have completely changed.

Patrick cringed. "Yeah, I'm glad we have this 'urgent case' to keep me busy at the beginning of the week. I think her dad believes I'm going to have a sudden change of heart and leave his daughter in a foreign country. She has a job here. We've been together for almost two years, but it's all still a whim to him. I'm hoping he'll ease up once we've walked down the aisle."

"Fingers crossed."

Patrick leaned back in his chair and locked his gaze on James and grinned. "So, any progress with you and Tessa? Are you two going to be next down the aisle?"

James scoffed. "She's still a client, and I'm sticking with my morals and not dating a client. However, we have been talking a lot, and it's been nice. We've been texting a bit in the evenings before she heads to bed for the night. She's hilarious and can hold her own in a pop culture reference battle."

"You're smitten."

"I will admit. I am."

Patrick did a fist pump. "Finally. You're going to make Evelyn so happy with this news. Especially if things work out well with you and Tessa."

"Because she makes delicious cake, and she would bring it to our get-togethers?"

"No, because she's been worried about you."

"Worried? Why would she be worried?"

"Because you're alone. She cares a lot about you and she wants you to be happy. She wants you to have what we have. We love you, mate, but you've been a workaholic for quite some time and have really neglected your social life. Knowing you're going out of your comfort zone and at least flirting with Tessa was good enough for us. To learn you're actually getting feelings for her? We're thrilled for you. We want you happy."

James reflected on the last few years. Not just the last year and a half with the business booming, but before that, he could definitely see where Patrick was coming from. Yes, he flirted. He was great at flirting. But it never really went beyond that. The last time he was in any sort of relationship was back when he was on the force, before he and Patrick left to start their business. Even then, it was kid stuff. They were so young, and it wasn't very serious. He hadn't been thinking about marriage or the future. That was stuff for adults. Then the business started, and he put all his efforts into it. Starting it, maintaining it, helping Patrick as he navigated grief, the Fitzgerald fiasco. Life merely got too busy for him to slow down and try to give himself what he wanted. Except, he didn't know he wanted it, until recently. Until Tessa.

"I think I am happy. I mean, I was never *unhappy*. I love what I do, what we do, and I love spending my time with you and Evie. The times we lived together in the flat were some of the best times I've ever had. I guess I never stopped to think about how I could get that outside of you two. I know you guys are going to want to spend more time just you two, and eventually you'll have kids, but I guess I took for granted you would always be here. I never thought about what it would be like to be left here, alone."

"You know we would never abandon you, and you know we aren't trying to get you married off so we could go off into our little world. Evelyn wants another girl at movie nights to even the score a bit. She loves it being the three of us, but she would also love it being the four of us. You know what I'm saying? She has all these elaborate fantasies of us double dating, going on couples' holidays, our kids growing up together and going to primary school at the same time. Nothing we talk about involves us all going our separate ways. In fact, it involves us getting even closer."

James hadn't even considered it a possibility that they would get closer. He always assumed he was going to be left behind as his friends moved on. He liked the vision of the future Patrick laid out for them. The funny thing was, he could picture it. Double dates, couples holidays, all of it. Funnily enough, he could picture it all with Tessa by his side. He shook his head. He was really getting ahead of himself now. He knew he liked her, and he could assume she felt the same way. At the very least, she flirted right back at him, but did she picture her future with him in it?

"That all sounds really nice. Makes me want to try hard to solve this case so I can ask Tessa out on a date."

"Just ask her out. It's such an arbitrary rule, not dating your clients."

James shook his head. "I made this rule and I'm going to keep it. And this way it doesn't interrupt your wedding. You will have an unproblematic cake. And then we will solve the case and I will ask her out for a proper date."

Patrick smiled. "I like it. Now that you've calmed down and have something to look forward to, can we get back to finishing this footage so we can move to the next step?"

James nodded and turned back to his computer. He was feeling better about the future, and more motivated to catch this bastard than ever before.

CHAPTER 10

TESSA

JAMES: CCTV footage was a bust. Have you seen anyone watching your shop?

TESSA: No. Everything feels normal here.

JAMES: What are you wearing to the wedding on Saturday?

TESSA: Why?

*JAMES: Seeing as you'll be sitting next to me, thought you might want to coordinate. *winky face**

Tessa smiled as she set her phone down. Taking the time to visit her father the previous Thursday provided a welcome distraction and was beneficial for her mental health. Her week started off a little lighter because of it. Also, the random texts from James helped. Although, his hinting at meeting his mom sat with her all weekend. She could barely concentrate on making Patrick and Evelyn's cakes throughout Sunday. And now he wanted to know what she was wearing to the wedding?

She was a little out of practice on the dating scene, but knew he was flirting with her. She was a hundred percent open to it, but was now really the time to be thinking about being in a relationship? Was it OK to date the guy you hired to handle your stalker situation? Maybe it would be a bad idea to get into a relationship with James right now. It would feel too much like she was paying someone to be her boyfriend. She should wait until he caught her stalker.

TESSA: What color are you wearing?

She tucked her phone into the back pocket of her denims and turned back to the several batches of pumpkin bars she was frosting. She'd started making several large batches in the mornings before the shop opened and another round about halfway through the morning in order to have enough to last until close.

The kitchen was hushed, but she could still make out the faint buzz of conversation from the customers at the front of the shop. Freddie was no longer just the numbers guy. He was full time behind the counter boxing up customer orders while Mariel rang everyone up. It was a good thing Brits knew how to queue. Less chaos in her shop. Didn't have to go out and buy ropes to contain the crowds. Not only were the pumpkin bars selling out, nearly everything was. She was used to making some of her items in batches that lasted a day or two, and now she was having to make things daily. The whole thing was mad.

On the one hand, it was good her business was succeeding in ways that she never could have imagined. On the other, if this continued, she was going to need help in the kitchen. She could barely keep up with demand as it was. If the demand continued to rise, she would either need to hire another baker, or cut hours at the shop. Less time the shop was open, the fewer items being sold, the less she would need to make.

Hopefully, once autumn ended, and she retired the pumpkin bars for the year, things would slow down. At least she hoped it would work that way.

Her phone buzzed in the back pocket of her denims, and she willed herself to not check it. She needed to finish the baking and go upstairs and take a nap, not banter with James.

The phone buzzed again. And again.

She frowned.

Grabbing a towel, she wiped her hands from any of the cream cheese icing that found itself on them and reached behind, pulling her phone out of her pocket. She laughed. In a series of texts, James had sent her several pictures of what he was going to be wearing to the wedding on Saturday. Screen shots from the website. Pictures of the tux laid out on his bed. And finally, some selfies of him wearing the tux in the mirror, making silly faces.

She shook her head and typed a reply, telling him she would go through her own wardrobe to find something suitable that would match his tux, and for good measure, she turned on the camera and took her own selfie. Her hair was up in a messy bun, with tendrils frizzing out around her head in almost a halo, and there was flour smeared down her face she didn't know was there, most likely from her adjusting her glasses as they slipped down her nose. She stuck her tongue out the side of her mouth and snapped the picture, sending it before she changed her mind.

James' reply came almost immediately, and it was only one word: stunning.

Blushing, she returned her phone to her back pocket and focused on her baking. She glanced at the clock and sighed. There was no way she was going to leave at her normal time today. Not if she was going to finish everything she had planned for the day and get slightly ahead for tomorrow.

She looked toward the door to the bakery, knowing Freddie was out there working the till. When the store closed, she was going to need to talk to him about their finances and see if they could afford to hire some more help. Logically, they should be able to with this uptick in business, and it didn't need to be permanent. It could just be through the Christmas rush, and then, when things settled down, they could go back to the way it was before. Just the two of them.

The part of her that liked control didn't like the idea of having someone else in her kitchen, but the part of her who liked sleep really needed to have some help so she could have a functioning brain.

Her phone buzzed again in her pocket, and she was determined to ignore it. She knew it was probably James, sending her more teasing texts. Or telling her about whatever they were doing today. He had warned her over the weekend the case would be a little slow going this week. Patrick had taken the week off to spend time with Evelyn's family and to prepare for the wedding, and James was also going to be spending time with his best friend's fiancée's family. He had explained they were practically his family, too, and he rarely got to see them, so he was going to do some touristy things. She had assured him it was fine. Her case was at a dead end anyway.

The phone in her pocket was vibrating again and despite this, she reminded herself that she had to ignore it. She needed to finish her baking so she could go upstairs and collapse until she could talk to Freddie about the shop.

As if her very thoughts summoned him, Freddie walked into the kitchen. His usually slicked into submission hair was out of control and the natural curl was very prominent. He looked exhausted.

"Mariel and I flipped the sign so we could go for lunch. I hope you don't mind."

Tessa shook her head. "Good for you. You deserve a break. Was it mad out there?"

"Mad would be an understatement." He walked over to the stool sitting in the corner and collapsed on it. He leaned back against the wall and closed his eyes. "When I close my eyes, all I see are pumpkin bars. Sometimes they have little wings so they can fly themselves off the shelves."

Tessa laughed. "Pumpkin season is ending soon and so will your nightmares of pumpkin bars."

"Don't get me wrong, Tess. I'm positively chuffed with how these bars are selling. The cafe is well into the black. But bloody hell am I exhausted."

"I've been thinking we should hire some more help." Tessa suggested as she frosted another set of pumpkin bars. "Another person for the front and maybe someone to help me back here. If things don't slow down after pumpkin season, I'm never going to keep up."

Freddie opened his eyes and set up a little straighter. "Absolutely. That's a brilliant idea. We can sit down with the book on Sunday and see what we have in the budget, but if things continue to go as well as they are, I don't see why we couldn't at the very least hire someone to help back here."

"If we only have the budget for one person, we should honestly hire someone for the front-"

"No," Freddie interrupted. "I can always help in the front. We should focus on finding someone for back here. You work hard enough as it is, you deserve the help. You don't need to martyr yourself over sticky toffee pudding."

Tessa smiled. "Thank you, Freddie. For not only believing in me enough to risk everything to open this shop with me, but for also caring for me when I would just let myself go."

"You're welcome, but you really don't need to be thanking me. I love you, Tess. You're my best friend, practically my sister. You know I have your back, no matter what."

Comfortable silence fell between them as Tessa cut the bars and placed them on the sheets to go into the display case and Freddie sat resting.

"Has your detective found anything more?" Freddie asked, breaking the silence.

"No. He messaged earlier to tell me they have hit a dead end. They couldn't get anything from the video. Whoever it is must know where the cameras are because they kept their face turned away."

"Fuck, I'm sorry, Tess. Has there been any other contact between you and the stalker?"

She shook her head. "No, I haven't heard from them in a couple days. Not since James caught them across the street hidden in the alley watching the shop."

Freddie sighed. "Are you sure you're fine staying here? I have an extra room in my flat. You're more than welcome to it until they catch him. I am worried about you staying here alone."

"Thank you for the offer, but I think I'll stay where I am for now. Nothing has been outright threatening, and they have stayed outside the shop for now."

"Except the time they bought something here and then used the receipt to write a threatening letter to your PI."

"Touche."

"Can I at least install some cameras inside your flat? They are inexpensive and it will make me feel better if you had something vaguely resembling security."

"How would cameras inside my flat help you feel better?"

"I would have access to the cameras and get an alert when they go off. Then I can—"

"Ew, Freddie, listen to what you just said. All of it together."

Freddie contemplated in silence for a moment, but then it seemingly all made sense to him and he involuntarily shuddered. "Yeah, I heard it, so, we won't be doing that. Maybe on the outside of your flat? The front door? That's less creepy and stalkery, yeah? And you would also have access so you can arm them at will. Think about it, please."

Tessa nodded. "I will. I'll think about it. Thank you for being so concerned about me."

Her phone dinged in her back pocket, signifying another text message. She ignored it and kept lifting the pumpkin bars from the pan to the trays. It dinged again.

"Aren't you going to see who that is?"

She shook her head. "I'm sure it's only James. He was texting me earlier about what he is wearing to the wedding on Saturday so we can coordinate since we're sitting together. I'm sure it's just him."

The mobile dinged again.

Freddie stood up from the stool and walked over to her, picking the phone out of her pocket. He looked at it and frowned. "Does James have an unlisted number?"

It was Tessa's turn to frown. "No, he should show up as himself."

Freddie turned the phone to face her. Three unread text messages from an unknown number.

"That's odd." She reached out to take her phone, but looked down at her cream cheese covered fingers and frowned.

"Your passcode still the same?"

"Yes."

Freddie input her code and the way his eyebrows drew in almost made her heart stop.

"What is it?" she asks.

"You'll want to call James."

"What is it?" she repeated, grabbing a towel to wipe her hands off.

Freddie turned the phone toward her, and she could feel her legs collapsing from under her as she read what was on the screen.

UNKNOWN: I can see you.

UNKNOWN: Why are you talking to him?

UNKNOWN: STOP IGNORING ME!!!!

CHAPTER 11

JAMES

"Is your mobile number on your website or tied to anything with the shop?" James asked.

Even though he technically had the week off to prepare for Patrick and Evie's wedding, he dropped everything at Tessa's frantic call, letting him know her stalker had escalated yet again.

"It's not. I set up a phone line only for the shop so I wouldn't get calls to my personal line. It's not on my business cards, it's not on the website, it's not on my Google search results. Nothing."

James held out his hand, and Tessa immediately handed her phone over. They were sitting in Tessa's flat to give them some privacy. He was sitting in an armchair upholstered in a burgundy and gold floral pattern and bloody comfortable. It was sitting directly across from a matching love seat on which Tessa sat perched with Freddie, who draped his arm over her shoulders.

James had to remind himself he had no business being jealous of the casual way Tessa and Freddie interacted. Tessa had told him she and Freddie were just friends. Besides, he didn't date clients.

He looked at the messages. He pulled out his phone and copied the number to his phone. Then he forwarded the messages to himself.

"When I get back to my flat, I'll run the number through my software. However, I'm not very optimistic I'll be getting any hits."

"You think the bloke used a burner phone?" asked Freddie.

"Yeah. I'm almost certain of it. He's been covering his tracks so far. If he used his own number to send this, it would be a huge mistake on his part."

"And he doesn't seem the type to make mistakes," Tessa filled in.

"He does not," James agreed.

Tessa ran her hands through her hair. James took the time to actually notice her for the first time since coming in. Her normally put together appearance was anything but. Her curls, usually pulled back into some sort of bun, were riotous and seemed to have a life of their own. She was still wearing her apron from the kitchen, and there was flour on her face, right below her left eye on her cheek. She had dark circles under her eyes, which were red from crying.

"I don't understand. Why me?" Her voice was tight, as if she were trying not to cry again.

"Stalkers are narcissistic people who want something and go for it," James explained. "Someone noticed something in you they liked and latched onto it. It became an obsession."

"But what could I have done to encourage him to do something like this?" she gestured to her phone.

"It could have been something as simple as being nice to someone. Giving them a smile, saying hi. People like this are attention starved. They live an unhappy life, or they're treated unfairly by people around them. Any sort of kindness sent their way will feel like a lifeboat," James explained.

"And they latch onto that string of hope and become obsessed, yeah?" Freddie asked.

"Yeah."

Tessa took off her glasses and handed them to Freddie before bringing her hands to her face and groaning. "I'm trying to think of people who I would have been nice to in the last couple months who I see regularly enough that seem suspicious, but I can't think of anyone." Her hands muffled her words, but James could easily hear the emotions getting the best of her in her voice.

"It may not even be someone you see regularly. Your stalker could have come in once, bought a cake. You would have smiled and thanked them, told them to have a good day, and thought no more of it. And that one interaction could have meant the world to them." James wasn't sure if his words were making things better or worse at this point. Would it be better if the stalker were a regular customer or a one off? He didn't know, honestly.

Freddie moved his arm so he could rub Tessa's back. "You have an amazing smile. Lights up the whole bloody room, always has. Ever since we were kids. I can see someone becoming obsessed if you were to smile at them and they had no one else in their lives who smiled at them."

Tessa removed her hands from her face. "Oh, God," she muttered.

"What?" James inquired.

"What if it isn't a customer at all? What if it's someone from my past who was a little sketchy?"

Freddie stopped rubbing her back and sat up straighter. "Who are you thinking..." His eyes widened. "Oh fuck, I think I know who you're thinking of."

James leaned forward, opening the notes app on his phone. "What's his name?"

"Bruno Nelson," Freddie declared, without hesitating. "He was our friend, well, former friend, and he had this weird obsession with Tess."

"I wouldn't call it an obsession—"

"You caught him fucking spying on you in the loo, Tess," Freddie practically yelled. "He was a tosser. Her dad thought about pressing charges after the loo incident, but his parents begged him not to."

"He was my friend," Tessa explained. "He, Freddie, and I were all best friends in primary. In the summer before year nine, he went on an extended holiday on the continent and when he got back, he was different. Freddie and I had sort of grown apart from him. We were still friendly. We just weren't hanging round him much anymore."

"He became a bit of a loner. Very stereotypical, early 2000s goth and emo sort of thing." Freddie continued. "Except he would always make sure he was sitting next to Tess in every class they had together."

"He was my friend. We hadn't been hanging out outside of school very much, but we were still friends."

"Except he would get really fucking weirdly jealous at parties."

"Explain," James pulled out his phone and began frantically taking notes. This was the most promising lead they had. He didn't want to miss anything.

Freddie handed Tessa her glasses, leaned forward, and began talking with his hands. "So, whenever we were at a party or a club and some bloke would come and talk to Tess to try to pick her up, Bruno would walk up, looking like Richmond from the *IT Crowd*."

"And he would just stand there." Tessa took over. "He would just stand there and hover. He wouldn't say anything and inevitably, whoever I was chatting with would simply walk away."

"Tell me about the loo incident." James opened his voice recording app. Since it seemed the 'loo incident' was a significant event which seemed to have a stalker tendency to it, it seemed important to make sure he didn't lose one word.

"I was in band, and so was Bruno. We would have practices after school. And being kids, we would mess around. One day, I was doing a dance with a friend before practice, and bumped into someone drinking a red drink. Spilled it all over my shirt. Naturally, I went into the loo to try and salvage my white shirt. I had just taken my shirt off when I heard a sound from inside one of the stalls. I knocked on the door to ask if the person was okay and they hadn't shut it. It was slightly ajar. It opened even wider after I touched it."

"And when it opened, there was fucking Bruno, his trousers around his bloody ankles, having a wank," Freddie finished.

"What happened after you caught him?"

Tessa and Freddie were both quiet for a second as they turned to look at one another, neither seeming to want to talk about the next part.

"I need to know what happened next. It could be important. This is the first lead we've had in this case. Whatever you tell me, I will only share with Patrick in the context of solving the case. I won't tell Evie or anyone else."

Tessa closed her eyes and turned her head back toward James. "He didn't say anything. He looked so embarrassed. He sort of tucked himself away and made a run for it. I sort of stood there, baffled."

"Our teacher caught him coming out of the girl's loo, and when the teacher walked in to make sure everything was okay, she noticed Tessa there and raised fucking hell."

James stopped the recording. "Well, I would say we have a suspect."

"Really? It was so long ago," Tessa remarked. She was skeptical, he didn't blame her. "And it was all most likely a misunderstanding. I kept telling people there was no way he could have known I would be in there changing. But, no one would believe me. They thought I was covering for a friend."

"Do you still have any contact with him?"

"No, that was the last time either of us talked to him. His parents took him out of college before he could get expelled, and Tess's dad didn't press charges, but he didn't want him to come near her. And then we left school and went to university and that was that," Freddie answered.

Tessa drew her bottom lip between her teeth and looked down.

"Tessa?" James inquired.

Freddie turned, so he was looking at Tessa. "Tess? That was the last we saw of him, yeah?"

"Well," she started.

"Tess!" Freddie exclaimed.

"He reached out after my dad died. And we're sort of friends on social media now."

Freddie closed his eyes and allowed himself to fall back onto the couch. "Oh, my God, I can't believe you're in contact with fucking Bruno. Bruno!"

"I know! But he seems okay now. At least from what I've seen on his socials. He's not dressed like a vampire anymore."

"Appearances can be deceiving," James pointed out. "Forward me links to his socials. I'll check them out. And I'll do a thorough background check on him as well. We'll either rule him out as a suspect or he may very well be our guy."

Freddie immediately perked back up, pulling himself into a sitting position. "You really think he could be our guy? Like we catch him, and Tessa will be safe?"

"Possibly," James explained. "Or he could simply be a bloke you knew from school."

"Even just having this lead makes me feel a little better," Tessa affirmed.

James checked the time on his phone before tucking it back into his pocket. "At the very least, I now have something tangible to follow up on, rather than just spinning circles with faceless people in black on surveillance tape."

James stood from the chair. He needed to get back to Patrick and Evie and the wedding preparations. He and Evie's sisters had a lot of items on their lists as best man and co-maids of honor. "Are you alright staying here?" he asked. "Because the Stevensons are paying for us to stay in a hotel for the next few nights leading up to the wedding, so we're all together. My flat is empty if you would rather stay somewhere else."

"I'll be fine," Tessa insisted. "I will not let some arsehole scare me out of staying in my home."

"Are you sure?" Freddie asked. "If you're only being polite because you don't want to impose on James, my spare room is empty. Alice moved all her stuff out this past weekend."

"I'm not only being polite. I'm really, really sure. As long as he's not breeched my door, I feel safe here. I want everything to stay as normal as possible."

James gave her a smile. "If, you're sure."

"I've said, I'm sure! Now go. I talked to Evie this morning to finalize a few things, and it sounds as if you are in for a busy week. So, go. Run nothing through your programs until after the wedding. This can wait."

James locked his gaze with hers. The fear and defeat he saw mere moments ago seemed to have vanished. It was as if the promise of a lead, the idea this could all be over sooner rather than later, invigorated her.

"I can't promise to wait until after the wedding, but I'll at least wait until my duties for the night are finished."

"After the wedding. I'm going to be busy with wedding baking. I won't have time to worry about whether you found anything. Promise you'll wait until the wedding is done?"

Her eyes never left his as her mouth quirked up into a smile. He shook his head, returning her smile with one of his own. It was impossible to tell her no. "Fine. I promise to not look into anything until after the wedding."

"Thank you."

"You're welcome."

James was the first to break away as he moved toward the door. "Keep an eye out round here, yeah?" he asked, directing it at Freddie.

"Always," the man James now respected answered.

James gave them a nod and opened the door and left.

As he made his way out of the shop and began his walk down the sidewalk toward the underground entrance, he couldn't shake the feeling he was being watched. But as he turned around to check behind him, there was nothing.

CHAPTER 12

TESSA

The door had barely closed behind James before Freddie turned toward Tessa.

"Are you sure you'll be okay here?"

"Yes, I'm sure. Please stop worrying."

Freddie shook his head. "As long as this person is out there threatening you, I'm going to worry. You're my best friend, my sister. It's my job to worry about you."

Tessa smiled. "Well, try not to worry too much tonight. So far all he's done is leave notes and text. He's never tried to approach. I don't think he'll choose tonight."

"If he does, please call the police, and then either me or James," Freddie urged. "I'll come as quickly as possible."

"Okay. I will."

Freddie looked at his watch. "I better go. I promised my mum I would be home so she could pick up Alice's something borrowed."

Tessa frowned. "How are you doing? I feel like we swept your crisis aside for mine."

Freddie shrugged. "Dunno. I'm alright, I guess. Alice came by while I was working at the shop to clear out the rest of her things so she wouldn't have to see or talk to me. It feels surreal. We were supposed to be married, yeah? And now we don't even talk."

"I can't help but feel a little responsible for your breakup. It was me she didn't like."

Freddie shook his head. "Don't. Everything is on her. Giving me a fucking ultimatum. She had to know what I would choose. She was looking for an out and used you as a scapegoat. Ten quid says she was fucking around with some other bloke."

"You really think she would cheat on you?"

He shrugged. "She accused me of cheating on her with you. Usually, accusations reflect the actions of the accuser."

"Well, either way, I'm sorry. Were you able to get any of your money back?"

"Most of it. Turns out vendors feel sorry for a bloke left at the altar. Played up the wounded soul a little."

"At least something good came out of the mess."

"Yes, the glass is half full or whatever. Now I really must be going. You know my mum. If I keep her waiting, I will never hear the end. And I'll already have to have an earful of her telling me all the ways this wouldn't have happened if I had simply let her set me up with a nice Indian girl."

Tessa gave him a sympathetic smile before walking to her fridge and pulling out a container. "Would some gulab jamun take a little heat off?" She gave the container a little shake.

"I'm not going to ask why you have a secret stash in your fridge, but yes, it would. It absolutely would. You know my mum takes pride in teaching you how to make all the traditional Indian sweets and loves that you carry them in your shop. Of course, the flip side is instead of lecturing me about not accepting an arranged marriage, she's going to spend our time waxing poetically about how she wishes you were her daughter-in-law and why I haven't I married you already."

"Well, I don't have to give this to you." She turned to make it look like she was going to put the dessert back in the fridge.

"No, wait, I'll take it. Listening to the monologue about you is preferable to the arranged marriage one."

Freddie walked over and took the container from her hands. He leaned forward and gave her a quick peck on her cheek. "Thanks, Tess. I owe you one. And I was serious. Call. Any time." He gave her a little wave and walked to the door. "Lock up behind me." And then he was gone.

And she was alone.

She walked over to the door and flipped the lock into place. The click sounding louder than it should.

Had her flat always been so quiet?

She glanced around.

Seriously. Had it always been this quiet?

Her phone buzzed in her hand, and she jumped.

She tentatively looked down at her hand. Was it him? Was he messaging her again?

When James's name was on the screen, she sighed, letting out the breath she was holding, her heart still beating a kilometer an hour. She opened the text.

JAMES: Just making sure you're doing okay. Don't forget to send me the socials for Bruno when you get a chance. See you at the wedding... X

Tessa closed out the message. Her hands were shaking. Was this going to happen every time someone texted her from now on?

First, she feared the post. Then she couldn't have her curtains open, lest she have her picture taken. Now she couldn't even get messages on her phone? What would be next? What else would this arsehole steal from her?

She threw her phone at the armchair and let out a primal scream as she fell to her knees onto the carpet. Hot tears spilled down her cheeks, causing her vision to blur behind her glasses. She had never felt so helpless and trapped before. Never in her life did she think she would become a prisoner in her own home. A prisoner in her life. Fearing shadows, always wondering if the customer she was serving was the one making her life a living hell.

All she wanted was to live her life. For everything to go back to normal.

***

The next morning, Tessa was in the kitchen at her normal time. She'd barely slept the night before. Every time she drifted off, she would relive that moment in the loo during school. Telling

James about it must have drudged up her suppressed emotions about the entire ordeal. She hadn't slept more than a handful of hours.

She put her hands under her glasses and rubbed her eyes, immediately regretting it.

She had forgotten she had moved the pumpkin bars onto the display tray. Now she had cream cheese icing all over her face.

She walked over to the sink and washed her hands and her face before grabbing the tray and carrying it out into the store. She placed it in the position of honor, front and center. Over half the display was with pumpkin bars, and she had even more in the back. Plus, another batch in the oven. She really hoped she had enough.

She walked to the front door and turned the lock and flipped the sign, officially open for the morning.

As soon as she made it back to the counter, the bell sounded, announcing a customer.

She turned around to see Fraser walking in.

"Good morning!" he announced, sounding way more chipper than anyone should at six thirty in the morning.

"Good morning, Fraser. You're not usually in so early."

"Yes, well, mum had a rough night, so she asked if I would run over and pick her up a couple pumpkin bars. She was worried if I waited until the afternoon, they would be all gone."

Tessa smiled. "Well, I think I made enough pumpkin bars to last through the afternoon, but with the way things have been going, it's probably a brilliant decision to come so early."

She moved behind the counter and pulled out a box. "How many?"

"Four. Mum was very specific. It needs to be four, and I can't eat any," he moved toward the register, pulling out his wallet.

Tessa smiled. "Well, I'll throw in a fifth one, on the house, so you can have one. I'll even put it in a separate bag. It'll be our little secret." She gave him a wink as she carried the bars over to the register.

"Are you sure? I can pay for it. It's not a big deal."

"It's fine. You and your mum are some of my best customers. So, on the house."

Fraser smiled his crooked smile, his right side going higher than his left. His blue eyes twinkling. "Thanks, Ms. Lopez. I really appreciate it. You know me mum loves you, and loves coming here for tea."

"Well, I look forward to seeing her every week."

She rang him up, and he handed over his credit card.

"Are you doing, okay?" Fraser asked as she handed his card back.

"I'm fine. Why do you ask?"

He shrugged. "You don't seem like yourself. You look tired."

"I had a rough go at sleeping last night. Pumpkin bars are showing up in my nightmares. At one point I dreamt there was a riot in my shop because they had sold out." She fibbed, not wanting the others to know the real reason. All they would do was worry, and she didn't want that.

Fraser let out a low whistle. "Sounds rough. Well, I will cross my fingers no one riots over pumpkin bars in your shop today."

Tessa laughed. "Thanks."

He reached into his wallet and pulled out a card. "If you need any help, or just want to talk about anything, this is my number."

Tessa picked up the card. Fraser Hudson, Software Developer.

"I work from home, so I'm almost always available," he continued.

She tucked the card into the pocket of her apron. "Thank you. I will definitely keep this in mind. I appreciate it."

He gave her one more smile. "Well, I better be off. Take care, Ms. Lopez."

"Thank you. Have a good day."

He gave a little wave and walked out the door.

Tessa turned back around and walked back through the kitchen. Mariel would be there soon, and until then, the bell would alert her to any customers. She needed to get started on Patrick and Evie's wedding cake preparation, since the wedding was this weekend.

She was pulling down her large mixing bowl, when she had an epiphany.

She pulled out her phone and the business card. She snapped a picture of it and sent it to James.

TESSA: Could be nothing, but he's a regular. Do you think it's worth checking out?

She was about to tuck her phone away since it was still early. She wasn't expecting a reply when it dinged.

JAMES: It's worth checking out every lead. I'll look at him when I look into Bruno.

TESSA: Thanks. What are you doing up so early?

JAMES: Wedding stuff.

JAMES: How many pumpkin bars did you make this morning?

TESSA: Too many. Counting the days until December.

JAMES: It'll be here soon enough.
JAMES: Counting the days until I see you again.

Tessa smiled down at her phone. All the stress she was carrying in her shoulders melted away, and she was relieved. She was falling hard for this man. And she was hoping he was falling for her, too.

TESSA: Me, too.

CHAPTER 13

JAMES

The sun wasn't even up yet, but James couldn't sleep. He spent the last couple of days worried about Tessa and her stalker. He knew he was supposed to be on "holiday" so to speak, but it didn't stop him from worrying.

He sat on the couch in the living room of the hotel suite he was staying in. It was early, so no one else was up yet. He opened the laptop he had retrieved from his flat and booted it up.

"You're not supposed to be working," a voice from behind James spoke up, causing him to jump.

"Fuck," he muttered under his breath after he turned to see Evelyn standing behind him.

She was wearing Patrick's old robe and holding a cup of coffee wrapped in her hands. She hadn't brushed her hair, and she was smirking.

"I'm honestly surprised. I know you've been throwing yourself into work lately, but this feels like a very Patrick move," she pointed out as she moved closer to the couch.

"You know I wouldn't normally be sneaking in work on holiday like this, but there was a development in the case."

Evelyn stiffened. "You're kidding. You have a lead?"

"I have a lead."

Evelyn quickly moved around the couch, sitting herself down next to him. "Patrick mentioned the CCTV footage was a bust."

"It was. This lead came from talking with Tessa the other night. After she received the text message threat."

"What did you find?"

James quickly filled Evie in on what Tessa and Freddie had told him about Bruno and the loo incident.

"I honestly don't know what I want to do more right now, hug Tessa or punch this Bruno bastard in the face," she seethed once James finished.

"Yeah, well, Tessa gave me this Bruno bloke's socials to look into. Apparently, they reconnected after her father died."

"We can circle back to the fact Tessa friended him on social media after everything he did. First, tell me what you're hoping to find? Do you think he's posted declarations of love to Tessa? Posted pictures of his black hoodies?"

James shook his head. "No, nothing like that. Mostly, I'm hoping to grab a picture or two to plug into our facial recognition software."

"And run it against the CCTV footage." Evelyn filled in. "Smart."

"Yeah, hoping he's been hanging around the shop without his full regalia. If I can catch him at the shop as Bruno, then maybe I can compare him to the person in black."

Evelyn leaned her head on his shoulder and watched while James began inputting the URLs Tessa sent him into his search engine.

"What are you doing up so early?" James asked. "What's on your mind?"

Evelyn let out a soft laugh. "You know me so well."

James shrugged. "We lived together for a year."

"It's more than that, and you know it." She grew quiet as she watched him scroll through Bruno's Facebook page. "I guess I'm a little nervous about tomorrow."

James stopped scrolling, turning his head to look at her. She was looking down at her coffee, so all he could really see was the top of her head.

"What do you mean?"

She shrugged. "I don't know. Something about standing up in front of everyone I love and committing to someone I've only known for a year and a half for the rest of my life."

James frowned. "You're not having second thoughts, are you?"

She shook her head. "No?"

"You don't sound very sure."

"No, I'm sure. I just...I don't know. I love him, and I moved halfway around the world for him, but...you don't think we're moving incredibly fast, do you?"

James set his laptop down onto the table and moved so he could wrap his arm around Evie, pulling her into a side hug.

"No. I don't. If it were anyone else, I would be hesitant to say you were moving anything but fast. However, I was there. I was there when you two first met. I've watched you fall in love, and I will say, with absolute certainty, you're not moving too fast."

Evelyn looked up at him, her eyes shining with unshed tears. "Yeah?"

"Yeah." He bent his head down to place a kiss on the crown of her head. "Has anyone been telling you otherwise?"

She shrugged. "My parents have spent the last four months asking why we were moving so fast. Repeatedly asking, 'What's the hurry?'"

"Citizenship? Visas?" James enumerated.

"I told them as much, and they worried I was marrying him *only* to stay in London."

"Your parents have completely lost the plot."

"They're just concerned—"

"Mate, they've been fucking 'concerned' about all of your choices you've made in the last year and a half."

"That's not fair," she argued, lifting her head from his shoulder.

"It is. You're forgetting, I lived with you, and I was around for your video calls."

Evelyn closed her mouth and frowned.

"During the trial, they were 'concerned' about how long it was taking. When you transferred to finish your masters here in London, they were 'concerned' about whether you were making the right choice. When you called to announce your engagement, they were 'concerned' you were being too hasty."

"Alright!" Evelyn whisper shouted. "I get it. They are very concerned."

"I'm wondering if that concern is creeping into your head, making you have doubts. You're not planning to stand Patrick up at the altar tomorrow, are you?"

"Absolutely not," she rushed to say.

James smiled. "See. Nothing to worry about. If you weren't sure about your choice, or thought you were moving too fast, you wouldn't have answered that question so quickly or so surely."

Evelyn smiled at him. "Thank you."

"For what?"

"For listening to my neurotic thoughts before the sun is even fully up."

"You're welcome."

James bent over and picked his computer back up.

"Anything interesting on Bruno over there?"

He shook his head. "It's all innocuous. He doesn't seem to be extremely active. I'm going to nab this picture of him and upload it to the facial recognition software and let it do its thing."

"How long until you get any results?"

"Probably not until after the wedding."

"That's so long."

"It's a lot of footage. A lot."

Evelyn pulled a face. "At least this time you won't have to comb through it all yourself."

"Silver lining."

He finished inputting the settings into his software and minimized the screen. He opened the text from Tessa he got the other day and looked at the picture of the business card she sent him.

"Who's Fraser?" Evelyn asked.

"A regular of Tessa's at the shop. He comes in every week with his mum."

"Oh! I think I know who you're talking about."

James turned, so he was facing her. "You do?"

"Yeah, they come in on Wednesdays for tea. His mom is the sweetest. She helped me decide which floral design I wanted on my cake."

"What about this Fraser bloke?"

"Friendly. He's a little older than us, maybe late thirties, possibly early forties. Dotes on his mother. Makes great conversation. Seems like a genuinely nice guy."

James nodded. "Good, good."

"Why did Tessa send you his card?"

"Since we've hit such a brick wall with this case, we discussed potential suspects. What to look out for. I told her and her business partner to look for people who may be from the past, or people who are regulars at the shop, but not necessarily someone who would be overtly suspicious."

Evelyn nodded. "And Fraser Hudson is a regular, who spends a lot of time in the shop, but he doesn't act as if he's stalking Tessa."

"Exactly."

"What are you going to do with this information?"

"Same as with Bruno. Head to his socials, get a picture, put it in the facial recognition."

"Won't he show up if he's a regular?"

"Yes, but we'll also be looking for him if he shows up and does something weird."

James typed Fraser's name into all the social media apps and came up empty.

"Is that a worrying sign?"

"Nah, Patrick and I don't have social media. Many people don't. It's not a red flag. It's just disappointing because I can't get a picture of him to run through the software."

"You should dance with Tessa at the wedding," Evelyn blurted out.

James' head turned so quickly in her direction he was pretty sure he gave himself whiplash. "What?"

"You should dance with Tessa at the wedding," she repeated.

"I heard you the first time, but I don't understand why?"

"Because you like her."

James opened his mouth to reply.

"Don't deny it." Evelyn interrupted. "It's written all over your face when you talk about her. And you've all but admitted it in the past. Dance with her."

"I don't date clients. It's unethical."

Evelyn held up her left hand and wiggled her left finger where her modest engagement ring sat. "Is it though?"

James shook his head. "You were different."

"Was I? You both helped solve the case of the notorious crime family who wanted to murder me."

"You weren't paying us. We did it because we're kind and generous..."

"And you could tack me onto the case someone else was paying for you to solve," Evelyn finished.

"Exactly. Not a client. An adjacent client."

Evelyn shook her head. "James. For the last year, you have been working yourself to your bones. You never go out. You're not allowing yourself to live your life outside of the agency."

"We've been really busy."

"Not too busy to take a break. I know. I'm marrying your partner."

James sighed, running his hand through his hair. "I don't know. I guess I have been feeling down lately."

"About what?"

"You and Patrick."

Evelyn gasped. "What?"

"Not like that. It's just, I guess I'm feeling left out. I knew it was inevitable. The three of us couldn't live together forever, but ever since you moved out, it's been a little lonely? We picked that flat out together. And then you two just...left."

Evelyn gave him a sad smile. "I'm sorry. We didn't know us moving out would be that big of a deal. Honestly, we moved out because we didn't think you enjoyed being the third wheel. Maybe we should have talked to you about it before moving forward with our plans."

"I've never thought of myself as the third wheel, for the record."

"I know. But don't you want to have something of your own?"

"I do, but—"

"Then why won't you let yourself be happy with Tessa?"

James shrugged. "I don't know. Because you're right. I do really like her."

"Then why won't you do anything about it? And don't feed me some bull about not dating clients."

"Because what if she doesn't feel the same and rejects me?"

"Then she rejects you, and you move on. But you'll never know for sure until you do something. Ask her to dance with you tomorrow."

James looked into Evelyn's face, which was so sincere in her desire to see him happy that he could feel himself caving.

"Fine," he sighed. "I'll ask her to dance."

Evelyn's face broke into a wide smile, and she was practically bouncing in her seat. "Yay! I'm so excited."

James shook his head and stopped fighting the smile spreading on his face.

Evelyn moved to stand up. "I need to head into the shower before someone else claims it. Everyone else will wake up soon and we have a busy day."

"That we do. Rehearsal and the hen and stag parties."

Evelyn wrinkled her nose. "Yes, don't remind me. I tried to finagle my way out of having a hen party, seeing as I don't have very many girl friends here, but my sisters insisted, and I'm not entirely sure what we're doing tonight."

James laughed. "It will all work out. I promise. You'll have fun."

Evelyn's eyes widened. "You know what they have planned."

"I do. But before you ask, they've sworn me to secrecy."

"Traitor," Evelyn whispered, narrowing her eyes.

James laughed. "Go. Take your shower. You're not getting anything from me."

Evelyn started walking toward her room, and James turned back to his computer.

"James?"

He turned around.

"Thank you." Evelyn gave him a sincere smile.

"Thank you," he replied.

Before he could get back into doing what he was going to do, his phone went off. He picked it up and there was a text from Tessa. He opened it and laughed.

TESSA: May I present to you, wedding cake! Think they'll like it?

Attached was a picture of Tessa, sitting on the counter in her kitchen, two tiers of cake on either side of her. She was gesturing to the cake, her arms wide open, presenting it to the camera, and her face had a streak of blue icing down one cheek, and there were multiple colors of icing staining the front of her white apron. She was wearing a traditional chef's hat, which she must have put on for the picture because, unlike the rest of her, it was pristine. The cake tiers looked amazing, with their cascading blue and purple flowers on white icing, but he only had eyes on the baker.

James continued to stare at the picture on his phone.

This was a side of Tessa he hadn't been able to see through most of the case. She looked happy and playful. Everyone was right. He had it bad for her.

He touched the box to type in his reply and didn't even stop to think before he hit send.

JAMES: Beautiful

He tucked his phone into his pocket and stood from the couch. He ran a hand through his hair and for a split second worried about what he sent.

Almost immediately, a reply sounded, and he rushed to take the phone out of his pocket.

TESSA: (Heart Eyed Emoji)

James smiled.

Satisfied, he tucked the phone back into his pocket and whistled lightly as he sauntered to the bathroom to claim the first shower.

He had forgotten what it was like to start something new with a girl. He could get used to this feeling.

CHAPTER 14

TESSA

Tessa carefully set the cake topper Evelyn and Patrick had picked out on the top layer of the cake and stood back. She let out a sigh of relief. The cake was straight, and it looked sturdy. She smiled to herself. She had lined the flowers up perfectly on the first try.

The cake was white, with a line of dark purple and cerulean flowers cascading down the right side of the top layer and moving across the other three layers in a way that made them look like they were swirling down the cake. Placed on top of the elegant cake she and Evelyn had designed sat two cartoon characters Patrick had paid someone to make to look like him and Evelyn.

She bent down and picked up the boxes she had carted the cake in and walked to the back of the reception hall where the kitchen sat. She stowed the boxes and quickly untied her apron and tucked it away with the boxes.

She ran her hands down her navy dress to make sure everything was sitting right. The men were wearing the cerulean color, so Tessa thought the navy would pair well with what James was wearing without making it look like she was part of the wedding party.

There was movement at the front of the hall and Tessa peeked out the door of the kitchen to see guests already arriving.

She took a deep breath and let it out slowly.

Why was she so nervous?

She waited as everyone filed in and began mingling as waiters walked around hors d'oeuvres for people to snack on.

Finally, the DJ came on and announced the wedding party. She watched as the first couple walked in. She assumed it was Evelyn's youngest sister and James' roommate, Joseph, the police officer. Next, James walked in with Evelyn's other sister. He had the biggest grin on his face. His red hair slicked to the side, showing off his blue eyes. He looked fit. Really Fit.

Finally, Patrick and Evelyn came in, and everyone cheered. He was wearing a tux that matched the others, black, with a cerulean waistcoat and tie. She was in a simple white dress. It was floor length, with a small train, a lace sheath overlay on the white silk underneath. Her hair was curled and a small veil perched on her head. Both wearing the largest smiles possible.

The wedding party made their way to their separate tables, and when James got to his, he stopped and looked around.

Tessa took another deep breath and stepped out of the shadows of the kitchen. As soon as she moved into James' eye line, he noticed her and froze. His grin widened as he moved his gaze along her figure. When his gaze returned to hers, he drew his bottom lip between his teeth and shook his head.

As she walked to the table, she could feel her cheeks warm under his scrutiny. If she didn't know better, she would swear every eye in the room was on her. Everyone was talking amongst themselves, waiting for their dinner to be served.

She finally made it to her seat at the table the rest of the wedding party was sitting and looked up at James.

"You clean up nicely," she complimented.

"Oh, this old thing?" He joked as he pulled on the lapels of his suit jacket. "You look amazing. Hardly recognize you without the apron."

Tessa grabbed hold of her skirt and held it out. "Turns out I exist outside of the bakery and have fancy dresses."

"Who knew?"

"Who. Knew."

James moved and pulled out a chair for her. "Milady."

She laughed, shaking her head. "Thank you, my kind sir."

He pushed in her seat and then took the seat next to hers. "Let me do some introductions. Everyone, this is Tessa. She's the owner of Cake Me Home Tonight, and she made the cake we'll get to partake in later. Tessa, this is Joe, my flat mate and our friend. Next to him is Michelle, Evie's youngest sister, and next to her is Elizabeth, Evie's middle sister."

Everyone greeted her with smiles, and she held up a hand in a small wave back.

"How was the ceremony?" she asked.

"Beautiful," Elizabeth answered. "Evelyn cried during the vows, which made Patrick cry."

"Which made me cry," James pointed out. "Not a dry eye in the house."

"Are you ready for your speech?" she asked. He had texted her the night before, worried about it. Couldn't decide if he should go funny or serious. She had convinced him to mix it up and do both.

He patted his breast pocket. "As ready as I'll ever be. I bloody hate public speaking."

Joseph let out a guffaw from next to James. "You? Hate public speaking? The most extrovert of extroverts I know?"

"Hey, just because I'm extroverted doesn't mean I'm okay with hundreds of eyes on me."

Elizabeth made a show of looking around the room. "Hundreds of eyes?"

Tessa glanced around and noticed that the "big crowd" of guests she had seen come in earlier was really only fifty people.

"Each of these people has two eyes, don't they?" James emphasized.

The table laughed and then settled into comfortable conversation. Tessa had turned to Elizabeth and was talking to her about Uni. She was getting ready to graduate. As she chatted, she could feel the warmth radiating off of James' arm, which he had slung on the back of her chair. Her heart thrilled at the proximity. It was the second time they had been so close, and it still thrilled her as much as it did the first time. She found it hard to concentrate on her conversation with Elizabeth.

She had to stop herself from pouting when the food arrived and he moved his arm from its position.

"Does this meat look dodgy to you?" he asked, poking around his plate with his fork.

"It looks fine." She picked up her knife and cut through the piece of chicken in front of her.

"Are you sure? I don't want to get food poisoning and miss out on giving my speech."

"For fuck's sake, James, eat the fucking chicken," Joseph stated, not bothering to look up from his own food.

"Alright, alright."

She shook her head. "Are you always this difficult?"

"Not always. Must be the nerves."

They ate and chatted, and before she knew it, someone was clinking their glass, announcing it was time for speeches.

James leaned into her, whispering in her ear, "Wish me luck," but before she could answer, he was already up and moving toward the front of the room.

Tessa grabbed her wineglass and turned so she was looking at James.

James took the microphone from someone and turned so he was facing Patrick and Evelyn.

"I thought really hard about what I was going to say today, and I couldn't decide if I was going to be funny or sincere. But when I looked back on our friendships, I thought, of course I need to be sincere. You two are my best friends. And I'm so happy for the two of you finally making it to this moment right here.

"Patrick, you're my brother, mate, no question. Evie, you're the little sister I've always wanted. Together, we're the Three Musketeers. All for one and one for all."

Patrick and Evelyn said that last line with James, and the room erupted into laughter.

"As you move on to this new chapter of your lives, remember where you came from. And all the trials you faced at the beginning of your relationship. You've already tried out the 'sickness and in health' portion of your vows and made it through. Anything else you face will be a breeze comparatively."

Patrick raised a hand to his forehead while Evelyn brought her hands to touch her ribs. Tessa noticed a large scar on Patrick's forehead she hadn't noticed before. They must be remembering the injuries they got while fighting the Fitzgeralds last year.

"You two are the perfect example of what love should be," James was wrapping up his speech. He turned his head until his gaze met hers, holding it as he said the next part. "I could only dream of having what you have." He turned back to Patrick and Evelyn, raising his glass. "To Patrick and Evie."

"To Patrick and Evie," everyone repeated.

As Tessa raised her glass to her lips, she could feel butterflies in her stomach.

As she lowered her glass, she glanced up as James passed Elizabeth the microphone. As he caught her gaze on him, he gave her a wink and a smirk, and her face warmed.

Shit. She had it bad.

***

The music blared over the speakers, and everyone was dancing to the latest pop hit.

The cake had been cut and enjoyed. The important dancing had happened, and now the party had truly begun.

Tessa was sitting on a chair and swaying back and forth to the music. Laughing as James and Patrick were doing some weird half break dance, half secret handshake, she wasn't sure, but it was very physical, and the men had shed their suit jackets two songs ago.

The song stopped and everyone who had gathered to watch the men do their dance applauded and they took dramatic bows.

The next song queued up was a much slower song than the previous one.

When the initial notes of Ed Sheeran's "Thinking Out Loud" began, Patrick and Evelyn found each other on the dance floor, as if they were two magnets that couldn't help but be attracted to each other.

As everyone on the dance floor paired off, she watched as James made his way over to her.

His shirt sleeves rolled up to his elbows, his tie hanging loose around his neck, his once perfectly styled hair, hanging damp across his forehead, he kept his predatory gaze on her as he made use of his long stride to move quickly to her side.

He held his hand out, and didn't have to say anything. She knew what he wanted, and she wanted the same thing.

She reached her hand out and grabbed his.

He pulled her out onto the dance floor, pulling her into his arms. She wrapped her arms around his neck while he placed his hand on her waist, pulling her in close.

As Ed Sheeran sang about people falling in love and kissing under the stars, they moved together. She brought her hand to play with the hair at the back of his neck as his hands moved from her waist up her back, pulling her in even closer.

He laid his cheek onto the top of her head, and her heart skipped a beat. Just as Ed sang about finding love where he was, she couldn't hold it in anymore.

"James?"

"Hmm?"

"I like you. I really like you, and it's okay if you don't feel the same. It was something I thought you should know…"

James pulled back from her, moving one of his hands from her waist until it was under her chin, lifting her face until she was looking at him.

As he looked down at her, she could see everything he was thinking written on his face, and she didn't need his next words to know he felt the same way she did.

"I like you, too," he murmured.

Her breath caught in her throat, and she barely noticed they were no longer dancing, but standing still in the middle of the dance floor.

But it didn't matter. Nothing did. Not when he was bringing his face down to meet hers.

She held her breath in anticipation as his lips stopped a fraction from hers, waiting for her to make the last move, waiting for her to grant consent.

And grant it, she did.

She closed the gap, bringing her lips to his, sharing their first kiss.

CHAPTER 15

JAMES

They were kissing.

Tessa's lips were on his.

That's all his brain could think of as they stood in the middle of the dance floor, connected at the lips.

When his brain began working again, he moved the hand that had been cupping Tessa's chin until it was behind her head, pulling her in closer.

She wrapped her arms around him tighter, pushing her body flush against his.

He ran his tongue along the seam of her lips, and she opened to him, deepening the kiss.

It had been so long since he had kissed a woman, let alone made out with one. It had been even longer than that since the last time he'd had sex, and his body was reacting in ways he was unprepared for.

He could feel himself swell against her and adjusted his lower body. He didn't want her to think he expected more.

They were kissing on the dance floor, which was surprising all on its own.

The song changed, a loud bass began beating out of the speakers, causing the two of them to jump apart, breaking the kiss.

With everyone around them jumping around and dancing to whatever song was playing now, James and Tessa stood there.

James watched her chest rise and fall as she tried to catch her breath. When he moved his gaze back to her face, he could see her eyes widen behind her glasses, uncertainty creeping in.

"C'mon." He reached for her hand.

She didn't hesitate. She took his hand, linking her fingers with his.

He turned and pulled her from the dance floor, dragging her along with him. He pulled her toward the back door into the kitchen, weaving them through the counters where the caterers were busy cleaning up.

"Slow down," she panted from behind him. "I'm going to twist my ankle, moving so fast in heels."

"Sorry," he apologized, slowing down.

He pushed through the door, and they emerged outside, the cold air a shock against their hot, sweaty bodies.

"Wait." She stopped them. "I've left all of my things."

"We'll be back." He tugged on her hand and led them further into the alley.

Once they were far enough away from the door and ensconced in the shadows, he pushed her gently against the wall, immediately trapping her lips with his.

She returned the kiss with as much fervor as he gave.

He moved his hands up her body, and she rewarded his touch with the most tantalizing moans he had ever heard. He grew achingly hard. When he tried to move away from her, she moved her hands to his hips and held him there against her.

It was his turn to moan.

He reached down and tugged her by her thighs, lifting her so her legs wrapped around his waist. He moved in closer, pressing her firmly against the wall.

He pulled away from her mouth and moved his lips down her neck. One of her hands gripped his shoulder while the other threaded its fingers through his hair, holding tightly as they moved against one another.

He pulled back, looking at Tessa, her head thrown back against the wall, her eyes closed, panting.

"We need to stop," he breathed out.

"What? Why?" She opened her eyes, meeting his gaze. She looked distraught at the thought of stopping what they were doing.

"I don't want the first time we fuck to be in the alley."

She nodded her head vigorously. "Good point. My place or yours?"

"Yours," he answered, without hesitation. "You're closer."

He gently placed her feet on the ground and reluctantly stood back from her. They took a second to straighten out their clothes and fix their hair before James took her by the hand and led her back toward the reception hall.

"We should say goodbye to Patrick and Evelyn before we disappear." James looked back at her, his mouth curling up into a sly smile.

"And I need to get my things. I have cake boxes and my apron."

James nodded. "We won't forget those."

They made it back to the door that led into the reception hall, and James stopped them before they entered. He turned, so he was in front of her. "Before we go any farther, I wanted to check and make sure you're okay with all of this. You're a client, and you're paying me to catch a stalker. I don't want to cross any boundaries." Tessa smiled up at him. "I told you I liked you first, remember? Of course I'm fine. Are you okay with this?" James nodded before leaning down, capturing her lips in a searing kiss.

She instantly responded.

James didn't think he would ever grow tired of kissing her.

Reluctantly, he broke the kiss and led them into the reception hall.

Inside, he parted from Tessa and went in search of Patrick and Evelyn. He found them talking with her parents.

Evelyn noticed him first, her face brightening. "James! Where have you been? I need you to settle an argument for me."

James returned her smile. "What?"

"My dad thinks the best Doctor was Smith, but we all know the best is clearly Tennant. Right?"

James laughed. "What did Patrick say?"

"Whitaker, obviously," Patrick scoffed. "She and her fam made the show amazing."

James rolled her eyes. "Well, I'm sorry to say you're all wrong, because the best Doctor is Eccleston. Hands down. That is, if we're strictly speaking of New Who. If we open up the discussion to all time, the answer is completely different."

Evelyn playfully shoved James' shoulder. "Ugh, you're so annoying. You couldn't once agree with me?"

"Evie, my dear, sweet Evie, if the three of us were ever to agree on the best of anything, I'm certain the world as we know it would end. You don't want us bringing upon the apocalypse now, would you?"

Instead of answering, Evelyn launched herself at him, wrapping her arms around him, placing a kiss on his cheek. "I love you, you know."

James, taken aback, hugged her back just as tightly. "Of course I know that."

"Thank you for the beautiful speech, and for being here today, and just for everything in the past year. You're my best friend."

"You're most welcome."

She gave him one last squeeze, but before she moved away, she put her mouth up to his ear and whispered, "Now say goodbye and get back to snogging Tessa."

As she pulled away, he stared incredulously at her, his mouth moving, but no words coming out.

"Oh, don't look so surprised," she whispered. "I saw you two kiss on the dance floor and then run out of here like horny teenagers. I'm honestly surprised you're still here."

James shook his head and leaned down, placing a kiss on her cheek. "Can't get anything by you. You're not annoyed?"

"Annoyed? Why would I be annoyed?"

"It's your wedding."

She let out a stream of air and waved her hand. "I don't care. If you and her finally are acting on your feelings and it happened at *my* wedding, I get to take full credit and have bragging rights. And I'll never let you two forget I was the one who brought you two together."

"But—"

She held up her hand, stopping him. "I get full credit."

He shook his head, his grin widening. "You get full credit. Which I guess isn't too far off from the truth. I don't think I would have acted on my feelings right now without the aid of your wedding reception." He paused and thought for a second. "And if we're giving credit where credit is due, we should also credit Ed Sheeran. Because it was his song—"

"Oh, be quiet." Evelyn laughed. "Now, go. Don't keep Tessa waiting."

"Where's he going?" Patrick asked, moving to put his arm around his bride's shoulder.

James opened his mouth to answer, but Evelyn beat him to the chase.

"He and Tessa are leaving, so they can go shag like bunnies."

He caught the glint in Evelyn's eye and heard the words come out of her mouth, and wondered how long she had waited to pay him back for the teasing he'd thrown on her and Patrick way back at when their relationship was just beginning.

Patrick smiled. "Alright, James. But what happened to," Patrick held his hands up and made air quotes, "I never sleep with a client?"

James shrugged. "Something Evelyn said yesterday, combined with seeing her here tonight, made me rethink everything."

"Good. I'm glad. Now go. We'll see you when we get back from our honeymoon," Patrick drew him into a hug, "and if you need anything—"

"I'll ask Joe, because you're on your honeymoon and your mobile will be off while you spend the next two weeks relaxing and shagging your wife," James finished, giving Patrick a pointed look.

Patrick shook his head, and Evelyn laughed.

"Have a safe trip, and I'll see you in two weeks," James waved to them before turning around.

He made his way back to the kitchen and walked through the door to see Tessa standing there, wearing a large coat and holding a bag. Boxes were sitting at her feet.

"Ready?" she asked.

James bent down and picked up the boxes. "Ready."

"Brilliant, I parked Freddie's car out back. We can take it back to mine." She smiled.

James returned her smile. "Lead the way."

***

Later, James lay in the dark of Tessa's flat looking at her. She lay on her side, facing him, asleep. They hadn't pulled the blankets all the way up, baring her shoulder and most of her back to him. He smiled as he ran a hand down her bare skin.

They had come back to the flat and had barely made it across the threshold before they were shedding clothes and moving toward her bedroom.

The sex was everything he could have hoped for and more.

The pillow talk, even better.

She was in the middle of a sentence when she drifted off, and just the sight of her made his heart flutter.

They'd only known each other for a week, but he was falling in love.

His bladder took the opportunity to make itself known, so, reluctantly, he stood up from the bed, careful not to disturb her. Bending over, he picked up his boxers from the floor and pulled them on.

Quietly, he opened the door to her bedroom and made his way into the main living room. It was pitch black, and he struggled to see anything.

He moved to the curtains and opened one, letting the streetlight flood into the flat, allowing him to see the furniture. The room was still unfamiliar. He didn't want to pull a Dick van Dyke over an ottoman. He scampered around the chair and headed to the loo.

After doing his business, he moved back into the living room and walked to the window.

He took the curtain in his hand so he could draw it, but stopped short when something outside caught his eye.

It was late, and the pavement was clear, except for one lone figure standing directly across the street.

James squinted, moving closer to the window, trying to make out who it was.

The figure was all in black, with a hood pulled up over their head. They either had something over their face, or the shadows covered it, because James couldn't make out any features.

They were standing still, looking in his direction.

James cursed under his breath. His phone was in his trousers, somewhere in the flat. He glanced behind him. They were right outside the door to the bedroom. Two feet away.

He wondered if he went and got his phone, if the figure would still be there.

He turned back to look out the window.

The figure was still there, but now had something in their hand.

James frowned. He couldn't make out what it was. It seemed rectangular and thick.

He turned back and ran to his trousers, fumbling with the pockets, trying to get his phone out.

"What's going on?" Tessa asked, her voice scratchy with sleep. She moved into the doorway, her sheet wrapped around her body. She was not wearing her glasses and her hair was in an absolutely beautiful state of disarray.

"There's someone outside. Watching your flat," he told her.

She stood up straighter. "What?"

"They're dressed all in black, just standing there."

"What are you going to do?"

"I'm going to take some pictures," he stood, moving back toward the window, "and then I'll call down to the CCTV office and have them send me the footage right away." He was standing at the window, his back to it. "Maybe we can—"

A loud crash sounded through the flat, cutting him off.

"James!!" Tessa screamed.

He turned toward the window, but it was too late.

Something had flown through the window. He was alert enough to think "brick" right before it impacted his head.

The pain seared through him and knocked him off balance. As he fell, it was like he was moving in slow motion. His body hit the floor, and everything went black.

CHAPTER 16

TESSA

Tessa's heart stopped as she heard the sound of shattering glass and watched as James fell to the floor. It all happened in a flash. In a single moment, James went from walking towards the window to being thrown to the ground as glass exploded in her living room.

She moved toward him to make sure he was okay, but stopped before she even started. There was glass everywhere, and she wasn't wearing any shoes.

She also wasn't wearing any clothes.

She turned as quickly as she could and ran into her bedroom, throwing off her sheet. Before she did anything, she grabbed her glasses from her bedside table. Now she could see. Next, she ran to the wardrobe and grabbed the first thing she found and pulled it over her head. She reached in and grabbed some slip-on trainers and ran back out to the living room.

She went to the window and looked outside. She knew James would want to know if the person was still there.

They weren't. The street was empty.

She turned back and knelt down next to James.

He had been hit in the head with whatever had flown through the window. Blood was pooling next to his head, and he was unconscious.

She reached down and felt for his neck pulse. It was there, and it was strong.

She let out the breath she was holding.

His face was pale and his red hair stood out against it more starkly than normal. Blood pooled from his head onto her floor at what seemed like an alarming rate.

She ran into the kitchen and grabbed a towel.

She knelt back down next to him and pressed the towel firmly against the wound on his head.

"You're going to be okay," her voice was tight in her throat, "you're going to be okay."

Satisfied with her first aid attempt, she reached down and picked his phone up out of his hand. She scrolled through the contacts and stopped at Joe's name. She moved her finger over his name and then hesitated.

She looked at the clock. It was after two in the morning. She drew her lip into her mouth. He should be back from the wedding, but how much had he had to drink?

She called him anyway.

She pressed call and brought the phone up to her ear.

"'Lo?" a groggy voice came through the speaker.

"Joe? It's Tessa. Someone threw something through my window and hit James in the head. He's on the floor of my apartment unconscious. There is a lot of blood, and I don't..."

"Call 999 and touch nothing," Joe sounded more alert than when he first answered the phone. "I'm going to get dressed and I'll be right there. Don't panic."

The call disconnected before she could say anything else.

She immediately called 999 and told them what had happened. They told her they were sending an ambulance around at that moment.

She set down the phone and stood up. Looking down at James, with the bloody towel against his head, she decided he would be okay for a minute. She went into her room and picked up her phone and hit the first name in her contacts.

"What's wrong?" Freddie answered on the first ring.

"James." Her voice broke at the sound of her best friend's voice, and she was unable to say anything more.

"What did he do?"

"He didn't do anything. Someone threw something through my window, it hit him..."

"I'm on my way."

"The police and ambulance are on their way—"

"I'm on my way," Freddie repeated.

"Okay."

"Tessa?"

"Yeah?"

"Everything is going to be okay."

The call ended and Tessa set her phone down. She needed to go down and open the shop door so the emergency services could get in. Looking at James, she threw open her door and ran down the back stairs entering into the shop. She rushed through the shop to the front door and flipped the lock before hurrying back upstairs into her flat, immediately back into the living room to kneel next to James.

Joe told her not to touch anything, but stopping James' bleeding didn't count. She pressed her hands against the towel again, hoping pressure would stop the blood.

Tears rolled down her cheek. She tried to wipe them away with her shoulder, but it didn't really help.

Lights flashed through her windows and the sirens grew louder. The ambulance. That was quick.

She listened as the door to the shop opened and there was a rhythmic pounding coming up the stairwell. Followed by a knock on her front door.

She stood and rushed to the door, throwing it open.

She stepped aside and everyone rushed in. There were two EMTs. Following them were two police officers, followed by Joe, who was still wearing his tux pants and dress shirt.

"Tessa," he stopped in front of her, "this is PC Randolph and PC Davies. They're going to move around your flat and collect evidence. I'm going to take your statement."

"You're still in your wedding clothes."

Joe looked down at what he was wearing. "I am. And you're in an oversized t-shirt with a Tardis on it."

Tessa looked down at what she was wearing and noticed she had grabbed a shirt dress with the Tardis and the Tenth Doctor on it.

She shrugged. "I don't see a problem with what I'm wearing."

"And I don't see a problem with what I'm wearing."

The two stood there looking at one another, neither one wanting to voice what the other suspected the other of having done.

Joe gestured to the hall. "Let's stand out here and talk."

Tessa looked around him at where the paramedics were lifting James onto a stretcher to move him from the flat.

"He'll be fine," Joe reassured her.

Tessa nodded absentmindedly and moved out into the hall, not taking her eyes off of James.

"Tell me what happened."

"I was asleep, and I heard something moving in the living room. I noticed James wasn't in bed with me anymore, so I got up to look for him. When I moved into the doorway of my bedroom, I saw James digging in his trousers to get his phone. That's when he told me he could see someone on the pavement watching the flat. He wanted to take some pictures and then call the CCTV people to send him the footage. He had just turned around to walk back to the window when the glass sort of imploded into the room. And something, whatever caused the glass to break, hit James in the head and he fell to the ground."

Joe looked up from the notepad. "Did you see what broke the window?"

Tessa shook her head. "I didn't. Just heard the glass breaking and then I watched James go down. After that, I was too concerned about James to bother looking. Especially after you told me not to touch anything."

Joe nodded. "You did the right thing."

"Tess!"

Tessa turned around to see Freddie jogging up the stairs and down the small hallway to her flat. He was wearing pajama bottoms and a shirt that matched hers.

"Freddie." She met him halfway and embraced him.

"Scuz us."

They moved apart to let the paramedics by as they carried James away.

Tessa tried to follow them, but Joe stopped her with his hand. "They'll let us know which hospital he's taken to, and I'll bring you with me when I go over there."

Tessa nodded, turning back to Joe. "Is there anything else you need to know?"

"Did you see anyone on the street?"

She shook her head. "No, um, I went to look as soon as I put shoes on, since I know James would have wanted to know, but the street was empty."

"Why didn't James say he was going to call the police on the person watching your flat?"

"Oh, c'mon, you know why," Freddie stated. "You all are bloody useless when it comes to stalking. Tessa and I called about the letters multiple times."

"I was told the police couldn't do anything until the stalker escalated and actually threatened me," Tess wrapped her arms around her body.

Freddie stepped forward and wrapped his arm around her shoulder, pulling her close. "And they told us sending letters was technically not against the law."

"And I'm pretty sure standing on a public street in the middle of the night isn't breaking any laws either." Tessa's fear started transforming into anger. "The whole reason I had to hire James and Patrick in the first place was because the police were no help. So, I'm guessing that is why calling you was the last thing on James' mind before someone destroyed my flat."

"So, has the situation escalated enough for you lot to finally get off your arses and do something about this tosser?" Freddie asked, malice in his voice.

Joe held his hands up. "Look, I'm on your side. I even talked to James about your case the day he took it on. My hands were tied. But, you're right. This has escalated enough to warrant me to sign on and work the case from an official capacity."

Tessa perked up at what he said.

"However," Joe continued. "Unfortunately, this is going to be categorized as a vandalism case, since they threw something through your window. James and Patrick, when he gets back from his honeymoon, are going to still need to work on the case from a stalker angle. But since we're obviously looking for the same person, we'll be working on the same case."

"That's fucking bullshit," Freddie bit out. "Her fucking life is in danger, and unless the stalker is in here holding a gun to her head, you can't do anything. Throw something through her window, and we've got vandalism when it's obviously tied to the stalker. The law is shit."

"Yeah, well, take it up with your MP and get them to change the law," Joe stated with infinite patience. He was probably used to people going off on him.

Freddie and Joe stood in the hall, staring at one another. Their eyes locked. Tessa could sense the palpable tension radiating between the two men.

Freddie opened his mouth, like he wanted to say something else, but PC Davies stepped into the hallway holding a plastic bag in his hand. Inside the bag was a brick.

"What's that?" Tessa asked.

"Looks like it was what smashed in your window and smacked into your boyfriend's head."

"A brick? Where would he even find a brick?"

"We're in London. I don't think he would have had to go very far to find one," Joe stated.

Tessa and Freddie shrugged.

"What's interesting about this brick is it's no ordinary brick. It's an angry brick," Officer Davies explained.

Tessa tilted her head. "I'm sorry. Did you say it's an *angry* brick?"

"What on earth makes a brick angry?" Freddie asked.

PC Davies turned the bag around in his hands until the opposite side was facing them. "When someone scrawls cruel words on them."

Tessa brought her hands to her mouth as it dropped open.

Scrawled in black ink in big block letters spelled the word 'WHORE.'

CHAPTER 17

JAMES

James opened his eyes to be met with a bright light that was so intense it made him instinctively shut his eyes. He was obviously not in Tessa's flat anymore.

Shutting his eyes, he used his remaining senses to assess the situation. The air smelled of sterility and antiseptic, and his head fucking hurt.

Slowly, everything started coming back to him. The wedding. Tessa. The stranger on the street. The window smashing.

His eyes flew open. "Tessa," he whispered, struggling to sit himself up.

"Whoa there, mate. Let's lay back down. Tessa is fine."

James turned to see Patrick next to his bed.

"What are you doing here?" James asked.

"I'm your emergency contact."

"Shit," James muttered, settling back on the bed. "You're supposed to be on your honeymoon."

Patrick laughed. "It's four o'clock in the bloody morning, the day after my wedding. I'm supposed to be in bed with my wife. We don't leave on our trip until tomorrow morning, remember?"

"I'm sorry."

Patrick scoffed. "Sorry? What do you have to be sorry for? You didn't put yourself in the hospital. It's the arsehole who threw a brick through Tessa's window who should be sorry."

"A brick?"

"A brick."

James lifted his hand to his head, feeling the bandage on the left side of his forehead.

"You know," Patrick dragged the chair closer to James' bed before sitting down, "getting a head injury is completely unnecessary in pursuing a mate."

James looked over at Patrick. His scar from when he got shot last year was still red, not quite to the point of fading. Before the accident, Patrick had kept his hair short, but ever since, he had grown it out, wearing his hair over his forehead, covering the scar. The publicity surrounding the trial made them minor local celebrities, and everyone wanted to see the scar left by a top police officer in their borough.

"It's not like I tried. Didn't expect a brick to fly through the window at me, did I?"

"No one expects a brick to be thrown through a window." Patrick laughed. "Why would you?"

"How bad is my injury?"

"Four stitches and a minor concussion. You'll be fine."

"Tessa?"

"Uninjured, but extremely worried for you. She was here for a little while, but Freddie took her back to his to take a nap. She'll be back in a couple of hours."

James closed his eyes. "I didn't get a picture of the bastard."

"Joe is getting the CCTV footage as we speak. We'll be able to see the person standing there and throwing the brick. If we're lucky, other cameras caught him through the city."

"He had his face covered, and he was wearing a hoodie. We won't get anything."

"His face was covered at *Tessa's*," Patrick explained. "There's a possibility he could have uncovered his face at any time to and from the shop."

James opened his eyes. "When did you become the optimistic one?"

Patrick shrugged. "I think Evelyn is rubbing off on me."

"Was she angry you had to leave?"

He shook his head. "Nah, mate. She was worried about you. She wanted to come, but we didn't know if they would allow her to come back. We didn't know how serious your injuries were. She and her sisters are going to clean out the suite and take our stuff back to the flat. Your stuff will be at ours. You can let yourself in with your key and get it whenever you need. After, she's helping her family get off to Heathrow, and then she'll stop by here."

"My laptop was running the facial recognition software."

"It was done by the time we got back to the suite. I saved the files before I shut your computer down. I packed it into your bag."

"Is there any way you can convince Evelyn to bring the computer with her when she comes to visit?"

Patrick frowned. "Mate. Do you really think you should work right now? You're in hospital. Someone hit you in the head with a bloody brick. You should be resting."

James shook his head. "I just need to check the facial recognition. It's going to bother me if I don't. I want to make sure Tessa is safe."

Patrick didn't say anything. He just pulled his mobile out and typed something into it. "I'm only doing this because if it were Evelyn in danger, I would make the same choice." After he tucked his phone back into his pocket, he looked at James and smirked. "So, you and Tessa..."

James smiled while shaking his head. "Me and Tessa."

"That's great news!"

"Thanks. But don't be getting ahead of yourself and planning double dates. It was one night, and it ended with her window shattered and me in hospital. She's probably already told Freddie what a mistake it was to bring me home."

Patrick shook his head. "Quite the opposite, actually. Bringing you home caused the stalker to escalate to committing a crime the police can actually investigate. She was telling Freddie she should have made a move on you sooner."

"The police are investigating? Who's in charge?"

"Joe."

"Thank God."

"My thoughts exactly."

"How long until they let me out of this place?"

Patrick shrugged. "They didn't say. Considering you've been unconscious, my best guess is you'll be stuck in here for a while longer. They'll probably set you free later today."

James leaned his head back on the bed and closed his eyes. He was exhausted. "Sounds great. I think I'm just going to rest my eyes for a bit, if that's okay with you?"

He didn't hear Patrick's reply. He was already asleep.

***

When he woke again, someone else was sitting in the chair next to his bed. He smiled once his eyes adjusted, and he could see who it was.

"You're here."

Tessa looked up from the book she was reading and smiled. "I'm here."

"Where's Patrick?"

She set her book down on her bag next to the chair. "Evelyn called, saying she was on her way and bringing food. He went to meet her so they could eat before coming up. How're you feeling?"

"Like a brick hit me." He looked up at her and grinned.

Tessa shook her head, not cracking a smile. "Not. Funny."

"C'mon, it's a bit funny."

She shook her head again, still not smiling. "Someone threw a brick through my window with the word 'whore' scrawled on it. The same someone they're thinking who has been stalking me, although Joe can't comment on it in any sort of capacity. My flat no longer has a front window. You're in hospital because said brick smacked you in the head. And you're sitting here, cracking jokes."

James sobered. "I'm sorry. I'll stop if it makes you feel better."

"Thank you."

"Wait, did you say they'd written on the brick?"

She nodded. "They did."

"So, it's my fault."

"What do you mean?"

"He must've seen me go home with you. In a fit of jealousy, he hurled the brick through your window."

"Or, he was angry I'm not appreciating his advances and lashed out." Tessa reasoned.

James sighed. "You're right. That's the more logical explanation."

Tessa tilted her ear toward him. "I'm sorry. I don't think I heard you clearly. You said that I'm what?"

"You're right." He chuckled.

"That's what I thought. Now seriously, how is your head?"

"It aches. Patrick told me I have a concussion. I don't know how much longer I'll need to stay in here."

"I'm staying at Freddie's for a bit. I don't want to stay in my flat right now."

"I don't blame you. What about the shop?"

"It's Sunday, so we're closed today, but I'll open as normal tomorrow as long as the police say it's okay."

James nodded. "I can work from the shop tomorrow, if you'd like."

"If you're not here, you should be at home resting."

"I just want to make sure you're safe."

"I'm an adult, James. I don't need anyone watching out for me. Besides, I won't be there alone. I'll have Freddie and Mariel. And about five hundred people in search of pumpkin bars. Whoever this is won't try anything whilst I am working at the shop."

"I know, but—"

"No," Tessa interrupted firmly. "No. If we're going to move forward in some kind of relationship, then we need to have an understanding. I'm not some fucking damsel in distress and you're not a white knight riding to my rescue."

James sat up taller in his bed. "Look, I'm not trying to be a white knight, I'm just concerned—"

"Then be concerned. That's fine. Don't hover. I am thirty years old. I don't need a babysitter. If you're going to be concerned, do it from afar."

James frowned. "So, you don't want me around at all? How will that foster any sort of relationship?"

"You can be around. I would love for you to come 'round and hang out. But I can't have you just sitting in my bloody shop hovering."

"When Patrick was protecting Evie—"

"I don't need protecting, though, do I?"

"You have a fucking stalker! You are in danger!" James worked hard to keep his voice down, being mindful they were in a hospital room.

"He's *never* threatened me outright," she defended, using her pointer finger to emphasize her point.

James' face tensed, and he had a powerful urge to shout. He closed his eyes and inhaled deeply, feeling the tension in his face dissipate. "The brick through your window would beg to differ."

"Calling me a whore is not a threat," she argued.

"It's not the word, it's the action that is the threat."

Tessa drew her lips in tight, forming them into thin lines, her nostrils flaring. "If we can't agree on this, I don't think we are going to work as a couple. And I may need to request Patrick take over the case full time, and you step back."

James opened his mouth to argue, but she cut him off.

"No. This is non-negotiable. And before you invoke Patrick and Evie, their situation was completely different. Completely. There was no other choice other than her living with you, and there were active violent threats against her. My stalker seems to just want to be with me, not want to kill me, as that would be counterproductive to their agenda."

James was silent. He wanted to argue, but she was making some good points. Their situation differed from Patrick and Evie's.

He really wanted to protect Tessa. His gut was aching to keep her safe. However, he also wanted to see where whatever this thing between them was would go. He didn't want to lose the case.

The only solution would be to put away his chauvinistic instincts to protect, and to just stand back and give her the space she needs.

"Okay," he stated.

"Okay?" Tessa asked, her body relaxing as the anger seemed to drain from her body with that one word. "That's it? Okay? No more arguing?"

James shook his head. "No more arguing. If we're going to explore whatever this is, then we need to listen to each other and trust one another. So, okay. I won't set up a spot at your shop to work. I will text you periodically throughout the day to make sure you're doing okay."

"But not excessively texting." Tessa tacked on, holding her finger up, giving him a pointed look.

"Not excessively. Maybe when I know you're winding down for the day at the shop? And when I finish up at the office? And before I know you go to sleep?"

Tessa smiled. "Sometimes before I go to sleep and when you leave from the office is the same."

"True. So that would mean only two messages a day. Reasonable?"

Tessa pretended she was thinking it over. "It's good for now. We'll give it a trial run and reevaluate in a few days."

James relaxed as he laughed at Tessa's negotiation skills. "I can still come in for sweets, yeah? Before pumpkin season is officially over, I would like to get one or five more pumpkin bars before you bring in the different treats for Christmas."

Tessa leaned forward until her arms were resting on his bed, folding them perpendicular to her body, tilting her head, her gaze locked on to his. "Or," she started, her voice low, "I could come to yours and bake you an entire batch of pumpkin bars of your very own, and..." she trailed off, raising her eyebrows, looking pointedly into his eyes.

He caught her meaning.

"Yeah," he cleared his throat. "I like that plan. Come to my house and we can," this time he paused, tilting his head forward, almost conspiratorially, really leaning into emphasizing the next word, "bake."

When Tessa's face colored at his declaration, his chest swelled with pride. Along with other parts of his body. He leaned back into his bed, relaxing into his pillow and willed those other parts to calm down. They were in no position to do anything. They were in hospital, for fuck's sake.

Tessa practically jumped in her seat when they heard the knock on the hospital room door, like whoever it was had caught her in the act.

The door swung open, revealing Patrick and Evie, the latter with James' laptop bag slung over her shoulder.

"You look a lot better than I imagined when we got the call in the middle of the night," Evie walked over to give him a quick peck on his cheek.

"'Tis but a scratch," James teased.

"Well, I didn't know that when Patrick got called to go to A&E. All I could picture was you lying in a pool of blood, bleeding out from a gunshot wound."

"To be fair, he was lying in a pool of blood," Tessa spoke up. "There was *so* much blood."

Evie moved into the room until she was standing next to Tessa. She gave the other woman a quick, tight hug before pulling back into her own space. "It was the same when Patrick got injured. Head wounds bleed so much."

"I think I remember reading about him being injured during the trial," Tessa said.

Evie nodded. "During the Fitzgerald hoopla, his mentor shot him in the head."

"The bullet grazed me," Patrick clarified, lifting his hair to show off his scar. "Same spot as this bloke, only deeper. Now we match."

Tessa shook her head. "Thank goodness it was a brick and not a bullet."

"The way the glass of the window exploded, for a split second I was worried it was a bullet," James said.

"Me, too," Tessa agreed.

The four friends grew somber thinking about the close calls both men had.

"Hand it over," James gestured to the computer hanging from Evie's shoulder.

Evie slid the strap of the bag down her arm before handing the bag over to James. "Let the record show, I completely disagree with you working from your hospital bed."

"Noted," James extracted the computer from the bag.

Tessa removed the bag from the bed, setting it on the floor while James balanced the computer on his lap, booting it up.

Patrick moved to the head of the bed so he could see the computer screen. "So, are we hoping the software found something or not?"

James shrugged. "Honestly, I don't know."

He pulled up the files Patrick saved and opened them.

Patrick let out a low whistle.

"What is it?" Tessa asked, leaning forward in her chair again.

James turned the computer so both she and Evie could see the screen.

"Apparently, your old friend Bruno is a regular at your shop."

CHAPTER 18

TESSA

Tessa stared at the computer screen.

There was her old friend, Bruno. He looked almost exactly like he did when she had last seen him back in school. Except older. His blond hair, which he wore long and messy in school, was cut shorter and styled nicely. He was wearing slacks and a button-down shirt. The video was a profile, but she would recognize his Roman nose anywhere. It was a feature he was very insecure over when they were teens.

She struggled to find her voice, or any words to convey what she was feeling by what she saw.

James' facial recognition program found two dozen instances of Bruno visiting her shop.

Two. Dozen.

"Have you ever seen him come into the shop?" Evelyn asked, quietly.

Tessa shook her head. "I haven't seen him in person since we left school."

"How? If he's been coming to your shop so many times?"

James turned the computer back to face him. She watched as he clicked around before turning it back to face them.

He clicked on a video. "So, I went back to the video feeds where the program pulled these photos. And look at this."

The video played, and they all watched as Bruno would approach the shop, stand staring in the front window for a few minutes before turning and walking away.

"He didn't go in." Tessa couldn't believe what she was seeing. "Why didn't he go in?"

James read the date and time. "Do you remember if you were working the counter?"

Tessa shook her head. "I don't know. It's been so mad in the shop the last few weeks. I can't pinpoint whether I was in the front or back at that exact moment."

James peered over the top of the computer and clicked another video.

It was the same as the first. Bruno walked to the shop. Stopped. Spent several minutes looking through the shop window before walking away without going in.

James clicked through all twenty-four videos. They were all the same.

"He's never been in the shop," Tessa commented. "Not once."

"In some videos, he seems to spend longer looking in the window than others," Patrick pointed out.

"Do you think those times he spends longer are when Tessa is working the counter?" Evelyn posed.

"It seems logical," James answered.

"I don't understand why he would stop by so often, only to *never* step foot inside to talk to me. What reason would he have?" Tessa asked.

James looked at her over his computer, and the way he was looking at her, she didn't even need him to say anything else.

"Is this proof he's my stalker?" she asked, pointing at the computer.

"I mean, it's not definitive proof, but it's pretty compelling," James stated.

Tessa let out a breath. Bruno. Really?

"What do we do with this?"

"James can stake out his flat. Follow him around a little. See if he's the one coming and snooping around your flat at night. We can pass this lead along to Joe and he can question him," Patrick explained.

"So, you will stalk him, like he's been stalking me?" she asked.

"I wouldn't phrase it like that, but basically, yes."

Tessa bit her lip. "How long until the police will have CCTV footage of last night?"

James shook his head. "Dunno. I can call Joe and get an update on the case. Or I'm sure he or another officer will be here to question me about last night."

Tessa slumped back in her chair, throwing her head back against the headrest. She closed her eyes.

Most of the time, she could tuck this whole stalker thing to the back of her mind and carry on. But now? Now it was taking over her life.

She was supposed to wake up this morning curled up in James' arms before getting out of bed and making Chelsea buns.

Instead, she was sitting next to his hospital bed.

"When will this all be over?" she asked without opening her eyes.

She felt Evelyn place a comforting hand on her shoulder. "These things take time."

"I know," she took a breath, calming herself. "I know. But I just want everything to go back to normal."

"And they will," Evelyn gave her shoulder a squeeze. "Or, if not normal, maybe something close."

Tessa opened her eyes and looked up at her new friend. If anyone knew even remotely what she was going through, it would be Evie.

And as she looked at Evie, she could see someone who was happy.

Tessa sat up and looked at James, and smiled.

Maybe this entire experience would have one positive outcome after all.

***

Tessa knocked on Freddie's door.

She was exhausted, and all she wanted to do was go to sleep.

She had stayed at the hospital until it was clear James was going to be released.

The police had come and questioned him and after he told them the same things she had; they had also informed them they had just received the CCTV footage, but it would be several hours until they heard anything about it.

Once the hospital released James, Patrick and Evelyn had taken him home and she headed to Freddie's.

Freddie's door swung open, revealing her friend. He was wearing a t-shirt and sweats, his feet bare. Sundays were lazy days when you worked at a bakery.

"You could have used your key." He stood aside so she could enter.

"I didn't want to just barge inside in case you had a girl, or a guy, here." She entered his flat, undoing her coat as she walked.

Freddie scoffed as he closed the door, and dead bolted it. "I am far from ready to be entertaining any paramours. Especially when my best friend is in crisis."

Tessa dropped her bag next to the couch before falling onto it. She waited for Freddie to sit before she dropped the bombshell on him.

"Bruno has been stopping by the shop, staring through the window and walking away."

"What?" Freddie exclaimed. "How often?"

"Two dozen times in the time frame of the CCTV footage James and Patrick have."

"The fuck?"

"You never saw him? All those times you were manning the counter?"

He shook his head. "No. Although to be fair, I started helping at the front of the shop once it became a madhouse, once word of your pumpkin bars spread. Mariel might have seen something. If he was coming to the shop during the summer, before the autumn rush, she might've noticed something."

Tessa perked up. "Freddie, you're brilliant."

She pulled out her phone and opened to Bruno's social media and took a screenshot of his picture. She then opened up her messages and sent the picture to Mariel, asking if she had ever seen this man around.

"How's James?" Freddie asked once she had tucked her phone away.

"He's fine. They let him go home with orders to rest."

"That's good. I'm glad he's okay," he paused. "How are you?"

"Frustrated," she answered immediately. "Angry. Scared."

Freddie looked at her, nodding. "These are all understandable and very valid emotions that you are feeling. I am also frustrated and angry. I really wish there were more I could do for you."

"You're doing plenty, letting me stay here."

"Well, it's the least I can do. Unfortunately, staying here is going to be a huge inconvenience to you tomorrow."

Tessa groaned. "Oh, fuck. I'd forgotten. You live so far from the shop. I'm going to need to get up so fucking early," she moaned.

"Hopefully, it will only be for a few days. I've left a few messages with some window people and with insurance. Since your flat is part of the shop, we should be able to cover fixing it through the insurance."

"Thanks for taking care of everything. You didn't need to."

"I'm the money guy. It's my job. Besides, I needed to keep myself busy, otherwise I would be worried about you and James, or pacing around angrily wanting to punch whoever it was who threw the brick."

"Don't go beat up, Bruno. We don't even know if he's the one stalking me." Tessa cautioned Freddie, shooting him a look that left no room for argument.

"I'll promise I won't seek him out, but I can't guarantee I'll leave him alone if he walks into the shop."

"You can't just accuse him of stalking me."

"I won't. But I will tell him to get the fuck out of our shop. He's not welcome there after what he did in our last year of school. I'm glad I haven't run into him since we left. I would have probably already walloped him. Fucker deserves a beating for what he did."

"You already beat the shit out of him while we were in school, immediately after the incident," Tessa pointed out.

"Yeah, well, I didn't get it all out of my system. Teachers pulled me off of him way too quickly."

Tessa shook her head. "You're mad."

"What I can't understand is what happened to him. We were all such great friends, and then he drifts away, and comes back into our lives inappropriately obsessed with you. How many times had he watched you in the loo before you noticed?"

She made a face. "I try not to think about it."

Her phone buzzed, and she picked it up, checking the texts. It was from Mariel. When she read her reply, her stomach dropped.

Mariel: Oh, yeah! He used to stop by the shop all the time! Hasn't been in a for a while though.

CHAPTER 19

JAMES

James answered the phone on the first ring.

"You just spent all day with me in the hospital. Are you missing me already?"

"Bruno used to come into the shop all the time, but stopped once it became too crowded," Tessa's voice came through his phone. She was speaking hurriedly, a panicked edge to her voice.

"He what?"

"I sent his picture to Mariel, and she told me he used to come in and have a chat. When the shop started becoming busy, he stopped," Tessa repeated, slower this time.

"Did she say what he would come in and chat about?"

"She said it was small talk, mostly. He would come in and buy something and chat about the weather or which football team was playing. Then, a week before he stopped, he started asking questions about me."

"What sorts of questions?"

"Dunno. Mariel couldn't remember specifically. All she said was she didn't answer any of them because he was acting dodgy."

"Have you ever told Mariel about your stalker?" James asked.

"No. I don't know her well enough to tell her something like this. And with Freddie working the counter once the stalking escalated, I never saw the need to fill her in."

"Which would explain why she never thought to tell you about the man who was coming 'round the shop asking questions," James surmised.

"Exactly."

"This new information is pretty damning. He's been around the shop a lot. He very well could be the one dropping off pictures and letters."

"Is there any way to know for certain?"

"I'm on my own for the next couple of weeks while Patrick is on his honeymoon. There are two things I can do, and I'll do them in whichever order you would like. First, I can compare the images and video we have of Bruno to the ones we have of the stalker. See if they have any similar physical features."

"That sounds like a lot of tedious work." James could hear the pity in her voice.

"Yes, and it may be fruitless."

"What's the second?"

"The second is I can tail him. See where he goes. We know the stalker spends time outside the shop, watching it. I can follow him around for a couple of days and see where he goes and see if he favors dark alleys near your shop."

Tessa grew quiet on the other end of the line. He could tell she was weighing the two options, trying to figure out which one would help her life go back to normal the soonest.

"Do the second one," she answered after a minute.

"The stakeout?"

"Yes. I think that would give me the most definitive answer of the two, and you won't be stuck in front of a computer screen for hours."

"Thanks for looking out for my eyesight."

"You can't read a recipe if you can't see."

James grinned. "You're really going to teach me how to bake?"

"Of course. I can't be the only baker in this relationship."

Warmth spread in James' chest at the discussion of their relationship in terms that sounded long term.

"How about we hold my first lesson this week?"

"How does Tuesday sound?"

James tried to be stoic, but the thrill in his voice was unmistakable. "Tuesday sounds great."

"And I want you to know, I'm not just using you because your flat is closer to the bakery than Freddie's. I truly want to teach you how to bake the pumpkin bars." Tessa teased.

James had to bite his bottom lip to stop the groan from coming out. "I would never accuse you of using me."

"Glad we're on the same page. I better go. I need to get to sleep since I'm no longer living above my place of work, and Freddie's place is so far away it's like he lives on another planet."

James laughed. "Sleep well. I'll keep you posted on what I find out about Bruno."

"I appreciate it. Stay safe."

"You, too."

They hung up, and James couldn't help but perform a happy dance. As he spun around, stomping his feet, his gaze caught on the kitchen. He and Joe had been so occupied with their jobs and the wedding preparations, the dust and grime had started to accumulate in their flat. The kitchen would not pass a health code inspection in its current state.

"Oh, fuck."

He stopped dancing and walked into the kitchen, grabbing the cleaning supplies along the way.

***

James pulled the MINI-Cooper up next to the curb across the street from Bruno's residence.

According to LinkedIn, he worked from home. It took minimal sleuthing to find his house. Yes. House. Not flat. Whatever Bruno did, it must pay well.

James had woken early to make sure he arrived at the house before a normal work hour would have begun, just in case Bruno didn't work from home.

He settled in, making sure his camera with the long-range lens was ready to go and within reach in case he needed to grab it in a hurry. Reaching into the center console, he grabbed a breakfast bar, tearing it from its wrapping.

As he ate, he fought to keep his eyes open. He had stayed up pretty late, making sure the kitchen and the rest of his flat were immaculate before finally falling into bed to grab a couple of hours of sleep.

His phone buzzed.

TESSA: Good morning.

He smiled and looked at the clock. The shop had been open for a few of hours already, so that must mean Tessa had some downtime.

JAMES: Good morning. How's the shop?

TESSA: Just finished the morning rush. Mariel arrived minutes ago, so I'm back in the kitchen to get ahead on the baking.

TESSA: Are you at Bruno's?

JAMES: I am.

TESSA: Be safe.

JAMES: I will be.

TESSA: X

James smiled down at his phone. The kiss was a pleasant surprise. Without thinking about it, he sent one back.

He set his phone down and picked up his canister of coffee, taking a large sip. As he was setting it back down, the door to Bruno's house opened and the man in question stepped out, wearing track pants and an old T-Shirt.

James picked up his camera and snapped a few pictures as Bruno made his way to a red Corsa parked directly in front of his house. James smiled. A red car. Easy to tail.

He set the camera down on the passenger seat and turned the car back on. When Bruno pulled away, James pulled out into traffic and stayed a reasonable following distance behind him. Traffic was still a little thin, thankfully, so it should be easy to follow him.

The hunt was on.

***

The hunt was fucking boring.

James leaned his head back on the headrest of the Cooper and closed his eyes.

After Bruno left the gym, he had come straight back home and never left.

The curtains were all drawn, and all James could do was sit and wait. He planned to stick it out into the night, as Tessa's stalker seemed to watch her flat when it was dark.

But so far, Bruno seemed to live an extraordinarily boring, normal existence, and James was worried he was going to have to sit out here again another day to see if there was a break in the pattern.

But not tomorrow.

Tomorrow was for baking with Tessa.

The passenger door swung open, and Joe slipped into the seat.

"Oh, thank fuck you're here," James exalted.

"Being a bit melodramatic, are you?" Joe laughed.

"Mate, nothing has happened in the last four hours," James explained. "Nothing. He walked back into the house and hasn't left or opened any blinds. I'm starting to go mad."

"Only because you're hungry." Joe handed over a bag from The Deli Downstairs.

James immediately tore it open and pulled out his sausage roll, taking a big bite.

"Thank you so much. I was starving," he said, talking around the food in his mouth.

"Yes, I gathered that when I got your text, which read," Joe pulled out his phone and read, "Mate, bring me food. I'm feeling rumbly in my tumbly." Joe shot James a look that screamed annoyance.

James gestured out his window at Bruno's house. "Nothing has happened, remember? Bored. So, fucking bored."

Joe reached into the pocket of his jacket and dropped an old music player onto the dash. "Also, grabbed that out of your room and added the next couple of books in your Wheel of Time series onto it. Next time, be a better scout next time and come prepared."

"Thank you," James tried to sound sincere this time. "I honestly thought this would be a bit more exciting."

"The bloke works from home. What on earth did you think would happen?"

James shrugged. "Dunno. Maybe working from home was what he wrote on his profile and he lived some sort of torrid double life as an MI6 agent?"

Joe rolled his eyes. "Next time go into it assuming what you see is what you get and bring your fucking book player."

"Yes, mum," James took another large bite of his sausage roll.

"Before I head back to work, I should let you know we have been going through the CCTV footage, and while we have the perpetrator on film loitering in front of Tessa's and throwing the brick through the bloody window, we have yet to find any footage of them without the hoodie or the face covering."

"Bugger it all," James growled. "Did he bring the brick with him, or did he go off and find the brick after loitering?"

"See," Joe started, adjusting himself so he could fully face James. "That's the interesting part. He had been loitering near the flat for a full hour before you and Tessa arrived at the shop from the wedding. And when we watched him walking down the street, he was already carrying the brick."

James sat up straighter, setting the sausage roll down on the dash, before turning to face Joe. "What?"

"He had already been there. With the brick."

"That doesn't add up. Logically, the order of events should have been as followed: he's already there, we arrive together, he leaves to find a brick and scrawl whore on it, returns and throws the brick through the window when he sees me looking out at him."

"I agree. It doesn't make any sense. However, it is what happened."

James furrowed his brow, picking up his sausage roll. As he ate, he ran a variety of scenarios through his mind. As he was stuffing the last bite into his mouth, it came to him.

"Get more CCTV footage," he said quickly after swallowing his food.

"How much more? And what are we looking for?"

"I would go two nights back," James explained. "Look to see if the stalker has been standing outside the flat. Then track to see when he first brings the brick with him."

Joe pulled out his notepad and took notes. "What's your theory?"

"Three nights before the wedding Tessa called because the stalker had escalated to sending text messages. I went over to her flat and spent a while with Freddie and her going over scenarios in which the stalker could text her. I left alone. He might have seen me go in and out and started drawing conclusions."

"Why would he suddenly decide she was sleeping with you now rather than all the other times you had been over?"

"I had never been up to her flat until then," James explained. "She's always come to my office."

Joe nodded. "Fair point, but Freddie was also there."

"But I don't think he knew that," James explained. "Freddie typically arrives and leaves through the back entrance in the alley. There's no way he could have known whether or not Freddie was there."

Joe nodded again, making notes. "I'll have them pull CCTV footage from the street. What day does the footage you have end?"

James gave him the date.

Joe wrote it down. "I'll have them pull from that point forward. We'll see if we notice any patterns. Did you notice any in the footage you have?"

James shook his head. "It's all erratic. Nothing consistent other than he obviously knows where the cameras are and has been good at hiding his face."

"Do you only have the cameras around the shop?"

"Yeah."

"We'll pull from the shop to the tube station. He comes and goes in that direction. I'll have some rookies comb over all the extra footage and see if we can find anything."

"Do you have all the footage now for the night of the brick incident?"

"We do."

"And he has hidden his face in all of them?"

Joe nodded. "He knows where all the cameras are. He comes out from a building, we're not sure which one, and as he walks, he puts on the face covering, keeping his face away from cameras."

"I wonder when the face covering began." James mused.

"My guess is when Tessa hired you to find the bastard."

"Any other leads?"

Joe set down his pen and grinned. "That's what else I wanted to tell you. They got a print from the brick."

CHAPTER 20

TESSA

Tessa sighed as the strap on the canvas bag she had slung over her shoulder slipped down her arm again. She had had a successful journey to James' flat from Freddie's via the tube, yet the walk from the station to the flat was proving to be a challenge.

She had two tote bags with ingredients to cook dinner and bake pumpkin bars in addition to an overnight bag. Taking the overnight bag seemed a little awkward and presumptive, but all their texting and calls since the wedding implied that she would stay the night, and she didn't want to risk not being ready.

She made it to the door of James' flat and knocked.

The door swung open and Joe was standing there, his police shirt unbuttoned, exposing his white vest. He had a bottle of beer hanging from the fingers of his left hand.

"'Ello, Tessa," he greeted with a smile.

Tessa's stomach dropped. Had she completely misread the situation? Why was Joe here? And why was he the one answering the door?

"Hello."

"Come in. James is still getting ready."

Tessa pushed her way past Joe, walking fully into the flat. As she stepped into the living room, she was pleasantly surprised.

The flat was much cleaner than expected, considering two young bachelors lived there. It was also larger than she expected.

"I know you're probably wondering why I'm still here, but don't worry," Joe moved to perch himself on one of the stools set at the kitchen island to finish his beer. "I'll be out of your hair soon. Came home to clean up before heading out to the clubs."

Tessa frowned. "It's Tuesday."

"Yeah, but it's my Friday," Joe explained, taking a sip of his beer. "It kind of sucks being off in the middle of the week. The clubs are mostly empty, but I'm usually able to pull, so it all works out in the end."

"So, you're not in a serious relationship, I take it?" Tessa asked, moving into the kitchen to set down her canvas bags of food.

Joe shook his head. "Nah. I don't know if I'm the 'serious relationship' type, to be honest. Too many men out there to just commit to one."

Tessa smiled. "If you say so."

Joe took another drink of his beer before setting the empty bottle down on the counter and pointing at her. "Hey, your friend Freddie. Is he single? If so, think I could pull him? He feels a bit out of my league, but a man could dream, yeah?"

Tessa laughed. "He is single. He just got out of a long-term relationship. His fiancée broke off their engagement a couple weeks before the wedding, in fact. We were talking last night, and I'm not sure he's ready for a serious relationship."

Joe nodded. "Rebound sex is the hottest sex." He spoke those words as if they were a sacred mantra.

Tessa wrinkled her nose. "Boundary number one. Freddie is like my brother. If you pull him, I don't want to hear about it."

Joe laughed. "No problem." He mimed zipping his lips. "We'll keep our torrid affair under wraps."

Tessa shook her head, pulling out her phone. "What club are you starting at? I'll send a text to Freddie to meet you there. He could use a fun night out, and a good flirt from someone good looking."

Joe told her the name of the club and she sent it to Freddie. "Done."

"Thanks. You're making out to be a good wing woman."

"Don't thank me yet. He hasn't agreed."

Her phone dinged.

FREDDIE: Tell him I'll be there. I need a good night out.

"Well, he says he'll be there."

Joe did a fist pump and stood from the stool. Gotta get ready and put some extra thought into my look. Wish me luck."

Tess laughed. "Good luck."

She watched as Joe walked out of the kitchen and down the hall toward the bedrooms with a bit of a spring in his step, laughing and shaking her head.

Tessa had just started unloading groceries on the kitchen counter when she heard a door open from the back of the flat. She could feel her stomach flutter with anticipation.

Spontaneously sleeping with James after the wedding was last minute and unexpected. Coming over to his house to cook dinner and dessert together, knowing what the expectations were for the evening was different. This was a date.

Their first.

She could hear James' soft footfalls on the hardwood floors as he made his way toward her.

"Hello," she greeted, not turning away from her task.

James wrapped his arms around her waist from behind. His body stepped into hers and she could feel his heat on her back. He bent his head forward, placing a kiss on her neck before resting his chin on her shoulder, their cheeks touching.

"Hello," he breathed.

His cheek was scratchy against hers with his beard, and she couldn't resist rubbing her own against his.

"It surprised me when you didn't answer the door."

"Sorry about it. But to be fair, you are a bit earlier than I expected."

"I was nervous, so I left early."

"Nervous? We don't have to do more than cook together."

Tessa pushed on James' arms until he loosened his grip on her waist. Once they were loose, she rotated herself until she was facing him. She brought her hands up to rest on either side of his face, making sure she was looking directly into his eyes.

"I wasn't nervous about our night leading to sex," she asserted. "I was nervous because this is our first date."

She couldn't hold back the laugh that formed as James' eyes widened almost comically.

"Shit, it's our first date! And you're cooking in my flat, when I should have wined and dined you somewhere in the city!"

Tessa leaned forward and placed a quick kiss on his lips. "I don't want to be wined and dined in the city. I think this is the perfect first date."

James smiled and leaned forward to place a quick kiss on her lips. "You're right. This *is* the perfect first date."

He leaned forward and caught her lips with his again, but this time, it wasn't quick. He deepened the kiss as he pushed her back against the counter. Tessa opened her mouth, and he entered. She moved her hands from his face until she threaded her fingers through his hair.

She could feel the edge of the counter digging into her lower back, but she didn't care.

James pressed himself closer to her, using his knee to push her legs apart so he could slip his leg between hers.

She could feel his hardness against her hip as James' hands wandered until they rested on the curve of her arse. He clenched his fingers around her, and she broke away from the kiss with a moan.

"Don't mind me."

James and Tessa leapt apart as if they were on fire.

She looked around James to see Joe standing near the front door, putting his coat on with an impish grin.

"Fuck off, Joe," James growled, running his hands through his hair. He was breathing heavily and staring at the ground.

"If you didn't want to be interrupted, you shouldn't have been trying to fuck your girlfriend in the kitchen."

James grabbed something off the counter and threw it toward Joe.

Tessa cringed as she watched her bag of carrots slam against the wall inches from Joe's head.

All Joe did was laugh.

"I'm off. Stop throwing veg at my head," he laughed hysterically. "And don't wait up. I won't be sleeping here tonight. With any luck, I'll be at Freddie's." Joe waggled his eyebrows as Tessa groaned, covering her face with her hands.

She heard the door open and close quickly, and knowing Joe was already gone, she removed her hands in time to see James holding the double cream in his hand, ready to throw it.

"If you keep throwing our ingredients at your roommate, we won't have anything left to eat."

James at least had the decency to look embarrassed. "Sorry." He set the double cream down on the counter and moved to get the carrots from the floor near the door.

Tessa turned so she was facing the counter. She began putting away the foods she didn't need right away, before looking around to find the pans she would need to make their dinner.

"So, I'm guessing Joe officially killed the mood?" James asked, moving to place the carrots on the counter.

"Yeah, you could say that. You throwing our food around didn't help matters either. Besides, I'm famished. Stay here and be my sous chef, and I'll teach you how to make the best roast dinner you've ever had."

James smiled as he opened a drawer and pulled out two aprons, handing one to her. "Challenge accepted."

***

Later, as she lay in bed next to a dozing James, she smiled as she replayed their evening together. It really had turned out to be a really nice first date. They laughed, they cooked, they snogged while the dinner was cooking. Baking the pumpkin bars turned out to be more foreplay than anything. But at least they pulled the bars out of the oven before succumbing to their lust.

She looked over at the clock on James' bedside table. It was only seven, but she could feel sleep pulling at her.

"You can go to sleep," James wrapped his arm around her, spooning in behind her. "You won't offend me. I know what time you have to wake up to go into the shop, especially now that you're not staying above it."

Tessa snuggled back into James' body, closing her eyes. "Mmm," she hummed. "If I fall asleep, the day will be over."

"Yes," James whispered into her ear, "but the next day will begin, and we'll have a new adventure to explore."

"I like the sound of that." She paused, already feeling the pull of sleep dragging her down. "If I sleep, what will you do?"

"Good thing we're in my flat, yeah? I'll probably go catch the end of the Arsenal game on telly, and turn in myself. I have a long day of tailing Bruno tomorrow."

"Unless the fingerprints come back clearing him."

"Yes, that. Part of me is hoping it's not him, so I don't have to spend another day sitting outside his house."

"You're getting a lot of reading done."

James chuckled. "Yeah, that I am. Gonna make my way through the whole *Wheel of Time* series if I sit outside his house any longer."

It was Tessa's turn to laugh. "Well then, it will be worth it. Those books are amazing, especially the part—"

James gave her a playful squeeze to cut her off. "Eh, no spoilers."

She laughed. "Fine, my lips are sealed."

James planted a kiss on her bare shoulder. "Seriously. Go to sleep. I'm closer to the shop than Freddie's place, but not above the shop close."

"Come into the shop for tea tomorrow if you can get away from Bruno's.".

James placed another kiss on her shoulder. "I'll be there. Now go to sleep."

She lifted his hand and placed a kiss on his palm. Lying there in his arms, it took no time at all before she was asleep.

CHAPTER 21

JAMES

James rolled over in his bed and touched the space where Tessa had slept next to him. He sighed. He wished he could have woken up with Tessa in his arms this morning, but unless it was a Sunday or if he wanted to wake up in the middle of the night, that wouldn't happen.

He had brief memories of her leaving and saying goodbye, but he wasn't fully awake for it, so it was all fuzzy.

He ran his hands down his face, rubbing his eyes to wake up a little more.

Perk of running your own business was not having to get up before the sun. However, he needed to get to Bruno's early enough to catch him coming home in case he was sitting in an alley across from Cake Me Home Tonight.

That's why he was up at five in the morning.

He got out of the bed, threw on a pair of boxers and walked out of his room. He walked down the hall toward the kitchen, his stomach growling, knowing he had an entire sheet of pumpkin bars waiting for him in the kitchen.

He rounded the corner to the kitchen and stopped dead in his tracks.

"No," he breathed out.

Freddie turned from where he was pouring himself a cup of coffee at the counter. His brown eyes were wide, his mouth dropped open as he struggled to find words.

"What are you doing here?" James asked, even though he knew the answer.

Freddie's dark cheeks flushed with red, and he hung his head to hide his eyes behind his untidy hair. "Fuckin' 'ell," he muttered under his breath. And then quickly whipped his head up, locking his gaze with James'. "Oh, fuck, is Tess here?"

James shook his head. "Left around three to get to the shop."

Freddie visibly relaxed.

James laughed. "Ashamed of fucking my mate?"

"Ashamed? No. Embarrassed? Yes."

"Embarrassed? Why? Joe is a catch."

"Because I ended a long-term relationship with my fiancée a month ago, and now I'm in bed with the first bloke to flirt with me post-breakup? How sad is that?"

James shrugged. "Mate, it's been a month. You're allowed to move on. Have some fun. No one is saying you and Joe need to get serious or anything, and no one is expecting you to remain chaste until you're ready for a new relationship. We're young, we're allowed to live a little. Have some fun."

Freddie leaned against the counter, holding his coffee in his right hand. "Is that what you're doing with Tess? Having a little fun?"

It was James' turn to sputter. "What? No!"

"I mean, it's fine if you are. Having fun, that is. Just as long as you're both on the same page," Freddie paused and took a sip of his coffee, never removing his gaze from James. "If she thinks what you're doing is something serious and you think it's casual, she's going to get her heart broken, and I just can't allow that."

"It's not casual," James rushed to defend. "I'm not sure how serious it is, but I know for sure it isn't casual. At least not to me."

Freddie broke into a wide grin, "Oh thank fuck. I didn't want to have to give you a threatening speech."

"Threatening speech?"

"You know, 'if you ever hurt Tess, I'll find you and beat the shit out of you,'" Freddie intoned, deepening his voice and wagging a finger. "All a bit rubbish," he changed back to his normal voice, "innit? But as her non-brother brother, it's my duty to threaten the love interest."

"I'm pretty sure Tessa can take care of herself."

"Oh, absolutely, but I enjoy doing the speech. Tessa gets a kick out of giving hers to whoever I'm currently seeing."

This time, it was James' turn to smile. "So, is she going to need to give it to Joe?"

Freddie narrowed his eyes. "No." He paused with a frown. "Maybe?" He sighed. "I don't know. Last night is all blurry."

"You were drunk."

"Yes, I was drunk. We were at a bar. And Joe looked even hotter than he did in his uniform on Saturday night. One minute we were talking and drinking, and the next…" he trailed off and gave James a pointed look.

"I get the picture," he replied with a laugh. "If you're looking for something non-committal, then Joe's your guy. He has a phobia of commitment."

"Oi," Joe's voice came from behind him. "Don't be spouting shite." He walked into the kitchen, in just his boxers, and made a beeline for the kettle. He squeezed in close to Freddie to pour himself a cup, and as he turned back around, he placed a kiss on Freddie's cheek. "I don't have a phobia of commitment. I'm willing to commit to the right person."

He said all of that with his gaze locked on Freddie.

Freddie's cheeks colored.

He cleared his throat. "Well, I'd best be off. I hate leaving Tess to deal with the morning rush on her own."

"You have my number?" Joe asked.

Freddie nodded. "And you mine?"

Joe nodded.

"So, I guess I'll see you around?"

Freddie set down his mug and moved to leave the kitchen, but Joe stopped him. He placed his hands on either side of Freddie's face, pulling him in for a kiss. It didn't take long for Freddie to give in and reciprocate. The kiss grew heated, and James turned his head and looked away, giving the two men some privacy to say their goodbyes.

James heard them break apart and whisper something to one another before Freddie pushed past him on his way to the door.

"See you around," Freddie said.

"See you."

When Freddie had left the flat, James whipped around. "What the fuck was that?" He pointed his finger at the door.

Joe shrugged and brought his coffee up for a sip. "I don't know what you're talking about."

"Fuck off," James chastised him. "You and Freddie?"

"Don't know what you're talking about. Tessa asked Freddie to meet me at the club."

James shook his head. "And?"

Joe shrugged. "And it didn't go exactly how I had planned."

James laughed. "You caught feelings for the bloke after one night?"

Joe shrugged again. "Maybe. I don't know. When I met him Saturday, I was like, 'hmm, he's handsome, pretty sure he's queer, I would like to hit that.' And then last night, he got to the club, looking better than anyone ever deserves to look, and we hit it off. Confirmed he's queer, and after hours of talking, I brought him here for a shag."

"See, this is the part where I know you've caught feelings, because you never bring a bloke home. You always go to theirs."

"I know!" Joe asserted. "I know. This is completely out of character. And Freddie has just gotten out of a relationship with a bird he was going to marry. And I just ended things with what's his name,"

"Clint," James supplied

"Clint, yes. It must be some sort of punishment for my promiscuity for me to find a man I would like to have a relation-ship with, only to have that man be completely unavailable."

"I mean, I wouldn't consider him completely unavailable. He came home with you, yeah? And from what I know of Freddie, he doesn't seem like that one-night stand kind of bloke."

"What're you saying?"

"I'm saying keep an open mind. Don't write anything off yet. Text him later."

Joe cringed. "Same day? Seems desperate, doesn't it?"

James shook his head. "Not desperate. Interested."

"I'll keep that under consideration."

James moved into the kitchen to help himself to some of the coffee Freddie had brewed and cut himself and Joe each a pumpkin bar.

"What are you doing up so early on your Saturday?"

"Got a message from the lab about the fingerprint on the brick," Joe answered after taking a bite of the pumpkin bar.

"They got a match?"

Joe shook his head. "Inconclusive."

"Fuck."

"Yeah, sorry, mate. I really thought this would clinch it."

"Inconclusive because the print was rubbish or because the person isn't in the system?"

"The second one."

"So, if we can somehow get some fingerprints..."

"We can run them against the brick," Joe finished. "But and this is a *huge* but, we have to consider the person who threw the brick, that might not be his print. For all we know, he found that brick lying about and it's some random person's fingerprint."

James groaned, throwing his head back. "I know, I know."

"We still have all the CCTV footage still to look through. It's not completely hopeless."

"I'm not frustrated by the lack of progress. I'm frustrated because I need to go sit in front of Bruno's house again today."

Joe cringed. "Yeah, I can see why you're upset. You need me to swing by with lunch again today?"

James shook his head. "I'm meeting Tessa at the shop for tea. I'll just pack some snacks to tide me over."

"Think he'll do something more interesting today than Monday?"

James scoffed. "I highly doubt it. I'm prepared to sit in the car, listening to my book, one hand on the camera, waiting to take a picture of absolutely nothing."

"How long do you plan on sitting outside Bruno's?"

James shoved the rest of his pumpkin bar in his mouth and picked up his coffee so he could go get ready in his room. "For as long as it's going to take."

Chapter 22

TESSA

Tessa wiped the counters down in the shop and let herself relax for the first time all morning. It was their mid-morning slow down, and she'd let Mariel and Freddie take their breaks while she manned the counter.

She was literally counting down the days until November ended and she could switch to Christmas treats and retire the damn pumpkin bars.

She had hung a sign the day before declaring pumpkin bars were to end on the first of December, and people had apparently heard about it. She didn't know how it was possible, but business had increased. Originally, she thought this new uptick was because of the damn pumpkin bars, but now she was selling out of everything. People were coming in specifically for items other than the pumpkin bars, and she was wondering if this level of business was going to carry on through past the pumpkin bar phase.

She glanced over at Freddie, who was sitting at a table, smiling into his phone.

The day she had left James', he had walked into work and confessed that he had slept with Joe and there was *something* brewing between them. She had given her his blessing, which he felt she needed, and for the last two days he's spent every spare moment texting back and forth with Joe.

Which she loved for him, but she had to wonder if Joe ever worked.

Freddie must have sensed her gaze on him because he looked up from his phone, a sheepish look on his face. "Sorry."

She waved him off. "Don't be. I don't think I've ever seen you this happy."

Freddie frowned. "Really? Not even at the beginning of my relationship with Alice?"

Tessa shook her head, frowning. "Not that I can recall, although I spent most of the beginning of your relationship with Alice being interrogated by Alice."

"Why don't I remember any of this?"

"Probably because she did it when you weren't around."

"Weren't you dating what's his face when I started seeing Alice?"

"Ben? Yes. Did it matter to Alice? Absolutely not."

"The more you tell me about how Alice treated you, the more I wonder why you didn't back me into a corner two years ago and tell me to break it off."

Tessa shrugged. "You were young, and in love, and I didn't want to stand in the way of your relationship. No matter how many times she accused me of fucking you behind her back."

"Ugh, she was the worst, and I'm only noticing it now, because hindsight is twenty-twenty and all that shit, but fuck, I'm feeling much less sad she basically left me at the altar." He looked down at his phone again, grinning. He typed in a quick reply before glancing back up at her. "Okay, tell me. Are you seeing any red flags with Joe? Before I get in too deep?"

Tessa remembered back to the day before when the four of them had sat together in the I and enjoyed tea together. "None."

"Really?"

"Really."

"You're not just saying that because I'm happy and you don't want to crush me? Because I want you to be brutally honest with me."

"I am being brutally honest. I really like Joe. He's funny, he's nice, and he's not jealous of me. Honestly, I can't think of anyone better as a partner for you."

"You don't think I'm moving on too quickly?"

"Absolutely not. It's been a month. And if you think about it, probably even longer since you were remotely happy with Alice. You're allowed to move on."

Freddie smiled. "I'm really glad you're in my corner, because things are moving really fucking fast, and I don't know who I would have talked to about it if you were against it."

"Well, who better to talk to about going from zero to one hundred in a relationship than me?"

Freddie's eyes widened. "Oh yeah! You and James! Joe and I are you guys two weeks ago, except instead of just giving into your attraction, you denied it for weeks."

"Weeks? You make it sound like we danced around each other for months. It was two weeks, and, yeah, we were idiots. What do you want?"

"At least you can admit it now."

"Yes, well, to be fair, I've had a lot on my plate, can't be thinking about starting a new relationship when I've got a nutter stalking me."

Freddie frowned. "Joe said they're still going through the CCTV footage and he will get a full report when they're finished. He's thinking any day now."

"Are they really going through everything Patrick and James had already gone through?"

Freddie shook his head. "Not the same footage. They pulled from surrounding streets and from down by the tube, since they think he lives around there. They're hoping to catch the bastard's face on camera." He held up his crossed fingers. "Here's hoping they find something and this whole thing can end."

"Yes, please. I think the most unnerving aspect is the stalker hasn't reached out and made any contact since the night of the wedding."

Freddie sat up straighter, setting his phone face down on the table. "Really?"

"Nothing. No letters, no text messages."

"You're not staying here. Maybe he knows and doesn't know where to find you?"

"He has my number, remember? And the shop has been open every day like normal."

"Wait."

Tessa leaned on the counter in anticipation. "What?"

"James has been at Bruno's every day since the brick incident, yes?"

"Not round the clock, but off and on, yes."

Freddie leaned on his arms on his table, pushing himself closer to Tessa. "What if your stalker has stopped contacting you because he can't without James finding out?"

Tessa frowned. "Are you thinking Bruno is really my stalker? And because James is outside his house, he's stopped so he won't incriminate himself?"

"Why not? It feels like it could be logical."

"But Bruno doesn't live near our tube station. He lives elsewhere in the city."

"Maybe your stalker simply makes it look like he lives around here? Circles back around to hop on a train after taking his disguise off?"

"All that seems pretty logical. However, James assured me Bruno wouldn't notice him. He's a professional."

Freddie laughed. "The mini isn't exactly the most inconspicuous car, and James has had it parked outside Bruno's house for days. If Bruno *is* your stalker, I'm pretty sure he would recognize James, and know he's being followed."

Tessa moved around the counter and sat in the chair opposite Freddie, resting her elbow on the table and her chin in her hand. "Fuck, I was really hoping it wasn't Bruno."

"After everything he put you through in school?"

Tessa slouched back in her chair and crossed her arms across her chest. "Yeah. Mostly because of everything we'd gone through when we were younger. We were best friends, Freddie.

Best friends. We were inseparable for years. Even though we grew apart, there was some part of me hoping maybe we could reconcile, despite that one incident at school."

"That you know of."

"What?"

"One incident that you know of," Freddie clarified. "We don't know what else he was doing in school. And what if, all these years later, he is still not over whatever obsession he had for you in school, and it's escalated to full-blown stalking?"

"But if it is him, why now? Why start now? Why wait so long?"

"Fucked if I know."

Tessa was about to open her mouth to answer when the door to the shop flew open.

In walked the subject of their conversation.

"Bruno?" Tessa exclaimed, leaping up from her chair, almost causing it to topple over.

Out of the corner of her eye, she could see Freddie typing something on his phone frantically. She knew he was messaging Joe, who would message James, to get the fuck over here.

They had decided James could take the day off from tailing Bruno and work on another case. And now he's here in her shop.

"Why are you having me followed?" Bruno shouted as he approached where Freddie and Tessa were standing.

"What?" Tessa asked, truly at a loss for what to say.

"The bloke parked in front of my house in the mini. He's the ginger detective who brought down the Fitzgeralds last year. He's fucking famous. I recognized him the minute I saw him. What I want to know is why are you having him watch me?"

Tessa found her voice. She stood up taller and crossed her arms in front of her chest. "What makes you think I hired him to watch you? We haven't even spoken in ages."

Bruno reached into his back pocket and threw down a copy of The Mirror on the table. The tabloid was open to one of the center pages. There was a picture of Patrick and Evelyn at their wedding. Behind them stood James and Tessa sitting at their table, James leaning over and whispering something in Tessa's ear.

"Because you were with him at this wedding. Plus, I can't think of anyone else in my life who would hire a fucking private detective to follow me around. But, like you said, we haven't spoken in ages, so I can't seem to figure out why you would do it."

"You know why," Freddie spoke up.

Bruno wrinkled his brow, his dark eyes narrowing. "Because of the incident in the loo? I've apologized for that. And it was over a decade ago."

"Not the loo incident," Freddie dismissed.

"I honestly don't know what you're referring to. I've done nothing."

"You haven't? Then why are you so worried about whether James is following you? If you have nothing to hide, then it shouldn't matter," Tessa spoke up.

"Of course, it bloody matters!" Bruno shouted, running a hand across his shortly cropped black hair. "Like I said, he's not exactly unknown, and my neighbors are talking."

"Why do you come to the shop and never walk in?" Tessa blurted.

Bruno stopped short, looking at her like she lost her bloody mind. "What?"

"You come to the shop, and just stand here, staring in, but you never come in. Well, at least not anymore. The girl who runs my register says you used to come in all the time."

Bruno looked truly confused. "Are you accusing me of something? Because last I checked, looking in the window of a public place is not a crime."

"Just answer the fucking question, Bruno," Freddie practically growled out.

Bruno raised his arm and pointed a finger at Freddie. "Because of this. Right here."

"What? Can't take a bit of disagreement?" Freddie challenged.

"You beat the shit out of me before we left school. I've had no desire to be around you since."

Tessa shook her head. "Enough," she scolded the two men before turning her attention back to Bruno. "You didn't come in because you were worried Freddie would beat you up?"

"Not exactly. But I knew there would be some sort of confrontation. I stop by the shop to talk to you, Tessa. Ever since we reconnected through social media, I've wanted to reconnect with you in person. I learned about the shop, but every time I came in, you weren't here. And then the shop grew busy, and every time I stopped by after, Freddie was working the counter."

"You could have called," Tessa threw out.

"I don't have your number, and it's not listed anywhere. How could I call you?"

Before Tessa could answer, the door to the shop flew open and James strode in, followed closely by Joe, who despite it being his day off, was wearing his full uniform.

James didn't stop until he was standing right next to Tessa.

She was really proud of him when he didn't put his arm around her like he was trying to claim her for his own. Their talk over the weekend really did a number, and she really appreciated it.

"Is this man bothering you, Tessa?" Joe asked.

"Um, not really?" she answered truthfully.

Joe turned to face Bruno. "Sir, do you mind if I ask you a few questions?"

"What the fuck?" Bruno was stunned. "You called the police on me? For coming into your shop? Are you mad?"

"I didn't call the police," Tessa reassured him. "This is Officer McCleary. He works closely with James."

"He's the lead officer investigating who threw a brick through Tess's window Saturday night," Freddie filled in.

Bruno sputtered. "And you think I had something to do with that?"

"Where were you Saturday night?" Joe asked. "Between the hours of midnight and two a.m.?"

Bruno shook his head. "I'm not answering that."

"Why not? Guilty?" Freddie taunted.

"Freddie, don't," Tessa chastised him.

"Am I under arrest?" Bruno asked.

"You are not," Joe answered.

"Then I don't need to answer any of your questions. I'm out of here. I don't need any of this." Bruno turned to walk out the door, but stopped and turned back. He marched back, stopping inches away from James.

"You stay the fuck away from my house. Stop. Following. Me."

James didn't say a thing. Tessa was pretty sure he didn't even blink.

Bruno turned on his heel and marched out the door.

No one stopped him.

CHAPTER 23

JAMES

James watched Bruno storm out of the shop, his eyes narrowed.

He couldn't say with a hundred percent certainty Bruno was innocent, but he couldn't say he was guilty either. The only thing he *could* say was he seemed really fucking shady.

"Can Bruno have you arrested for loitering?" Tessa asked, her gaze still locked on the door where Bruno had just exited.

"No," James and Joe answered at the same time.

"Loitering isn't a crime in the UK," Joe explained.

"So, he can call, but all it will do is allow me to have a nice social break in the middle of my observations."

"Are you still going to watch him?" Tessa asked.

"I wasn't going to, but after this exchange, I kind of want to just to spite the bastard."

"He was really pissed," Freddie piped up. "Like really pissed."

"Did he say why he's been loitering at the shop window?" James asked, turning toward Tessa.

"Told me he wanted to reconnect with me," she answered, finally turning away from the door.

James frowned. "If he wanted to reconnect, why stay out-side?"

"He said he was worried I would knock his head off," Freddie answered, crossing his arms in front of him.

"Would you have?" Joe asked.

Freddie shrugged. "Dunno. Before the stalker stuff? Probably not. I would've just given him the stink eye. After the stalker stuff? Maybe."

"What do we do now?" Tessa asked. She was antsy. Crossing and uncrossing her arms. Tucking stray hairs behind her ears.

James stepped closer to her, wrapping an arm around her shoulder, pulling her in closer. "Now, we wait for the CCTV footage to come in. And from there we'll decide the next steps. Has he contacted you at all since Saturday night?"

Tessa shook her head. "Nothing."

"Maybe the police presence has spooked him," Joe offered.

"Never thought of that," Freddie said. "Police investigation feels more serious than a PI poking his nose about. No offense, James."

"None taken, because it's true. We can do a lot of legwork, but we still need to turn suspects in to the police. We don't have arresting power."

Tessa rested her head on James' shoulder. "Part of me hopes the police have scared him away. The other part doesn't."

"Why is that?" James asked.

"Because if the police have scared him away, I'll never know who it was. I'll always wonder who had the nerve to stalk me. If he's not caught, could he come back? Could he simply start again once the scrutiny is off?"

"Always looking over your shoulder," Freddie added.

"Scared of the bogeyman in the shadows," Tessa finished.

James dropped a kiss on the top of her head. "We won't give up. If he stops, the urgency is gone, but I promise I'll keep trying to figure out who this is."

"Don't make promises you can't keep," Tessa's voice was quiet, almost forlorn.

"Oh, I bloody well intend to keep this," James almost growled. "The bastard threw a fucking brick at my head. It's personal."

The bell above the shop's door rang, announcing someone entering the shop. Tessa pulled away from him, smoothing her hair, and plastering on a smile for her customer.

"Good afternoon," she greeted brightly. "Welcome to Cake Me Home Tonight."

"Afternoon, Tessa!" the man who entered greeted.

He was about their age, maybe a little older, brown hair combed smartly to the side, a half-smile on his face. He was escorting an older woman on his arm.

"Fraser! Mrs. Hudson! We missed you yesterday!" Tessa moved to the counter and pulled out a plate.

Fraser. This was the man whose card Tessa had sent him. The one who Evie didn't think was worth looking into.

James watched him as he led his mother to a table and helped her sit down.

"Mum was feeling poorly on Wednesday. I couldn't even get away to pick up our treats. I was worried about her breathing."

"He worries too much," Mrs. Hudson answered as she set herself down in a chair, trying to prop her cane against the table next to hers.

"Let me take that, please, Mrs. Hudson," Freddie moved to take the cane and set on the floor next to their table.

Tessa brought over a large plate with a few of their most popular items, placing them on the table.

"I'll be right back with the tea. Fraser, you should have rung ahead. We would have had everything ready for you."

Fraser flashed her a smile. "Although it would have been a kind thing to do, I wasn't certain we would make it. I was worried mum wouldn't be able to handle the walk, and if I had called ahead and we'd had to turn around, I would have felt guilty having you go through all the work for nothing."

Tessa waved him off. "Call next time. We could always enjoy the tea for ourselves if you end up not making it. No harm done."

Tessa gave one more smile before walking into the kitchen to prepare the tea.

"I don't think we've met," Fraser addressed James.

"James Moore," he offered his hand.

Fraser shook his hand and gave him a wide smile. "Fraser Hudson."

"Your name sounds familiar," Mrs. Hudson queried, "have we met?"

"I don't think we have," James turned to face Mrs. Hudson, "I was in the news for a bit. My partner and I were instrumental in the takedown of the Fitzgeralds. The trial was on the telly a lot."

Fraser clicked his fingers and pointed at him. "I *thought* your face looked familiar, but I couldn't put my finger on where I could have possibly seen you. We have the BBC on most of the day. Mum likes the background noise, so I'm sure I saw you on the news."

James smiled. "Yeah, I'm sure that's it."

"Wow," bright smile spreading across Mrs. Hudson's face, "a celebrity in our local shop."

James chuckled. "A celebrity I am not. And it's my local shop, too. I live here in the neighborhood."

Fraser looked around at Joe. "You look familiar, too."

Joe stepped around James. "I'm Sergeant Joseph McCleary. You have probably also seen me on the telly, as I also had a hand in taking in the Fitzgeralds."

"Two celebrities!" Mrs. Hudson declared gleefully. "Fraser, you should have let me do my face before coming down here."

"Mum," Fraser chuckled. "You look fine. And as they mentioned, they're not exactly Prince Harry and Prince William. I'm sure they don't mind you looking the way you do."

"You look beautiful, Mrs. Hudson," Joe complimented.

Mrs. Hudson blushed.

"What brings you down to our little cake shop?" Mrs. Hudson asked. "Are the rumors true? The police fond of their cakes?"

Joe and James laughed.

"While it is true, we love our cakes, and this is the best place in the borough to buy sweets, we're just here to see our sweethearts," Joe answered.

James watched Fraser closely for his reaction. If he were the stalker, he would react to this statement.

Fraser narrowed his eyes and tilted his head to the side. "Sweethearts?"

"Yeah, James here is dating Tessa, and I'm seeing Freddie," Joe explained, slipping an arm around Freddie's shoulders.

James could see Joe out of the corner of his eye, and just by his stance, he could see what he was doing. He knew Fraser was a suspect. He was goading him to see if he could get a reaction. James kept his eyes on Fraser so he wouldn't miss the reaction.

The door to the kitchen opened, and Tessa came out with the tea tray.

"Tessa," Fraser said as she made her way to the table, setting the tea tray down. "You should have told me you were seeing someone."

"Oh," Tessa was a bit taken aback. "It's all new."

"Well, now I feel like a right twat, giving you my card, telling you if you needed to talk, to call me." He turned to face James. "Sorry about that, mate. I didn't mean to ask out your girlfriend. I'm not that sort of person."

James was surprised. "It's not a problem. Don't worry about it."

"James and I weren't even really seeing each other when you did that," Tessa explained. "We knew each other, but were just friends. Honestly, I didn't even know you were trying to ask me out."

Fraser let out a breath with a small laugh, placing his hand on his chest. "I'm thankful that you were single when I tried to hit on you, but I'm embarrassed that you didn't realize what I was doing. I don't get out much," he explained. "Working from home and taking care of me mum gives me little time to go out, so I'm rubbish at flirting. I feel like a numpty."

Tessa rested a hand on his shoulder, giving him a soft smile. "You're not a numpty. You're just out of practice."

"Yeah, mate, you just need to get out and interact with people your own age," Joe piped in. His eyes widened. "You should come out with Freddie and me."

Fraser shook his head. "I don't know."

"You should! We'll go to the straight clubs, find you some girls to pull, and we can be your wingmen!"

Freddie looked at Joe side-eyed. "You're way too excited. Tone it down a notch."

"I think your enthusiasm is scaring him," Tessa whispered.

James stifled his smile when he caught the deer in headlights look on Fraser's face.

"I don't know," his words were stilted, as he stammered a little. "With my mum—"

"Oi," his mom piped up, "don't use me as an excuse. I'm in bed by seven every night. Go out and have fun with your mates."

"There you have it!" Joe exclaimed. He pulled out his billfold and took out a card. He handed it to Fraser. "This is my number. We are going to go out on Tuesday. Let's make plans to meet up."

Fraser reluctantly reached into his pocket, pulling out his own card, handing it to Joe.

Joe looked at the card with a smile on his face. "Brilliant." He looked back up, locking his gaze onto Fraser's. "We're going to get you laid," he declared with full sincerity oozing out of his voice.

James watched as the color drained from Fraser's face, his expression clearly telegraphing he was certain he'd made a grievous error.

"C'mon, I'll walk you out. We're done scaring our best customer for the day," Freddie took hold of Joe's arm and began leading him outside, "G'day, Fraser. Mrs. Hudson."

They watched as Freddie led Joe outside and toward the tube.

"Blimey," Fraser muttered. "Is he always like that?"

James let out the chuckle he had been holding in during the interaction. "Yes. And believe it or not, this was pretty fucking tame for him."

Fraser ran his hands through his hair. "What have I gotten myself into? I can barely talk to a girl. And now he wants me to…" he swallowed. "I will have to tell him I'm not coming when he sends the information."

Tessa laughed. "You will be fine. Maybe it will be good for you."

Fraser turned. "Will you two be out with them? That's a thing, right? Double dates? I am so out of my depth."

James eyed Fraser.

He had been watching him this entire time, and nothing he was doing seemed to be suspicious. He didn't seem jealous. In fact, he seemed like a genuinely nice person. However, he had one more test.

"Sure," James answered. "We can go out with the lot of you on Tuesday. We wouldn't be able to stay too long. Tessa has to get enough sleep in order to wake up early to get into the shop to bake. She's staying with Freddie until her window can get fixed, and he lives eons away from the shop."

"What happened to her window?" Mrs. Hudson asked.

James kept his gaze on Fraser when he said the next part. "Someone threw a brick through it last weekend."

Fraser looked genuinely shocked. "Someone threw a brick through her window? Who on earth would want to a throw a brick through a baker's window? Was it one of those old ladies who couldn't get a pumpkin bar last week?"

James' shoulders relaxed. "We don't know. Joe and I are trying to figure it out."

"It's a good thing she and Freddie are dating men of the law," Mrs. Hudson expressed. "Hopefully you'll be able to catch whoever it is who would do something so cruel."

"That's our hope," James agreed.

"We won't keep you any longer. Enjoy your tea and let me know if you need anything else."

"We will, dear."

"Yes, thank you, Ms. Lopez. I'm sorry about your window," Fraser apologized.

"Please call me Tessa, Fraser."

"Oh, okay. Thank you, Tessa."

Tessa gave him a smile, and she and James moved through the shop and into the kitchen, since Mariel was back from her break.

"So," Tessa began speaking as soon as the door closed behind her. "What do you think?"

"Honestly?" James leaned against the counter. "I feel pretty good about him not being our stalker."

Tessa perked up. "Really?"

"Really. He seemed genuinely surprised about the brick. And he didn't seem jealous when he found out you were dating me."

"You can tell these things?"

"I'm fantastic at reading people. It comes with the job. I don't think he's the stalker."

Tessa let out a breath. "I'm so relieved to hear that, because I really like him and his mum."

"They seem like good people. When I talked to Evelyn about this before the wedding, she told me she didn't think it could be him, either."

"So, that leaves us with—"

"Bruno."

CHAPTER 24

TESSA

Tessa stood in Freddie's bathroom trying to finish her make-up.

She had pulled out all her "going out" outfits from her wardrobe and threw them in a bag Saturday night before leaving the shop for the night. She dropped them off at Freddie's before spending her Sunday with James.

He had really scaled down his tailing of Bruno. The man never left his house, and James thought it was mostly because he was sitting there. He talked to Joe, and this week they were going to stand down, and mid-week, grab the CCTV footage from his block and see if they could see any delineation from the pattern.

Her case was on the back burner for a while, and James was going to focus on a backlog of cases in their email, at least until Patrick got back from his honeymoon next week.

"You almost finished? I need to fix my hair," Freddie spoke through the door.

"Yes, I'm finished," Tessa called back, putting the lid on her mascara.

She rarely wore makeup, since it would all just melt off her face in the heat of her kitchen. But if she was going to go out, she was going to doll herself up. She briefly thought about trying out contacts again, but opted for her simple black-rimmed glasses.

She opened the door to let Freddie in.

He let out a low whistle. "Damn, you clean up nicely."

Tessa waved him off as she pushed past him.

"Seriously. You should go out more often."

"You know, going out is not my thing. I would much rather stay in, wearing sweats and going to bed by eight."

Freddie pulled her into a one-armed hug. "Yes, I know you revel in living like an old lady, but this will be good for you. And for you and James. Besides, I can't reign in Joe all by myself. I haven't learned how to control him yet. I need James."

Tess sighed. "Fine. For just one night I'll pretend to be a thirty-something rather than an eighty-something. But come ten, I'm out. I turn into a pumpkin if I stay out too late."

"More like the Wicked Witch of the West," Freddie muttered, not quite under his breath.

Tessa gave him a playful shove. "Be nice, or I'll cancel."

"You wouldn't," Freddie teased. "You like Fraser too much to sacrifice him to the whims of Joe."

"I hate it when you're right."

"Now, out, I need to make myself look beautiful."

Tessa laughed as she made her way back to the office, aka her room. She immediately went to the full-length mirror propped up against the wall.

She decided simple was better than going overboard. Especially after a full day of work. She was probably going to convince James to sit somewhere. Her feet were tired from spending the whole day standing on them.

She opted for dark wash skinny jeans, and a black asymmetrical tunic length blouse. She wore her hair loose, her tight curls fully on display as they cascaded down her back. Light makeup, no jewelry, and her black and white Chuck Taylor trainers.

She smiled.

She cleaned up nicely.

She opened her purse and pulled out her ID and a card, slipping them into her front pocket, and slid her phone into her back pocket.

One last look in the mirror before she turned off her light and walked to the front of the flat.

Just as she entered the living room, there was a knock on the door.

She opened it to see James and Joe standing there.

As soon as James caught sight of her, she could visibly see his jaw drop.

"Fuck."

She laughed. "I'll take that as a compliment."

"Definitely a compliment. Always a compliment."

"You're acting like you've never seen me in fancy dress before. When it's only been a week and a bit since the wedding, where I was in much fancier dress."

"Tessa, love, I'm going to let you into a little secret." Joe moved in closer, leaning their heads together. "He's speechless because while you looked brilliant in your dress at the wedding, it did not fit your body like a glove like your current outfit. Poor James here is short circuiting because that outfit makes your tits and arse look phenomenal, and that is coming from me, the gayest man in this group."

Tessa's cheeks warmed and her mouth dropped open.

"For fuck's sake, Joe," James growled. "You haven't even started drinking yet."

"Not true," Joe disagreed. "I had a beer from our fridge right before we left."

"You're incorrigible," James grumbled.

"Gonna go find my man." Joe pushed past Tessa into the flat.

"Hi," James drawled when they were finally alone.

"Hi," Tessa replied.

James moved closer and placed a hand to cup the back of her head, pulling her into him, capturing her lips in a kiss.

They broke away before things could get heated.

The beginning of a relationship was always her favorite. Getting to know one another, both in and out of bed, and the newness made it so they couldn't keep their hands off of each other.

"Are you sure you want to go out with these lunatics?" James asked, gesturing toward the back of the flat with his head. "We could stay in, watch a new episode of the latest MCU show on Disney, go to bed..." he lowered his voice as he trailed off, waggling his eyebrows.

Tessa laughed. "While your idea sounds like my ideal evening, we made a promise. And do you *really* want to leave poor Fraser alone with those two?"

She turned her head into the flat where Freddie and Joe were practicing some sort of coordinated dance to something Joe was playing on his phone.

"You're right. We're Fraser's only hope," James shook his head.

"Oi," Joe called over to them when he noticed they were looking at them. "What are you lot looking at?"

"We need to go if we're going to be at the club when Fraser arrives," James answered.

Joe picked his phone up from Freddie's counter and shoved it in his pocket.

"What are we waiting for?" He waltzed past them into the hallway, Freddie trailing closely behind. "Let's go."

Tessa and James exchanged a look before following the two men, Tessa closing and locking the door behind her.

The club's music was too loud for Tessa's comfort, but it wasn't so loud that it drowned out her friends' conversation.

As she settled herself at the table they found, she glanced over at Fraser.

He was wearing dark wash jeans and a dark grey button-up shirt, buttoned most of the way to the top, and French tucked into his trousers.

"You look nice," Tessa leaned in toward Fraser so he could hear her over the music.

She could see Fraser's cheeks color. "Thanks," he shouted over the music. "I wasn't sure what to wear, and even more unsure if I could even wear jeans. I'm glad you're also wearing them, so we can both be in this faux pas together if we were supposed to wear something nicer."

Tessa laughed. "It's not a faux pas. You're fine. You should relax."

Fraser took a deep breath, held it, and let it out. "I'm so nervous. This is my first time at a club."

Tessa tried to hide her surprise, but knew she was failing. "Really? Not even at school?"

Fraser shook his head. "My mum has been ill for most of my life. After my dad left, I was the only one who could take care of her. I've been a bit of a hermit, honestly. Finished my A-Levels and did most of my university courses online, worked from home. I don't want something to happen to my mum and not be there for her."

Tessa reached over and placed a hand on his arm. "You are a good man, Fraser, and an excellent son. But you deserve to have a little time for yourself."

Fraser dropped his gaze to where she had placed her hand on his arm before bringing it back up and meeting hers.

Tessa's gut clenched when their eyes met.

There was something in the way he looked at her that made her feel a little uneasy, but she couldn't quite place it.

She removed her hand and placed it in her lap.

Fraser kept his gaze on her, causing her to squirm a little in her seat.

He was socially awkward; she told herself. He's been isolated in his home. He didn't know how to act around others. That's all this is.

Tessa forced herself to smile, which caused Fraser's smile to widen, and whatever it was she saw in his gaze disappeared.

"We have booze!" Joe announced as he, Freddie, and James made their way to the table.

James had a pint in each hand, as did Freddie, and Joe, well, Joe was carrying a tray of shots.

"You don't have to take one," James muttered, as he took his seat next to her, placing her pint in front of her. "Don't let him pressure you."

"James, I don't like that you are always warning people away from me, as if I'm some sort of bad influence. I'm a well-respected London police officer."

"Who is very charismatic, and who likes to goad people into doing his bidding when out," James observed, "remember the night after the Fitzgerald verdict?"

Joe set the tray on the table and folded his arms, staring off into the distance before shaking his head. "No, I can't say that I do."

"Neither do I, and neither do Patrick and Evie. All I know is it started off with coming to a place like this, and you bringing over a tray exactly like this one, and then it's a blur."

"We were all equal participants in that night of revelry," Joe defended. "I will not take the blame for what you do and do not remember."

Tessa laughed, taking a sip of her pint. "I'm going to pass on the shots. I have to be up at three so I can get to the bakery in time to, you know, bake. I can't be hungover."

James sat back and placed his arm around her shoulders. "I'm out, too. Solidarity."

"Spoilsports," Joe teased. "More for the rest of us. Drink up chaps, we're in for a wild night!"

Freddie and Joe immediately reached for a shot. Tessa couldn't help but smile. This was the happiest and most carefree she'd seen Freddie in a while. Even if his relationship with Joe was short-lived, it was a wonderful experience for him.

Fraser moved a little slower, but he also grabbed a shot.

The three men counted down from three and threw back their respective shots before setting the glasses back on the table.

"Alright, lads, let's away!" Joe shouted, leading the charge, holding tightly to Freddie's hand as they made their way to the dance floor.

Fraser shot her and James a pitiful look before he, too, followed Joe into the abyss.

James tightened his arm around Tessa's shoulder and brought his head down. He used his nose to push aside her hair before planting a kiss on her neck.

"First date outside the home?" Tessa asked, her voice already taking on a breathy quality.

"Mmm," James hummed against her neck as he traced his way up to her ear, giving it a little nibble. "First double date, too." He captured her lips with his.

Tessa felt like a schoolgirl again, sitting in a club making out with a hot guy.

Freddie was right. Getting out was a good thing.

When James' hand traveled to her breast, she pulled away.

"Want to dance?" she gasped out.

"What I want is to leave this place and go home and get into bed with you, but I'll settle for dancing."

James stood and held his hand out for her. She placed her hand in his and he led her to the dance floor.

***

Dancing was not the activity she needed for her overactive libido.

The booming music cast a steady beat for the last half hour as she and James moved together on the dance floor.

Right now, he was behind her, and she could feel his erection digging into her ass as they moved together to the heavy bass line, and she finally had enough.

She knew it was earlier than she had promised, but she didn't care. She wanted to go home and fuck her boyfriend before going to sleep.

She turned around and draped her arms around James' neck, pulling him down to talk to her. "Want to get out of here?"

"Fuck, yes," James growled into her ear.

"I need to use the loo first. I'm bursting."

"I'll go tell the others we're taking off, and I'll meet you by the loos, so we're not wandering 'round trying to find one another and stuck here for eternity."

Tessa laughed. "Good idea."

James gave her one more quick, searing kiss before they parted. She watched briefly as James weaved his way through the gyrating bodies of the fellow club goers before turning herself in the loo's direction.

She pushed open the door and as it shut behind her; she breathed in a sigh of relief. The music was much quieter in here. Her ears still rang as she took care of her business and washed her hands.

She took a second to check out her appearance in the mirror. She had time. It would take a few minutes for James to find Joe, say their goodbyes, and make his way back to her.

As she scrutinized her appearance in the mirror, she couldn't keep the smile off her face. Things were going really well with her and James. They had only been a couple for a week, but boy, what a week it had been.

She tried to tame her hair, but decided it was fruitless, especially given what they planned to do back at his flat.

She bit her lip to hold back the smile.

She tucked her hair behind her ears and practically skipped to the door.

When she stepped back into the hall with the bathrooms, the music playing at its normal volume was too much for her.

She stopped outside the door and looked down the hall.

To her right, there was just a dark hall which led to an emergency exit, the left led back to the dance floor. Both ways were empty, so James must've still been talking to Joe.

She walked the few feet from the door of the women's room to where the hall met the main floor. From here, she would be more visible to James, and they could leave right away.

She stood on her tiptoes and looked around and she could see James' familiar red hair weaving its way through the crowd.

He broke through the crowd, looking around for the hall.

She raised her arm to get his attention, when something wrapped around her waist and neck.

Whatever had wrapped itself around her body jerked her backwards hard enough for her glasses to be knocked off her face.

Arms.

These things, wrapped around her, were arms.

And they were swiftly dragging her toward the emergency exit.

CHAPTER 25

James turned when he caught movement out of the corner of his eye.

He smiled as he caught Tessa signaling to him. He couldn't wait to get back to his place and have her to himself for the night.

He started toward her, but stopped short when he watched her suddenly jerk backward into the dark hall.

It only took a second for him to realize she was being pulled. His heart skipped a beat before he took off at a run.

He shoved his way around the drunk people in his way and ran full speed.

His feet skidded on the polished concrete floor as he made the sharp turn into the hallway. Something crunched beneath his feet as he entered the hall. Looking down, he could see Tessa's glasses lying on the floor. The pit in his stomach grew. How hard did the bastard grab her for her glasses to fall from her face?

He looked up from the floor to look for Tessa.

The hall was so poorly lit, and he could barely make out the two figures of Tessa and her assailant.

Whoever was dragging her was trying to be quick, however, dragging a struggling Tessa was slowing him down. Which was good for James.

As James ran toward them, he cursed to himself. He should have thought ahead and put his knife in his pocket. Given him some sort of defense if the kidnapper had a weapon.

James shook that thought from his head. His priority should be to get to them before they made it to the emergency exit and caused the alarm to sound, creating chaos in the club.

Running through the hall, it was as if he were in a dream. Everything seemed to move in slow motion, and the hallway never seemed to get shorter. He was convinced he wasn't gaining any ground. Like he was running in place on a treadmill.

As he got closer, his heart skipped a beat as he could see Tessa being dragged more clearly. Her legs were kicking out from under her, trying to find purchase on the polished concrete floor of the club. It was too dark to make out her expression, but he didn't need to see it to know she was terrified, because he was terrified.

He was just about to close in on them when they stopped, and the kidnapper let go of Tessa and thrust her at him.

James watched as Tessa, not prepared to stand fully on her own, fell, face first, toward the ground.

He sprinted across the gap between them and dove, wrapping his arms around her, holding her tightly as they both went down. As they got closer to the floor, James turned so he would make impact with his side, and rolled onto his back, holding his head up and not letting it smash onto the concrete.

Quickly glancing at Tessa to make sure she was okay, James rolled to his side to see if he could get a look at the kidnapper.

He caught the back of the man just as he reached the emergency exit.

The man turned around briefly, looking toward James and Tessa.

James couldn't make out any features, it was too dark.

And just as quickly as the man had stopped, he pushed through the emergency exit, which didn't set off any alarms, and ran out into the dark of the night.

As soon as he couldn't see the man anymore, he turned his attention to Tessa.

He could feel her shaking in his arms.

He sat them up and moved them so she was sitting on his lap, facing him.

James brought his hands up to her face and pushed her hair back so he could get a good look at her.

She was crying, her mascara running down her face.

"Are you hurt?" he asked. He almost asked if she was okay, which was a stupid question. Of course, she wasn't okay.

She shook her head. "Not really."

"What hurts?" James asked, looking her over, moving his hands down her body as he assessed for injuries.

"My neck and my stomach from where he grabbed me."

James brought his hand up to her neck, moving her hair out of the way. It was hard to tell in the dimly lit hallway, but he thought he could make out some bruising.

"We need to talk to Joe and make a report."

"Joe's drunk."

James shook his head. "Not a report to him. We need him to make the call to someone on duty to come and take the report. Can you stand?"

Tessa nodded. "Yeah, I think so."

James shifted them so he could help Tessa get to her feet, before standing himself.

She was a little wobbly, but that was probably more because she was still shaking than her actually being injured.

"My glasses."

"I'm sorry. I stepped on them when I chased after you. They're broken."

"It's okay."

"How poor is your vision?"

"I can see fine. I won't be able to read anything too far away, but you're not a blur or anything."

James wrapped an arm around her and helped lead her through the crowd.

He scowled at everyone who bumped into them as they weaved across the dance floor.

He'd been having so much fun tonight, and had been looking forward to what was going to happen next, and now, his mood was soured, and all he wanted to do was find the arsehole who tried to kidnap his girlfriend and beat the shit out of him.

Joe and Freddie were where he had left them, with the addition of Fraser. When he had said goodbye, Fraser had been off flirting with some bird, and Joe and Freddie wouldn't stop gushing like proud parents.

Freddie saw them first.

"What happened?" he asked as he rushed toward them, taking Tessa's hand in his.

James waited until Joe had joined them before answering.

"The stalker escalated."

James knew Joe wasn't as drunk as he had made himself out to be when the second he heard this information, he snapped into police mode. "Where?"

"Back by the loos," James answered.

"What'd he do?"

"He grabbed me, and tried to drag me out of the club," Tessa spoke up beside him.

"Fuck!" Freddie exclaimed, letting go of Tessa to run his hands through his hair.

He looked over at Tessa, who stood next to James as new tears ran down her face.

Freddie grabbed onto her and tugged her away from James, and wrapped her in a tight hug.

"Did you get a good look at the guy?" Joe asked.

James shook his head. "It was too fucking dark. Couldn't see a damn thing."

Joe pulled out his phone and dialed a number. "I'm going to call this in. You two will need to give a statement."

"Yeah, I thought as much."

Joe stepped away and walked toward the exit of the club so he could talk on the phone without the bass interfering.

"What's going on?" Fraser asked, reminding everyone of his presence.

James moved around Freddie and Tessa, pulling Fraser aside. "Tessa has had a bit of an incident. We're going to need to go out and meet with the police."

"The police? This sounds serious. Is she okay?"

"Physically, she's okay, but she's really shaken up."

"Does this have to do with what happened to her window?" Fraser asked, folding his arms and bringing one hand up to rest under his chin.

James frowned. He was getting a strong feeling, but he couldn't figure out what it was trying to tell him. "Yes," he drawled. "We're pretty sure it does."

"Oh my," Fraser intoned, "poor Tessa."

"Yes," James narrowed his eyes slightly, almost imperceptibly, "poor Tessa."

James waited for Fraser to say something else, to do something else, mainly to excuse himself from the situation. However, the man just stood there. Staring at him, standing up straight, his chin still resting in his hand.

That feeling in his gut came back.

Suspicion.

"Where were you about ten minutes ago?" James asked.

Fraser didn't even flinch. "I was over at the bar, trying to pull a girl. It didn't work out." He tilted his head. "You don't think I had something to do with this, do you?"

"I wasn't implying you did," James answered. "Trying to get an idea of where everyone was when it happened. Where were you a week ago Saturday? About two in the morning?"

"At home asleep. Like I've said, I don't go out much. This is my first time at a club."

"Can anyone corroborate your presence?"

"Me mum."

James watched Fraser's face and neck as he answered his questions. He wasn't exhibiting any of the tells of a liar. He was telling the truth. Then why was his gut telling him he wasn't?

Fraser uncrossed his arms and relaxed his posture, and just as suddenly James' suspicions rose, they dissipated. He shook his head, as if clearing the cobwebs.

"Right," he drew out, "since you weren't around, you won't need to stay and give a statement, and unfortunately, I think the night's done for the rest of us."

"Yeah, yeah," Fraser nodded, "I guess I'll just take off then."

"Don't let us ruin the night for you. Stay. Have some fun. Find a bird to go home with."

"Nah, I think I've had enough rejection for the night. Tell Tessa I'll see her at the shop tomorrow morning."

James must have looked confused.

"Me mum and I come in on Wednesday mornings for tea?" Fraser reminded him.

"That's right. I've got my days mixed up. Rarely go dancing in the middle of the week," James forced a smile and a short laugh.

Fraser returned his smile. "Same. I'll see you around, James."

James watched Fraser walk out of the club and couldn't shake the uneasy feeling he had.

When he could no longer see him, James turned toward Freddie and Tessa.

"We should head outside. Joe is calling in the attempt. They'll want to question us."

Tessa pulled back from Freddie and nodded. She stepped away from his arms and walked over and took James' hand.

He led them out of the club and into the frigid November night air.

Joe was standing on the sidewalk talking to the bouncer. He had completely sobered, which meant ninety percent of how he acted in the club was more for show, and he really hadn't drunk as much as he led people to believe.

Joe stopped talking when he noticed the group moving toward him. "Good news," he started once the four of them were together. "This bloke here says they have cameras in the alley, and they keep the footage here on the property. He's just called the manager and they're going to prep the footage for us now. PC Davies is on his way and will meet us in the manager's office."

"That was fast," James failed to keep the surprise out of his voice.

"Because it happened in the last hour, it's easy for the manager to pull up the footage. Let's head in."

Joe led the way, with Freddie following close behind. James took Tessa's hand and helped move her through the crowds.

Her grip on his hand was tight, as if she was worried someone could snatch her away from him at any moment.

He gripped her just as firmly, the same fear etched in his brain.

Watching her getting dragged through the hallway was the most helpless he had felt in a long time. He would be damned if he let anything else happen to her ever again.

They reached the manager's office and walked in. The room was small, barely big enough for everyone to fit, but they squeezed in and shut the door behind them.

"PC McCleary?" the manager, a thirty-something woman with a no-nonsense haircut and business suit, asked.

Joe lifted his hand. "That would be me."

She nodded. "I have the footage pulled up for the time in which the incident took place. But I'm afraid it won't be much help."

She turned her monitor around so the room could see. She pressed play, and they watched as the door to the club opened and a man ran out.

The footage was black and white and a little grainy. Because of the lack of color, you could only see that the man was wearing some sort of dark shirt and dark trousers, which was the dress of most of the men in the club. And he was wearing a dark knit hat, covering any identifying features, which weren't many, since he was looking at the ground as he ran.

"What the fuck is it with this guy and cameras?" James exclaimed, pointing at the video. "There's no fucking way he knew there was a camera in that alley."

"Maybe he scoped it out before tonight?" Freddie posited.

Joe shook his head. "We didn't even decide to come here until this morning. There's no way he could have known to come here and scout the alley."

"Then how did he know I was here in the first place?" Tessa asked.

"He probably followed you," Joe explained, "Followed us."

"So, he knows where Freddie lives?" she asked.

"It seems to look that way," Joe apologized.

"I can't go back there," she shook her head.

"You can come stay at mine," James offered, "if you want," he quickly added, remembering their conversation about him being overprotective.

"Yeah, I think I want that," she gave him a small smile, reassuring him he hadn't overstepped.

"I can bring round your stuff tomorrow," Freddie suggested, "after the shop closes."

"Thanks."

There was a knock on the door of the office before it cracked open. PC Davies poked his head in.

"Full house," he commented.

"I'll get out of the way. Stay as long as you like," the manager squeezed her way through to the door.

Everyone shifted and let PC Davies in.

"So," he pulled out his phone and turned on his recording app, "tell me what happened."

They took turns recounting what had happened, but hearing the story told back, James knew it was hopeless. No one had seen his face, or any identifying features.

They still didn't have a suspect.

James stood up straighter. If they were living in a cartoon, he was pretty sure a light bulb would flash above his head.

"Bruno Nelson."

"Who's that?" PC Davies asked.

"He's someone who went to school with Freddie and Tessa. He had an obsession with Tessa in school. I've been looking at him as a probable stalking suspect. I had been sitting outside his house, but obviously I wasn't there tonight."

"Do you think he could have done this?" Freddie asked.

"It's quite plausible. He has motive. He knew I was sitting outside and watching him, so he would have noticed I wasn't there today. Since he and Freddie used to be friends, he could have knowledge of where Freddie lives. It's quite possible he could have left his house, followed you from Freddie's and, when you went to the loo, escalated things."

"Why would he want to escalate things now? Over a week since he would have thrown the brick?" PC Davies asked. "Allegedly," he added quickly.

"He came into my shop and confronted me about having James following him," Tessa added.

"It's not hard evidence, but it's a lead. We'll go round and I'll question him myself."

"Thank you," Tessa said.

"My professional advice is to go home, get some sleep, and don't be too worried. Let us do our job," he made a show of turning off his recording. "My non-professional advice would be to be careful, be aware of your surroundings, and don't go anywhere alone."

Tessa nodded.

"I'll drive you to the shop," James offered.

Tessa shook her head. "I couldn't have you do that. It's so early."

James shrugged. "I can always come back home and go to sleep once you're in the shop."

"And I'll make sure you get to James' after you're done at the shop," Freddie spoke up.

"Looks like you're in excellent hands," PC Davies commented. "I'll be in touch. I'll let you know if anything comes from looking into this Bruno fellow."

He tucked his phone into his pocket and put his hand on the handle to open the door. "Oh," he said, turning around. "Before I forget, earlier tonight, the results of the CCTV search came in. They could find some shots of the bloke with his face uncovered. However, they're terrible shots. Blurry. I sent the files to you both," he pointed to Joe and James, "but I'm afraid they were inconclusive. We're back at square one."

CHAPTER 26

TESSA

Tessa took her glasses off and rubbed her eyes for probably the one hundredth time since she arrived at the shop this morning.

"Tired?" Freddie asked, walking into the kitchen.

"Yes," she placed her glasses back on her face before flapping her hands and jumping from foot to foot to wake herself up.

Freddie moved next to her and set a very large takeaway cup of coffee on the counter. "I figured. I went out and got one of these for each of us."

Tessa stopped her jumping and reached for the coffee on the counter. "You're a blessing."

"Did you sleep at all?"

She shook her head as she took a long drag from the coffee cup. "No. Every time I even drifted off for even a second, I found myself right there, back in the hallway with his arms around me, dragging me to who knows where, and then I would startle myself awake."

Freddie gave her a sympathetic smile. "And James?"

"He didn't sleep at all, I don't think. Every time I woke up, he was awake, watching me."

"He was probably worried about you."

"Yeah, I know. I hope he's getting some sleep now."

Freddie stared at her face, squinting his eyes, before breaking out in a long peel of laughter.

"What's wrong?"

"Have you been rubbing your face a lot?"

"Yes."

He pulled out his phone and opened the camera, flipping it into selfie mode and turning it toward her.

When she caught sight of herself, she about died. Flour and various other ingredients she had been working with all morning covered her face. Even the arms of her favorite purple glasses had flour fingerprints caked all over them.

"Fuck," she rushed over to the sink to wash her face and glasses. "I wonder how long I've looked a mess. I helped customers this morning before Mariel came in."

The admission made Freddie laugh harder.

"It's not funny."

"Oh, it absolutely is," Freddie wiped at the tears forming in his eyes from laughing so hard.

"I'm going to lose customers," she scrubbed her face.

"You're not. They're going to love you all the more because you look like you spent all morning baking delicious things for them to buy. They've probably gone and told all their little grannie friends, and we'll see an influx of visitors at lunch."

"You're trying to make me feel better."

"It's my job as the best friend. Is it working?"

"A little."

"Oh, before I forget, before I came in, I dropped your essentials in your flat so you can grab those when we leave. This way you won't have to wait for me to come back after the shop closes to clean your teeth."

Tessa smiled her first smile since the incident the night before. "Thank you."

"You're welcome. Now down the coffee and let's get to work. The pensioners will swarm this shop soon."

***

Tessa shut James' door behind her and leaned against it.

Freddie was right. Whoever had seen her looking like a mess this morning had spread the word, and they had double the customers they normally had.

She was exhausted.

Freddie was kind enough to walk her to James' flat before heading back to the shop to close it with Mariel.

All she wanted to do was go to sleep.

She took her shoes off by the door and walked through the flat. Joe's bedroom door was wide open, and he wasn't inside. She hoped he was out doing something for himself and he didn't go in on his day off. Not for something for her.

She looked in James' room. Also, empty.

He had probably gone into the office.

She dropped her bag on the floor next to the doorway and shuffled to the bed before falling on it face first.

She was asleep immediately.

***

When she opened her eyes, it was dark outside, and there were sounds coming from the kitchen. She rolled over and looked at the bedside clock. It was after six.

She stretched and sat up.

Her sleep pattern was going to be severely disturbed.

She stood from the bed and made her way out of the room. As she walked down the hallway, she noticed Joe's door was still open and the lights were out. She wondered where he was.

She made it into the kitchen to see James stirring something in a saucepan on the hob.

"What are you making?"

James jumped and turned around, his hand clutching at his chest.

"Bloody hell, Tessa, you're going to give me a fucking heart attack. Walk a little heavier next time."

She laughed. "Sorry, I didn't mean to startle you."

"Admit it. You enjoyed giving me a fright."

"I did."

James turned back to the stove, stirring the pot again. "I'm making ramen. Nothing fancy. I figured we needed a simple comfort meal after last night."

"Ramen actually sounds delicious." She walked over to the bar stools, pulled one out, and hoisted herself onto one, resting her arms on the counter. "What have you been up to today?"

"Spent some time outside of Bruno's. Nada, as usual. Then I went down to see if Officer Davies had found anything."

"Did he?"

"Went and talked to Bruno, and he said he never left the house last night. Which was then confirmed by the CCTV footage from his street. He never left his house. However, Davies pointed out there were no cameras in the back of the house, so they can only say with certainty he never left through the front."

Tessa put her head down on her arms. "We're never going to figure out who's stalking me."

"We will. We just have to be smarter than whoever it is."

"I feel like we're always one step behind them."

"We'll do some brainstorming. See if we can anticipate the next move."

Tessa picked her head up from her arms. "I love your optimism."

"I love you," James proclaimed.

Tessa froze.

James froze.

"What?" Tessa asked.

"Nothing. I said nothing. I love ramen?"

"That's not what you said."

"Just forget I said anything."

"So, you didn't mean what you said?"

James stood at the stove, his back to her. "Do you want me to have meant what I said?"

"We've only just started seeing each other," her voice was hesitant and unsure.

"I know. Just forget what I said."

Tessa watched James stirring the ramen with his back stiff. She thought back to the short time they'd known each other. She knew pretty quickly she felt something more than just friendly toward him. And even with only a couple weeks of dating between them, there was something here that was just... more.

"I don't want to forget what you said."

"What?"

"I said I don't want to forget what you said. Because I'm pretty sure I feel the same."

James set down the spoon he was using to stir and turned off the burner. It was a full five seconds before he turned around, sporting a wide, silly grin.

"You're not having me on, are you?" James asked.

Tessa shook her head.

"Well. Okay then. Let's table this revelation for after we eat our delicious dinner, and then we'll continue it say, in our bed, with less clothing?"

Tessa laughed. "I like the sound of that."

James turned back to the stove and whistled a jaunty tune she wasn't even sure was an actual song or something he had made up.

He dished up the ramen and walked the bowls over to the counter, placing one in front of her and the other in the spot next to his. He went to the fridge and pulled out a pitcher of squash, setting it down on the counter. He then went to the cupboard and pulled out two glasses and gave one to each of them before sitting down next to her on the other bar stool.

It all felt so fucking domestic. Combined with the words they both sort of said to each other, Tessa could feel a warmth spread through her body. This is what her future held for her. She could get used to this.

"How was the shop today?"

Tessa groaned. "It was a madhouse. I was so tired this morning, I kept rubbing my face. And apparently, I rubbed all sorts of flour and pumpkin and whatever all over it, I looked a right mess. Well, I served some grannies first thing. They thought I looked charming and spread the word, and I'm pretty sure every pensioner in London was in my shop this afternoon."

"That's wonderful!"

Tessa shot him a look.

"I mean, it's wonderful for your business."

"It is, it truly is, and I'll always be so grateful for all the people who come into my shop, but we really need to hire more people going into Christmas if this is going to be the normal flow of customers. I'll never be able to keep up with the baking on my own."

"Well, I hope you find someone worthy of working in your kitchen." James raised his glass to her in a toast.

She laughed and raised her glass, and they clinked them together before each taking a sip and turning toward their dinner.

"Did Fraser and his mum come in today?" James asked after they had eaten for a few minutes.

Tessa shook her head. "No. They didn't show. His mum probably wasn't having a good day today."

"I'm going to say something, and I don't want you to get offended. I know you like Fraser and everything, but last night—"

"He was acting strangely," Tessa interrupted.

"Yes, well, not exactly, but there was something strange about him. I don't know. My instincts were telling me to keep an eye on him, but he wasn't really giving me anything *to* suspect. He was telling the truth every time I asked him a direct question."

"It wasn't just you. We made eye contact last night, and there was something in his eyes that made me feel uneasy."

"Be careful around him, Tessa. I know he's one of your best customers, and his mum is really nice, but I don't know. Just be careful."

Tessa nodded. "I will be."

The door to the flat opened and Joe came walking in, carrying a large bouquet of flowers in his arm.

"Where've you been all day?" James asked.

"I went into the office and helped go over Bruno's CCTV footage, and then went around and looked at the alley in the daylight. Then I got peckish, so I swung by Cake Me Home Tonight. Freddie and Mariel were overwhelmed, so I jumped in to help them out until we closed. Freddie and I picked up a quick bite, and went our separate ways because we're bloody knackered after the last couple of days."

"And he gave you beautiful flowers to thank you for working hard in the shop all afternoon?" Tessa grinned.

"Actually, no. These were outside the door. They have your name on them, Tessa."

He walked over and put the flowers down on the counter next to Tessa and walked to the fridge, pulling out a beer.

Tessa frowned at the flowers. "You got me flowers?" she asked, turning toward James.

He shook his head. "I did not. And those weren't outside the door when I got home an hour ago."

Joe didn't even open his beer. He set the bottle down on the counter. "Touch nothing."

"What? Why?"

"Evidence," James explained.

"I'm going to get my kit so we can process everything." Joe left and walked toward his room.

"You think..."

"The stalker sent you these flowers? Yes."

Tessa stared at the beautiful arrangement. It had a variety of autumn-colored flowers and grasses. It looked expensive. And there, nestled amongst the flowers, was a large envelope with her name scrawled on it in red marker.

James must have followed her gaze, because he held onto her hand. "Remember, we can't touch anything, not until Joe processes everything."

Joe came back out into the room, holding a small bag and a camera. "I'll take pictures of everything, and dust for prints. Once I collect the prints, we can open the envelope and take pictures and prints on whatever is inside."

"I didn't think you could work my stalker case," Tessa pointed out.

"I don't fucking care at this point. The bastard tried to kidnap you. You're my friend, and I'm going to process this as evidence. And if I get shit for it, I'll point my superiors to you almost being abducted and your window."

Tessa watched as Joe moved through the motions of cataloging and fingerprinting everything. She had never seen him so serious before. She'd only ever seen fun, happy partying Joe. Watching him work, and seeing this other side of him, she instantly understood why Freddie was attracted to him and why they fit so well together.

"Alright," Joe finished his thorough investigation of the package, "let's open this and see what this bastard has to say now."

Joe plucked the envelope from the flowers, took a couple pictures, lifted a couple of prints and, with his gloved hands, opened the flap.

He pulled out one sheet from the envelope.

He unfolded it and set it down on the counter.

A chill rushed over Tessa as she looked at what came with the flowers.

It was a picture of her and James dancing last night in the club. Over her face, drawn in red marker, was a heart with an arrow drawn through it, bisecting her head. Over James' face, an 'x' had drawn angrily until it had ripped holes in the picture.

What really chilled her were the words scrawled across the bottom of the photo.

"Discard your redheaded twat, or you'll be sorry. If I can't have you, nobody can."

CHAPTER 27

JAMES

For the second night in a row, James couldn't sleep. Every time he closed his eyes, visions of something terrible happening to Tessa flooded his mind. All he could do was lay awake and stare at his girlfriend, and hope she wouldn't just vanish when he looked away.

He could tell she was having trouble sleeping again because she was restless, tossing and turning in her sleep.

He looked at his watch, noticing it wouldn't be long until they needed to be up to go to the shop, so falling asleep now would be fruitless. He debated getting up, but he would feel trapped without something to do.

He felt helpless. At least they had a purpose when they tried to save Evie. They knew who they were protecting her from. With Tessa, there was no suspect. He didn't even know where to start. Every lead they had seemed to come up empty. They had no viable suspects.

Except for Bruno. Who was a suspect, and a pretty good one. Nevertheless, there was no evidence that he was the one responsible for any of this.

"I can hear your thoughts. You're thinking so loud," Tessa whispered from the bed next to him.

James looked down at her and gave her a small smile. "I'm sorry. Didn't mean for my thoughts to wake you."

"I wasn't asleep, really, so there was nothing to wake me from."

James brought up a hand and ran it down her arm. "I'm sorry, love. I hate to be the bearer of bad news, but we need to be up soon to go into the shop."

Tessa groaned. "Another day of looking like a mess in front of customers."

James chuckled. "The upside? More. Customers."

"So many customers."

"Did you ever imagine being *the* bakery in East London when you opened Cake Me Home Tonight?"

"No. We both thought that we would barely make enough to cover our expenses. Which is what we were doing for the longest time. After a year, we were doing really well, and were actually making money for once. If I'd known all it would take were pumpkin bars to skyrocket our business to fame, I would have made them the first autumn we were open."

"They *are* fucking good pumpkin bars."

"They really are," Tessa laughed.

"What are you going to make for Christmas?"

"Well, mince pies."

"Obviously."

"I also usually make mini–Yule Logs, and mini trifles. Traditionally, I set up an order form on my website for Christmas Puddings. I'm hoping we'll have help by then because I'm worried too many people will order and I won't be able to make them all, which wasn't a problem I've had in the past, but with my newfound popularity, I think it very well might be."

"I have stopped at your shop so many times, but I have never gone in around Christmas."

"Do you do your own Christmas baking?"

James laughed. "No. No, I'm not the best baker. My mum usually does the baking and gives me enough to feed an army. Last Christmas, Evie was feeling homesick, so she made so many bakes. It was overwhelming."

"Evie can bake?"

"She can. And she's fantastic at it."

In the dark, he could see Tessa's eyes widen. "Do you think she would want to help at the shop? I know she is teaching at the university, but not during Christmas hols."

"She might. You should ask her when she gets back from honeymoon."

"I will! Thank you."

"For what?"

"Everything. Meeting you has been such a blessing. My life is different now because of you."

James smiled. "I could say the same to you."

"I guess it's a good thing I came into your office asking for help."

"And that I, the ever consummate over worker, had not left the office when Patrick ordered me to."

Tessa moved closer to him, wrapping her arms around his neck, pulling him in toward her.

He helped close the gap, capturing her lips with his.

The kiss was gentle, and he could feel everything she was feeling for him poured into this one kiss. He hoped she could feel everything he was feeling through his kiss.

He really meant what he had said the night before. He loved her. And it scared him how quickly and easily he could fall for her.

He finally understood Patrick and Evelyn and the beginning of their relationship. He never could figure out how they could fall so quickly for one another. And now he did. Sometimes, love needed little time to grow. It could come on suddenly, out of nowhere.

And it was fucking scary.

James broke the kiss and gazed deeply into Tessa's dark eyes. "I love you."

"I love you, too," she answered with no hesitation.

"Sorry I can't make it any safer for you, but we'll figure it out. I can lean on Bruno, ask him—"

"James?" Tessa interrupted. "No offense, but I *really* don't want to talk about Bruno right now."

She didn't wait for him to answer before pulling him down to kiss him again. This time the kiss was a little more heated, Tessa making it very clear what she wanted to do. And James was completely on board.

He shifted them until she was under him, and he could feel her curves against him.

They moved together in a practiced manner as if they had been doing this for years, peeling clothes off one another, pulling a condom out of the bedside table, and putting it on.

They had slept together almost every night since the first time the night of the wedding, but there was something different about this time. As if neither one was holding back. They didn't need to suppress their feelings, which James, at least, had thought had come on too early, too quickly.

James looked into Tessa's eyes as they came together and knew he would do anything for her. To make her happy. To keep her safe. Even if it meant sacrificing his own happiness. His own safety.

James rolled off of her, pulling her along with him, letting her settle on his chest as they caught their breath.

He ran his hand up and down her back as they caught their breath.

"Wow," Tessa's voice was airy as she tried to catch her breath.

"Yeah."

"I feel like I could sleep now. We should have done this earlier in the night."

James looked over at the clock on his bedside table. "We still have half an hour until we need to be up and at the shop. You should close your eyes and try to get some rest."

Tessa shook her head. "That's not enough time."

"It is. Close your eyes. I'll wake you when we need to leave."

He didn't have to tell her again, as he could hear her breathing grow heavier.

He tightened his grip on her as he, too, closed his eyes, letting her breathing lull him into his own slumber.

***

James looked around the small interior of Cake Me Home Tonight and couldn't believe it could hold so many people at once.

He chose to spend the day working at the shop. To his surprise, he didn't even have to list off his many reasons he should. Tessa agreed immediately. She was likely still rattled from the night prior.

However, after being at the shop for an hour, he realized he wouldn't get much work done. Not when he was watching Tessa try to juggle the influx of customers while finishing her baking in the back.

He set aside what he was failing to work on and sent her back into the kitchen. He handled the till, trying to ease some of the stress, until Mariel and Freddie came in.

And then at lunch, it was an all hands on-deck situation.

So many people.

James watched as the inventory dwindled.

Eventually, Tessa went back into the kitchen to prepare some baked goods to last until the store closed, and the number of customers decreased, and the area became still. James sat in his chair where he had placed his laptop and bag and sighed.

"You okay, mate?" Freddie asked, sitting down in the chair across from him.

"Is it like this, every day?"

"Ever since we put up the countdown to no more pumpkin bars? Yes."

"Fuck."

"I know. Tessa keeps thinking it will slow down once she no longer serves the thing that brought everyone in, but I don't have the heart to tell her this is more than likely our new normal."

"Hence hiring more people."

Freddie pointed a finger at him. "Exactly."

"I think she's going to ask Evie if—"

A scream from the kitchen cut through the shop.

James and Freddie leapt from their chairs and ran in the kitchen's direction. As they pushed through the door, Tessa was standing in the center of the kitchen, staring at the wall directly across from her, her hands up at her mouth, covering it.

James followed her line of sight and anger flowed into him.

Pinned on the wall using one of her knives was another picture, this time taken of them walking into the shop this morning, hand in hand, the knife going through Tessa's face.

"He's following us," Tessa whispered.

"He's escalating again." Freddie pointed out. "This is three days in a row. He's never done things three days in a row. And he's never outright threatened you."

"It's me. It's because of me." James stated.

"Mate," Freddie started.

"No. Look, the brick through the window happened the night we transitioned to a romantic relationship. The kidnapping, our first out of the flat date. The flowers and this now that you're staying at my flat. He upped his game when we started dating each other."

"We all know correlation is not causation," Freddie rationalized. "It could be a coincidence."

"He's jealous. He's jealous that I'm dating you and not him."

"I'm going to call Joe and tell him about this. Touch nothing. I know they're going to want to pull prints." Freddie pulled out his cell and walked to the front of the shop, dialing as he walked.

"When did he have time to do this?" Tessa mused. "He had to have come in the back."

"The shop was so busy all morning. He had ample opportunities to sneak back here. We never would have noticed," James pointed out.

His mind couldn't stay still. He caused the escalation. He just knew it. There was no other explanation.

"Do you even think CCTV would be helpful at this point?" Tessa asked. "We could look through the footage, and see if we can spot anything—"

"I think we need to break up."

The words were out of his mouth before he even realized what he was saying.

Tessa froze.

She stared at him, her eyes darting around his face to see if he really meant what he was saying.

"Wha-what do you mean? Break up? Why?"

"He's spiraling. It's obvious he's escalated because of our relationship. It will be best if we put everything on pause for now."

"Best? How is this the best solution? I love you." Tessa's voice broke. Which broke his heart.

He wanted to take everything back. But he knew this was the only way. The best way to keep her safe.

"I love you, too, but—"

"Then why are you ending things?"

"It's only temporary." James reassured her. "Only until we can catch the stalker. I think it will deescalate the situation. Make the overt threats stop. Once we catch him—"

"What if we never catch him?" Tessa shouted. "Huh? What then? Are we to never be together because some fucking arsehole threatened me? Am I never allowed to be happy as long as he's out there?"

Tears stung the back of James' eyes. He blinked them away. "We'll catch him."

"Is that all you have to say?"

James swallowed the lump in his throat as he nodded, not trusting his voice.

Tessa shook her head, swiping at the tears running down her cheeks, leaving a trail of flour behind.

"I think you should go," her voice was hoarse.

"Tessa..."

"No. I can't have you around. Not when," she swallowed, "not when you've broken my heart. I'll have Freddie come round and get my things."

"I'm sorry," James murmured. "I truly think this is the best thing for us right now."

"Yes. So, you've said. It doesn't matter what I want or what I think. You've decided."

"Don't be like that!" James shouted before wincing. He didn't mean to be that loud.

"Be like what? Upset that the man I love, who I told to not be an overprotective wanker, is doing exactly that? Pulling his man card like some fucking hero? Fuck you, James Moore!" by now she was shouting at him, practically sobbing her words. "When

Patrick gets back from his honeymoon, I want him on the case. I never want to see you again."

This time, James didn't stop the tears. He let them fall down his cheek. "If that's what you want."

"It is. So, please respect that."

He nodded. "I will."

The two of them stood there, silence enveloping the room.

James didn't know how things had gotten to this point. He wanted a temporary break, but it had spiraled into Tessa never wanting to see him again.

He needed to fix this.

"I won't bother you, but I'll keep working, and I'll send Joe round if I find anything. I love you, Tessa."

He didn't wait for her to respond. Instead, he turned on his heel and marched out of the kitchen.

He ignored Freddie and Mariel's stares as he gathered his things, and walked out of the door into the street.

He briefly glanced at the alley across the shop. He could have sworn he had seen a figure duck further in the shadows, but when he tried to get a better look, there was nothing there.

CHAPTER 28

TESSA

The only sound in the kitchen after James left was Tessa's sobs. The tears streamed down her face as her heart slowly broke apart.

The door to the kitchen swung open and she could already tell who it was by the sound of the footsteps.

She turned around and crashed into Freddie's chest as his arms wrapped around her, pulling her tightly to him.

"What happened? Mariel and I could hear you two shouting, and then James just stormed out of here."

Tessa tried to catch her breath. "He...he...he broke up with me."

"Are you fucking serious? Are you sure? Because I was talking to him right before we came in here, and he gave no sign he would break up with you. Quite the opposite, in fact."

Tessa swallowed, feeling her tears subside a bit. "He thinks being with me is what caused the stalker to escalate. So, he broke up with me to keep me safe."

"That is complete rubbish," Freddie growled. "Don't you get a say in the matter?"

"Yes. I told him as much. He brushed me off, saying it was only temporary. Once they catch the stalker, we can get back together."

"What if they don't catch the stalker? What then?"

"I told him I never want to see him again."

"Oh," Freddie whispered.

"Will you get my things from his flat?"

"I'll text Joe. I'll have him pack them up and bring them to mine." Freddie let go of Tessa and gave a quick text to Joe. "You're staying at mine again, yeah?"

Tessa shook her head. "I kind of just want to go home."

Freddie nodded. "Yeah, yeah. Right. So, I'm completely on board with whatever you want to do, but let me go buy and install a camera, okay? And clean the place up a little. The window still is just a board, but it's livable, after I hoover one more time to make sure we've gotten all the glass. Can you agree to these terms?"

"A security camera outside my door and my flat cleaned for free? Yes, I think I can be amenable."

"Brilliant. It's way past the time you clock off you should go back to my flat and take a nap, pack up whatever you want that you left behind, Joe will swing by with the rest, and I'll text you once I've finished."

Tessa tilted her head. "You're not going to walk me back and forth?"

"You've just had a man tell you what's going to happen in your life. Do you really want me to do the same? It's daylight, and you're in the middle of London. You'll be fine."

Tessa gave him a wavering smile. "Thank you."

"You're welcome. Now go. I have Ben and Jerry's in the freezer. It's yours."

Tessa moved forward and gave him a tight hug. "I love you."

"Love you, too," he paused. "I'm sorry you've had your heart broken."

"Thank you. I just wish I understood why he thought this was the only solution. He told me he loved me last night."

Freddie took a step back and held her at arm's length. "Here's the thing about blokes like James. He's the heroic sort. People like him are always wanting to do the saving, even if it means sacrificing their own happiness. Unfortunately, it means your happiness gets to be collateral damage."

"I told him not to do heroic shit."

Freddie gave her a wry smile. "And did you actually think that would work?"

She shook her head. "No, but I thought it would manifest in him moving into my flat, or taking up a part-time job at the shop. I didn't realize it would mean him breaking up with me for my safety. How fucked up is that? He actually used those words. For your own safety. Like we're in a film."

"Yes, he's a right twat, and I want to eat ice cream with you and dish about all of this. But later, after we've taken care of everything, yeah?"

She nods.

"Great. Go to my flat. Wallow, take a nap, take a bubble bath with the ice cream, and I'll let you know when it is safe for you to come back to your flat."

She took off her apron and threw it on the counter. She patted her pockets to make sure she had her mobile and keys, and walked out of the kitchen.

"Hey, Tessa?"

Tessa turned to see Mariel standing at the counter, holding her arm with her hand.

"Are you okay?"

Tessa gave her a small smile. "No, I'm not."

"If you want to talk, you have my number."

"Thank you, Mar."

Tessa pushed her way out of the door and made her way to the Tube and to Freddie's.

She was really proud of herself. She didn't cry on the train. However, she barely made it inside Freddie's before completely falling apart. She found her way to the guest room before collapsing completely on the bed and crying herself to sleep.

***

Tessa woke as the sun was setting. She sat up in the bed and stretched. She moved to the edge and listened.

It sounded like no one was here. She picked up her mobile and checked the time. It was a little after five, and she had a couple of missed texts from Freddie.

FREDDIE: All finished here. You can come home whenever.

FREDDIE: Joe dropped your things off here. Talk to you soon.

Tessa breathed a sigh of relief. She could go home.

Freddie was really nice to let her stay, but she just wanted to go home.

She stood from the bed, pocketing her mobile and walking out of the guest room.

She made her way into the bathroom and, after relieving herself, she looked into the mirror above the sink while washing her hands.

Fuck, she looked a fright.

Her hair was a frizzy mess from sleeping in a half bun, and her eyes were all red and puffy.

She took out her hair band and tried to smooth her hair and tame it back into a ponytail. Once she thought she could get on the underground and not be mistaken for a zombie, she dried her hands and exited the bathroom.

She went back to the guest room and threw her clothes into a bag. There were a lot. She didn't know she had brought so much of her wardrobe with her.

After everything was in her tote, she slung it across her chest and walked toward the door.

She hesitated for a second, contemplating whether she should text someone and let them know she was on her way to her flat, and stopped.

The person she wanted to text was James. He was no longer an option. Not anymore.

Tears immediately sprung to her eyes, and she blinked them away. She could fall apart at home.

Her hand reached for the door handle and hesitated. She turned back into the flat and walked up to the freezer and ripped the door open. She reached inside and grabbed a Ben and Jerry's and threw it in her tote. Freddie told her she could have it, and she knew she didn't have any at home.

Determined to make it home before becoming a mess again, she marched out the door and out into the evening.

After an uneventful train ride, she made her way toward the shop. As she turned the corner of her street, a chill ran down her spine. She shivered, coming to an abrupt stop across from her building.

As she gazed up at the window that was covered with boards, a feeling of unease began to settle in the pit of her stomach.

"C'mon, Tessa. Freddie said everything was fine," she muttered to herself.

She straightened her shoulders and quickly crossed the road. She pulled her key and inserted it into the front lock and froze.

She twisted her head and looked behind her into the alley. The one James said her stalker liked to hide in.

It was dark, but she thought it looked empty.

She spun back to the shop, unlocked the door, and pushed her way inside. She immediately locked the door behind her.

The shop had only been closed for an hour, Mariel and Freddie had only been gone maybe half that, but with the sun going down so early these days, the shop gave off an eerie, almost abandoned feel. Or was that just her fears projecting themselves into the atmosphere?

Keeping her keys in hand, she made her way through the shop, through the kitchen, and up the back stairs to her flat.

She made her way through the hall and stopped in front of her door.

She looked up to see if she could spot the camera Freddie had installed and give him a little wave, since she knew he must have activated it before leaving.

She frowned.

There was no camera.

She looked behind her.

Nothing.

The unease that had settled in her stomach earlier rose again.

Something wasn't right.

She pulled out her phone and checked it again.

The messages were there. She hadn't imagined it.

She moved to put the phone back in her pocket when it vibrated.

She looked at it again. A message from Freddie.

FREDDIE: Shop got busy after you left. Helped Mar close it. Just getting round to the shop with the cameras. Sit tight. I'll be back soon. Start eating ice cream without me.

Tessa took a step back from the door.

If Freddie hadn't texted her, who had?

She looked around and breathed a sigh of relief. She seemed to be alone in the hallway.

She looked down at her phone again.

The two texts from Freddie had come in different threads. Why didn't she notice it before?

She clicked on the one she received from Freddie earlier and forwarded it to Joe, telling him she didn't think this came from Freddie and if he could tell who it was from.

After sending the message, she put her hand on the handle to her flat and turned.

Locked.

Tessa let out the breath she had been holding. If the door was locked, she was fine. She was already here, she might as well go in.

She put her key in the lock and opened her door. She took about two steps in before stopping dead in her tracks.

Candles covered every surface in her flat. Hundreds of them, and they had all been lit. It must have taken whoever it was who put them there ages to light them all.

Tessa turned her head, her breathing speeding up as she took in the scene.

Playing over a wireless speaker, loud, but not so loud you could hear it from the hall, was Eddie Money's 'Take Me Home Tonight.' Her dad's favorite song. The song she had taken her shop name from.

The upbeat mood of the song contrasted with every feeling coursing through her right now.

She swallowed a lump in her throat as panic rose.

She fucked up.

She spun around, trying to see who was in her flat. But she couldn't see anyone.

She pulled out her phone and dialed the first number she could think of. One she dialed out of habit. The one person she hoped would come help her during this time.

James.

The phone rang as she brought it up to her ear.

Once.

Twice.

A third time.

The phone clicked as if he had answered it.

Behind her, the door to her flat slammed shut.

"Hello?"

Someone from behind her grabbed her phone out of her hand and threw it across the room. She heard it smash against a wall and cringed.

Whoever was behind her pressed himself against her back until she could feel the warmth of his body radiating against hers.

He wrapped an arm around her waist, pulling her in tight against him. His breath was warm against her ear as he leaned in, and in a voice she clearly recognized, sang along with the song, "Be my little baby."

CHAPTER 29

JAMES

James hadn't wanted to go home after Tessa had kicked him out of the shop.

After he had broken her heart.

It was still early afternoon, so he went into the office.

At first, he tried to distract himself with cases from his email. However, his brain couldn't stand it. If he was going to get the case solved quickly so he could get on his knees and beg Tessa to take him back, he had to focus on her case.

He opened his email and pulled up the one from PC Davies.

The blurry photos of the stalker.

He also pulled up the CCTV footage from Tuesday, the alley behind the club.

The clues to identify the person who was stalking Tessa had to be somewhere among these items.

His phone rang.

Joe.

"Hello."

"So, I'm here at Cake Me Home Tonight, because Freddie called and said the stalker had struck again, with another threat, and what to my surprise neither you nor Tessa are here. The two people the threat was aimed at. And when I asked why you two were missing, Freddie comes to tell me you broke up with her! What the fuck, James?"

"I—"

"Freddie told me. And look, I'm going to say this with all the love I can, because I'm your friend. This was probably the stupidest thing you've ever done."

"I know."

"She's perfect for you."

"I know."

"Now that we're on the same page, I wanted to let you know Davies came in and processed the scene, and took the prints back to the lab. I'm sticking around the shop to help Freddie and Mariel since they sent Tessa home. When the shop closes, I'm going to stick around and shop for cameras with Freddie and help him install it. Are you at the flat?"

"No. I'm at the office."

"Think you'll go home at all tonight?"

"Dunno. Why?"

"Tessa needs her things, so I was going to have you pack them up for me."

James sighed, rubbing his eyes with his free hand. "I can make time to go home."

Silence fell over the line.

"Hey." Joe broke the silence. "For the record, if Freddie were the one in danger, I would have done the same thing. It's the cop in us."

James bit his lip, his eyes stinging a little. "Yeah?"

"Yeah. We'll catch this bastard, and we'll help you do the biggest fucking grand gesture there is to win her back."

"D'ya think she'll take me back?"

"If we solve this within the week? Yes. Month? Probably. Years? Nah."

"Fuck, I hope it doesn't take years for us to solve this case."

"I give it a week. He's getting sloppy. We could pull a lot of prints off the knife today."

"Doesn't help if we have nothing to compare them to."

"Davies is going over to print Bruno."

James sat up straighter in his chair. "What?"

"Freddie told him about Bruno's confrontation in the shop the other day. Said that's reasonable grounds and went and got a fucking warrant. I'm feeling a bit like a proud dad at the moment. The new recruits I've been training up are fucking brilliant."

"So, we're going to have Bruno's prints to compare to all the other ones we have?"

"And we'll have an answer by tonight."

James threw his head back onto his chair, slumping down. "Fucking finally."

"We should thank the bastard for escalating to vandalism and attempted kidnapping," Joe pointed out, "without the escalation, no warrant."

"No warrant, no fingerprints."

"No fingerprints. You would still be sitting outside Bruno's house waiting for him to fucking leave and do something interesting."

"Do you think he's good for it?"

Joe sighed. "Look, he's the most likely suspect. He had that obsession with Tessa. He got caught wanking in the girls' loo while watching her change. He's been seen loitering outside the shop. The man shouted at her a week ago. The judge thinks it's enough evidence to get a warrant. I'm feeling good about the odds. It's Bruno."

"I hope you're right."

"I'm always right." James could hear Joe talking to someone on his side of the phone. "Hey, James, I need to go. The shop is getting its last rush, and I'm going to go and manage the till while Freddie brings things in from the kitchen. Send me a text once you've packed Tessa's things, and I'll come round and pick them up."

"Will do. And if you see Tessa...."

"I'll try to talk you up."

"Thanks mate."

"Bye."

"Bye."

James hung up the phone and turned back to the computer. He pulled up the footage from the alley and got to work.

***

As the sun was setting through the office window, James was pretty sure his eyes were going to fall out of his head in protest.

He had watched all the footage he had which showed the stalker so many times; he had each beat memorized.

No matter how many times he watched, no matter what resolution he had the footage at, he could not get a clear picture of his face.

The best he could determine was he was a white man, which in London, didn't narrow his suspect pool very much.

He leaned back in his chair, crossing his arms across his chest. There had to be something he wasn't thinking of. A different angle to look at things. If he couldn't see the bastard's face, how else could he identify him?

He sat up straighter.

James pulled up the footage he had of Bruno loitering outside the shop. He measured his height. He pulled up the footage of the stalker. Measured his height.

It wasn't a match.

"Fuck!" James yelled, his voice echoing in the empty office.

It wasn't an exact science, but it was pretty definitive.

There was a knock on his office door.

He frowned. No one came to their office, except...

"Come in!" he yelled, sitting up straighter, smoothing his hair.

The door swung open, revealing Bruno.

"You fucking bastard!" Bruno shouted, pointing an ink-stained finger at James. "I told you to fucking leave me alone, but today, in the middle of a very important meeting, I had police officers serve me a fucking warrant to get my finger-prints."

"Look, man, I'm sorry—"

"No! You don't get to apologize. They never even told me why. I've done nothing wrong. And now I've been humiliated in front of my employees."

"Someone has been stalking Tessa," James interrupted Bruno's rant.

Bruno froze, his arm sagging. "What?"

"Someone has been stalking Tessa for a few months, and it has escalated. That's why she hired me. To find out who it was. We'd run into a dead end, and I told Tessa to think of anyone in her life who she thought it could be. She and Freddie told me about what you'd done in school, and you were our only lead. You're *still* our only lead."

Bruno shook his head. "I can't believe someone is stalking Tess. I'll kill the bastard."

"Well, join the queue."

"I swear it's not me. I've only just reconnected with her. And I haven't even seen her in person. Well, except last week when I came to yell at her. But only then."

"I know it's not you. I analyzed the footage. You're too tall."

"There's footage?"

James gestured at the computer. "I've got the bastard on tape so many times, but he knows where all the cameras are and has successfully hidden his face. Every time."

Bruno walked over and dragged a chair next to James, sitting down.

"So, it's someone familiar with the area."

"That's what we're thinking."

"For the record? I was trying to go to see Tessa so I could apologize," Bruno kept his eyes on the screen, "when we reconnected after her dad died, I thought it was time to mend fences. I would go round the shop, but I could never really get the courage to go in and talk to her. I had finally resolved to write her an email when I noticed you hanging round outside my house."

"For the record?" James pulled up footage of the stalker. "I think she would be receptive to an apology. She never thought it could be you."

"That's Tessa. Always thinking about others. I'll make sure I take the time to apologize once this is all over."

"Join the queue," James muttered.

He pulled up the blurry images of the stalker.

"This is the best we've got."

Bruno leaned forward and squinted at the screen. "Can you zoom in?"

James zoomed in as far as he could.

His phone buzzed with a text from Joe.

JOE: Prints Not Bruno.

James typed back that he had already figured out it would be the case and set the phone down on his desk.

He looked over at Bruno, who was leaning forward, his hand over his mouth as he inspected the screen.

"I think I know him."

James sat up straighter. "How on earth can you tell from this picture?"

"The hoodie." Bruno pointed at what appeared to James a plain black hoodie. "It's very familiar. Do you have any clearer pictures? Of the hoodie?"

James opened up the stills he took from the CCTV footage of the stalker dropping the letters. He zoomed in.

Bruno leaned in closer.

James' leg bounced, and he brought his own hands up to his mouth.

Bruno leaned back and looked at James.

"I own a software company which is contracted out to several businesses throughout the city. I employ a small crew who I assign to different size companies throughout the city to help develop the software specifically for each company, so it's customized to them."

James nodded. "Are you saying this is one of your employees?"

Bruno shrugged. "I can't say with any amount of certainty, but I have someone who works for me who lives in the same area as Cake Me Home Tonight, and he has mentioned once or twice of frequenting the shop. And whenever I hold a virtual meeting, he's wearing this black sweatshirt."

"How can you tell? It looks like a black sweatshirt."

Bruno pointed at the screen. "See this, right here? There's a weird bleach pattern in the shape of France. I stare at it during all of our meetings. It's distracting."

James could feel the wheels turning in his head. The dots were connecting.

"You're in software development?"

Bruno nodded.

"And you have an employee who is a regular at the shop?"

"Yeah, goes there every week with his mum."

There it was.

James picked up his phone and scrolled until he found the picture of the card Tessa had sent him a couple of weeks ago. He turned his phone until it faced Bruno.

"Is this him?"

Bruno didn't hesitate. "Yeah, that's him."

"The *fucking* bastard!" James shouted into the empty office. "I *knew* there was something wrong with him!"

He dialed Joe, who picked up on the first ring.

"It's Fraser," he spat out the second Joe answered the phone.

"Who?"

"The stalker."

"How do you know?"

"His employer is sitting in my office and recognized his fucking hoodie on the video."

"Fuck!"

"You need to get to Freddie's and tell Tessa to stay there."

"Yeah, we'll head there next. We're at the camera shop now. I'll have Freddie send her a text telling her to stay put."

"Don't tell her about Fraser. We don't want to scare her."

"Good idea. I'll call Davies and have him try to get a warrant for Fraser."

They hung up without saying goodbye.

"Mate, you don't know how much we owe you for this."

Bruno shook his head. "It's nothing. But it's weird, yeah? That someone who works for me is stalking my old friend?"

James frowned. "Yeah, that is weird."

"Do you think there is a connection?"

"I don't know."

"He's odd," Bruno stated. "He has no social skills."

"Yeah, I'm familiar with him. We've spent time with him."

Bruno frowned. "He went out with you?"

"Yeah, to a club the other night."

"That's so strange. He's a bit of a recluse. Only goes out to take his mom to the shop to get sweets. Otherwise, he's got that weird fear of going outside his house. Tells me that when he thinks about leaving, he has panic attacks," Bruno explained.

"He didn't tell us any of that. And if he is the stalker, the bloke has no problem leaving his house. He's in the fucking alley across from the shop all the time."

James' phone rang again, this time Tessa's number came up. He hesitated.

"Aren't you going to answer?"

James swiped, answering the phone.

"Hello?"

Tessa didn't say anything. All he could hear was Eddie Money. He frowned. "Hello? Tessa?"

The next thing he heard was an enormous crash, and the phone went dead.

CHAPTER 30

TESSA

Tessa's head was pounding.

She opened her eyes and blinked.

She didn't remember going to sleep.

She looked around. She was lying on an unfamiliar couch in an unfamiliar room.

She closed her eyes, trying to remember where she was.

The last thing she remembered was walking into her flat after realizing someone had tricked her into coming home by spoofing her number. When she walked in, there were candles and music and...

"Oh, you're awake," a woman's voice said from somewhere above her head.

She turned herself until she could see who was talking.

Mrs. Hudson gave her a wide smile.

"Mrs. Hudson?" Tessa brought her hand up to her head. Her brain felt as if it were in a fog.

"Oh my." Mrs. Hudson set aside the knitting she was working on. "Do you have a bit of a headache?"

"Yeah. I don't know why, but my head is killing me and I'm finding it hard to focus."

Mrs. Hudson nodded. "Yes, Fraser said you had a bit of a swoon earlier. He said you weren't eating properly. I've sent him to pick up some takeaway. We'll do a proper shopping trip in the morning."

Tessa closed her eyes again, some of the fog lifting. She could remember Fraser coming up behind her, whispering in her ear, and then placing something over her face, and then nothing.

Her eyes sprung open. The fucker had knocked her out and kidnapped her. And brought her to...his house?

"I'm sorry, I'm confused. What am I doing here?" Tessa asked.

"Oh, you must have hit your head hard. You're finally moving in!"

"Finally?"

"Yes! Fraser has been asking you for ages, and you've finally agreed to move into our house. I'm so glad you finally came to your senses. There's so much to do before the wedding."

"The wedding?"

"Why yes, it's coming up quickly."

While Tessa's head was clearing, she was feeling more and more befuddled. Why on earth would Mrs. Hudson think she was marrying Fraser?

"I'm sorry, Mrs. Hudson—"

"You should call me mum."

"Mrs. Hudson—"

Mrs. Hudson's friendly demeanor immediately dissipated, as she narrowed her eyes, and the edges of her mouth curved down. "I don't think you heard me," she used a slow, measured voice. "You. Should. Call. Me. Mum."

Tessa's blood ran cold. "I'm sorry. Mum."

And as if someone had flipped a switch, her sweet grandma appearance snapped back into place. "Yes, dear?"

"I'm not marrying Fraser. I'm with James, remember? You met him last week at the shop." Technically, she wasn't seeing him at the moment, but as soon as she got out of here, she would sit down with James, and apologize for doubting him and his abilities.

"No, you're not," Mrs. Hudson contradicted. "You broke up this afternoon."

Tessa frowned. "How on earth do you know that?"

"Fraser and I watched it."

Tessa's heart skipped a beat. "What do you mean you *watched* it?"

Mrs. Hudson picked up the remote sitting next to her and clicked on the telly.

Tessa watched in horror as video of her shop filled the screen in four separate squares. The front of the shop, the kitchen, the alley, and the door to her flat, all displayed in color.

She leapt from her seat on the couch. "What the fuck?!"

"Language. I will not tolerate a foul mouth in my house."

"I'm not staying here. I'm leaving. And I'm calling the police." Tessa took two steps away from the couch and froze.

With everything going on, she didn't realize she had a chain on her ankle. She followed the length to see they had chained it to the foot of the couch.

Mrs. Hudson smirked. "You will not be leaving, and you will not be calling the police. Now, *sit* down like a good little girl, and wait for Fraser to get home."

Tessa walked back to the couch and perched herself on the edge. She stared at Mrs. Hudson. Sweet, fragile, Mrs. Hudson. It was all a fucking act. How long had she and Fraser been playing her? When did they get the cameras in the shop?

The front door to the flat opened, and Fraser walked in carrying bags of food. The scent of frying oil that wafted through the air made her stomach churn.

Fraser smiled at her as he walked over to the table, setting the bags down in front of her. "Oh good, you're awake. I was a little worried I may have overdosed you with the arsenic. The internet wasn't very specific about how much would be too much."

Fraser shrugged off his coat, and bent to give his mum a kiss on her cheek.

"I'm going to take my food in my room." Mrs. Hudson stood easily from her chair, scooping up one bag from the table. "She has a mouth on her, Fraser. You'll need to fix that."

"Yes, Mum."

"And she likes to argue. We'll need to fix that, too."

"We will."

"I'll leave you two alone to talk about the wedding. We have lots to plan." Mrs. Hudson walked through the hall and entered what could only be her room before closing the door behind her.

Tessa turned to Fraser. "Is your mom even ill?"

"Of course she's ill," Fraser argued. "She's been ill for my entire life. I've had to give everything up to take care of her. I didn't lie about that."

Tessa pointed toward where Mrs. Hudson walked. "She doesn't look ill to me. She looks perfectly fine."

"She's having a good day," Fraser moved to the couch and taking a seat right next to Tessa.

She tried to move away, put distance between them, but Fraser wrapped his arm around her, pulling her close to his body.

He stuck his nose in her hair, pressing it firmly against her scalp, and sniffed.

Bile rose up in the back of her throat as he pressed a kiss to her temple.

"Don't. Touch. Me," she growled out through gritted teeth.

Fraser sat back, but didn't remove his arm, chuckling. "Oh Tessa, you'll need to get used to me touching you. I'm going to be your husband."

"You and your mum keep saying that, but I hate to tell you, I'm not marrying you."

Fraser laughed. "Of course you are."

Tessa decided convincing this man she wasn't marrying him was going to be fruitless. Neither he nor his mum seemed to operate in reality. Then it came to her.

"How long?" she asked instead.

"How long for what?"

"How long have you been watching me?" She gestured toward the telly.

"A few months now."

"A few *months*?"

"July, I think."

"But the letters didn't start arriving until October."

"Yes, I decided it was time to start properly wooing you around then."

Tessa was at a loss for words. "I'm not following. Wooing me? Through anonymous letters?"

"It was my idea. Mum wanted me to just bring you home right away. But I thought it would be more romantic if I were to write you love letters. Let you know how much I loved you before you moved in. Delightfully old-fashioned."

"Can we please go back and explain why me? Why did you choose me for your weird obsession?"

"Don't call me weird!" Fraser shouted, moving away from her and standing from the couch. "I'm not weird."

"I didn't say you were weird. I was calling your obsession with me weird. Because it is. It's weird. And I just want to know what brought it on."

Fraser stared at her his eyes wide. "You were kind to me. And my mum."

"That's it?"

"You have the most beautiful smile. And you're the most beautiful person I have ever seen. That first time I stopped in the shop to bring mum a treat last summer, you smiled at me and asked how my day was. And then you told me you hoped I would have a nice day. Being flirted with by a woman as stunning as you was an unfamiliar experience for me. I fell in love right then."

Tessa's stomach dropped. It was as James had said. Something so mundane as showing someone a bit of kindness caused them to become obsessed with her. And Fraser told his story with so much sincerity, it broke her heart to think of how deprived he was of affection he thought her plastered on smile and the same greeting she gave everyone who entered her shop was flirting.

"I brought mum in the next day, remember?" he continued. "She thought you were lovely and agreed you would be suitable as a wife. We started coming in every week after that."

"Fraser," Tessa whispered. "I want to say, I adore you and your mum. You're some of my favorite customers. However, I wasn't flirting with you."

Fraser's face crumpled. "You were. You flirt with me *every* time I come in!" he shouts, his voice filled with emotion. "You tell me you look forward to our visits each week. You ask my mum how she is. We lock eyes and share smiles. We're in love."

"We're not."

"We are!" Fraser screams, spittle flying out of his mouth. "We. Are."

"You're a stalker."

"I'm not. I'm not a stalker."

"Explain the cameras? Or the hovering in my alley."

"Once a week wasn't enough. I have a job, and mum needs me all the time. Your locks are really easy to pick, so I went in after you were closed and installed the cameras. The company I work for designs security software for companies, so I designed my own for you. Every couple of weeks I have to go in and take the cameras for charging, which makes it so I can't see you for a whole day. But it doesn't matter anymore, because you're here."

After she gets out of here, she needs to buy new locks, more secure locks for the shop. She looked at the feed on the telly of her empty shop. She should at least be thankful he never entered her flat and put cameras there. But why would he need to? Her fucking giant window she always kept open was enough for him to just lurk in the alley and watch her.

"And the alley?"

"To see you in person. To make sure you weren't doing anything you shouldn't be doing."

"James said you weren't lying to us. He could tell you were telling us the truth when you said you knew nothing."

Fraser smirked. "You can learn anything from the internet."

"I'm not staying here."

"You are."

"James, Freddie and Joe are going to notice I'm missing. They're going to come looking. And you're top of their suspect list. They'll come round and ask questions—"

"Lies!" Fraser yelled. "All. Lies. I've been watching. I know everything. I'm not a suspect. They're my *friends*. Joe and Freddie like me. And I watched earlier today. You and James fought. You told him you never wanted to see him again. He won't come searching for you, not after the cruel words you said. When Joe and Freddie ask, I'll be concerned. I'll help them look. They will never think to look here."

Less and Less Tessa was seeing the sensitive man who came to her shop every week, and more and more she was seeing the conniving arsehole who stalked her and kidnapped her. "What about my shop?"

"Freddie can run it, or it will close. Mum and I agree, once we're married, you don't need to work. You'll live here, and my job pays enough to support all three of us."

"You're mad!"

"I'm not mad!"

"You are. You're mad to think that I'm going to live here with you, let alone marry you. You've completely lost the plot if you think I'm going to give up my shop, my *dreams* for you. And you're daft for even thinking I love you. I don't. I don't love you."

Fraser shook his head. "You're going to change your mind. When you've been here long enough, you'll see how compatible we are. We are meant to be. We're soulmates."

Tessa let out a frustrated screech. "We are not soulmates."

"We are. We are. Don't you remember the night I went to the club with you? You touched my arm, and there was a spark. I know you felt it, too."

"It was you. You tried to kidnap me at the club!"

"Kidnap is such a harsh word. I prefer 'bring you home.'"

"Kidnap. You tried to kidnap me, just like you've kidnapped me now, and now you're holding me hostage."

"You're not a hostage."

"I'm chained to the fucking sofa. You're not allowing me to call anyone, and you just told me you're going to keep me here indefinitely and force me to marry you. I'm a fucking hostage, Fraser."

"Language," Fraser growled. "Ladies don't swear. And they especially don't swear in my mum's home."

A noise on the telly caused them both to look at it. The door to the shop opened and Freddie went rushing in, followed by Joe, James and...Bruno?!

Tessa watched as they ran through the kitchen and up to her flat. At the door, Freddie pulled out his key, opened the door, and the four men went inside.

They were inside for a long time. They must be looking for them.

Hope filled her chest.

The phone call to James.

He must have heard something on the line, which caused them to go to her flat.

They knew.

"Why is my boss with them?" Fraser asked.

"What?"

"My boss."

"Bruno is your boss?"

"Yeah, I work for his software company."

"He's one of my oldest friends."

Fraser shook his head and ran his hand through his hair. "Bollocks!" he yelled.

The door to Mrs. Hudson's room opened. She came storming out.

"What's wrong?"

Fraser pointed at the telly. "Bruno is her friend. He's with them at her flat now."

Mrs. Hudson shook her head. "There's no way they know it was you. You were careful. We've heard them. They have no suspects. You're fine. We're fine."

Fraser's eyes widened. "I don't think we are. If they show him any of the footage, Bruno will probably recognize me."

"Impossible. We made sure you hid your face from all the cameras."

"Yes, but I wear the same hoodie in all my meetings."

Mrs. Hudson glared at her son. "Well, that's quite the pickle, isn't it? We need to move things up."

"The wedding?"

"Yes. I'll go and get the paperwork and the drug. We'll give her just enough to loosen her up so we can convince her to sign her name. And then we can file it in the morning. It will get the ball rolling. We need to find someone licensed willing to perform the wedding and forge the paperwork."

Tessa shook her head. She didn't understand why they thought if she married Fraser, everything was a done deal, unless…

All that talk about being old-fashioned. They still believed if she were to marry Fraser, she would be his property. Fucking idiots.

She looked around the room and settled her gaze to where Fraser had dropped the food. She frowned.

Keys.

Why hadn't she seen those before?

She looked at the key ring, and there was a small one. Looked like it would unlock the lock on her ankle.

Mrs. Hudson and Fraser moved quickly toward the bedroom.

Tessa quickly leaned forward and grabbed the keys off the table and brought them to her. She glanced up at the room and noticed they weren't coming back. She quickly undid the lock and threw the keys back on the table.

Mrs. Hudson and Fraser came back into the room. He was carrying a syringe of something. She didn't want to find out what sort of drug he had, or how he got it. And she definitely didn't want 'the internet didn't tell me the right dose' to inject her with anything.

She glanced up at the telly as more sound came out of it and her friends ran out of her flat and down the stairs out of the shop.

She had to have faith they knew where she was.

But she also had to be practical.

Her dad didn't raise a damsel in distress.

She waited until Fraser was close, leaning in with the syringe before jumping up and shoving him over.

He fell backward over the table, landing hard on the ground. The syringe falling from his hand and landing on the carpet.

Tessa put a foot on the table and hurdled herself over. She seized the syringe and held it out toward Mrs. Hudson.

Mrs. Hudson growled and drew a knife out from the pocket of her house dress. She came running toward her.

Tessa, shocked at how quickly the previously infirm lady could move, hesitated before turning and running toward the door and her escape.

Her hesitation cost her though, and the older woman bore down on her. Tessa's hand had just made purchase with the door handle when she felt the pain in her shoulder blade.

The bitch had stabbed her.

Tessa whirled around and, without thinking, stabbed the syringe into the woman and pressed the plunger.

She watched in horror as Mrs. Hudson collapsed to the ground.

"Mum!" Fraser screamed, scrambling to his feet.

This time, Tessa didn't hesitate. She ripped the door open, and she ran.

CHAPTER 31

JAMES

James looked around Tessa's flat. There were candles lit everywhere, and they looked like they had been burning for a while.

Freddie went into the bedroom to see if Tessa was there, but James knew she wasn't. This place was empty.

Joe looked around the flat and took out his phone. "Calling into Davies and reporting her missing."

"Tell him we know it was Fraser," James added.

Freddie came out of the bedroom. "Okay if I blow these out?"

"James, snap some pictures, and then yeah, blow them out. We don't want the flat to go up in flames."

James pulled out his phone and began taking pictures of the room.

He was taking pictures when he remembered something. "Music," he muttered.

Freddie looked at him. "What?"

"Music. When I was on the phone with Tessa, there was music playing in the background."

Freddie frowned and looked around the room. "There's a speaker here," he walked into the kitchen and pointed at the corner where the counters meet, "this isn't hers."

"Fraser must've brought it and forgot it when he took her," James observed.

He looked around the room at all the candles. How long had he been waiting here for Tessa to come home? His eyes landed on Bruno, who was still standing in the doorway to the flat, but instead of looking in, he was looking out into the hallway.

"What d'you see?" James asked.

Bruno pointed into the hall, toward the stairs. "That's one of our cameras."

"What?"

"That's impossible. We don't have any cameras installed," Freddie stated. "Joe and I were buying one when James called to tell us to get over here."

Bruno shook his head. "I didn't say you installed it, did I?"

"You think..."

"I know." Bruno pulled out his phone and typed a few things into it. He frowned. "This isn't the only one in here."

"The computer software you sell to companies..." James started.

"Security," Bruno finished. "We have an entire line of cameras, and we customize the software for each company, and each of my software engineers manages the company's system."

"Can you see the footage from the cameras here?" Joe asked, coming up to them.

"Yeah, it's easy. Fraser didn't put any sort of security on them, probably because he didn't think anyone would even notice they were here. Showing you would be easier on a tablet."

Freddie walked into Tessa's room and walked back out, holding her tablet. "Already unlocked it for you."

Bruno got into it and typed. Within two minutes, he had the feed up. He moved over to the kitchen counter and set the tablet down so they could all see.

"This is the current feed."

"Fuck," Freddie muttered.

"Took the words right out of my mouth." James stared at the tablet. There were four cameras, and he could see the entire shop.

"So, it was really easy to hack into the recordings, because he's a complete berk and stored it all on his work account. I'm going to back up the footage until we can confirm Fraser is the one who took her. I'm going to guess he's just arrogant enough to think no one would notice the cameras, and he didn't hide his face."

James watched over Bruno's shoulder as he backed the footage up.

"Stop." James pointed at the screen.

Bruno froze the video.

Walking through the kitchen to the alley door was Fraser, and he was carrying Tessa, who was lying limp in his arms. And the fucker, the arrogant *wanker,* looked directly into the camera and fucking smirked.

"I'm gonna kill him," James growled.

"How long ago was this?" Joe asked, pointing to the screen.

Bruno looked at the timestamp. "About an hour."

"Where do you think he took her?" Freddie asked.

"His home," James replied.

"You think?"

"I know. He's delusional. His letters have all implied he had feelings for her. That he saw and wanted a future with her. Logic dictates he would take her home."

"He's right," Joe agreed. "At the very least, it will be the first place we look."

"Where does he live? Somewhere close, yeah?" Freddie asked. "He comes here every day with his mum, who can barely walk."

Bruno read out an address. Everyone turned to look at him.

"Employee records." Bruno held up his phone.

"That's two streets from here near the tube station."

"What are we waiting for?" James asked

Freddie ran around the room like a madman and extinguished all the candles while Joe called PC Davies and read him the address, telling him to meet them there, with backup.

The four men ran down the stairs and out of the shop, Freddie stopping briefly to lock the door.

They took off, running down the sidewalk toward Fraser's flat.

As James ran, many scenarios flashed through his head. In every single one of them, Fraser had violated Tessa.

Anger coursed through his body, causing him to run faster, dodging in and out of crowds on the street.

As they got closer, the crowds thinned, and it looked as if there was a figure running toward them.

It was really hard to tell in the dark, but as they got closer, James could see that, yes, someone was running towards them.

As the runner moved under a streetlamp, James' breath caught in his throat.

Tessa.

She was running towards them, but he didn't think she knew they were there. She kept looking behind her as she ran. Her hair was down and flowed behind her in a chaotic stream, and he couldn't tell, but he thought she looked barefoot.

He didn't know it was possible for him to run faster, but he did.

As the gap narrowed between them, he could see the moment Tessa recognized him. Her eyes widened and her stride faltered. But not for long. She caught herself and she ran straight for him, no longer looking behind her.

When the two met in the middle, Tessa threw herself into James' arms, and he didn't hesitate to wrap his arms around her waist, tightly pulling her to his body.

"You're safe," he whispered repeatedly as she held on so tightly to him, she was almost cutting off his air, but it didn't bother him. His focus was on assuring the woman who was trembling in his arms that she was okay.

He felt more than saw when the other three men caught up to them. His focus was on the woman in his arms. Knowing she was safe.

"Tessa!"

James brought a hand up to push Tessa's hair out of his vision so he could see who was screaming her name.

Barreling toward them was Fraser.

"Tessa, you fucking bitch! I'm going to *kill* you for what you did to my mum!" Fraser screamed.

James reluctantly let go of Tessa, moving her behind him. She didn't argue. Bruno, Joe, and Freddie filled in around her, effectively putting her in a protective bubble.

"What happened to his mum?" James asked.

"I injected her with something they were going to inject me with," Tessa's voice was shaking. "She just sort of fell to the ground. I don't know what it was. They made it sound like it wasn't anything too terrible when they were going to pump it into my veins. But he also admitted he got everything off the internet and wasn't sure about dosage."

"They drugged you?" James growled, not taking his eyes off the large, angry man running toward them.

"He used arsenic to knock me out to take me to his house. Otherwise, no. I was able to find the keys and unchained myself from the couch before they could stab me with the needle."

"The fucking bastard," Freddie growled out. "I'm going to fucking chain him to the back of James' car and—"

"Get in line, mate," James snapped.

Joe got on the phone and was talking to someone, giving them directions to where they were, when Fraser made it to the group.

"What the fuck are you doing here?" Fraser growled when he was toe to toe with James. "You broke up with her. She's mine now. She's marrying *me*."

"I broke up with her five hours ago. I'm *pretty* sure she didn't just up and decide to marry you on a whim, so I'm going to go out on a limb and say you're full of shit."

"Kidnapping is a very serious offense, Fraser," Joe explained. "Much more serious than vandalism, but around the same level as installing cameras and spying on the shop."

"I didn't kidnap her," Fraser bit out. "She wanted to come with me."

"We watched the footage, mate. She didn't go with you willingly." James shook his head.

"How?"

Bruno poked his head around James. "Yeah, that would be my doing. By the way, I'm going to have to let you go."

Fraser stepped even closer to James, bringing his hand up and shoving his finger into James' chest. "This is all your fault."

"And how do you figure that?"

"Everything was fine until you turned up. I had a job, and Tessa was going to go out with me, and you came along and mucked it all up. Filled her head with lies."

"I dunno. Last I checked, you're the one who sent her creepy letters and installed cameras in her place of business. Oh yeah, and you kidnapped her. Can't force a person to do what you want against their will."

"She would have learned—"

"I'm going to stop you there, because I really have no interest in hearing whatever rubbish you have to say. We have the video of you taking her out of her flat, unconscious. And Tessa here'll testify about every little thing you've done to her. So, I don't really need to hear the whys of it, or listen to whatever delusions you have cooked."

The sounds of sirens filled the air, as the streets filled with police cars flying into the area.

"Oh, look, your ride has arrived."

The police cars stopped around them, and PC Davies stepped out of one car.

Fraser narrowed his eyes at James. "This is your fault. Your. Fault. Tessa! Tessa!" he shouted, trying to get a look at her from behind James. "I love you, and I know you love me," he babbled. "And I forgive you for what you did to Mum, you were acting rash. But tell them we're in love. Tell them I did nothing wrong."

Tessa didn't say a word. James felt her grab on to the back of his shirt with her fists, and press her head into his back.

PC Davies approached Fraser, handcuffs in hand.

Fraser, on his part, didn't put up a fight. He just stepped back, away from James.

"Can someone send an ambulance to mine and check up on mum? If she's not okay, we'll be pursuing charges against Tessa."

PC Davies ignored him. He walked up behind him and placed handcuffs on his wrists. "You do not have to say anything. But it may harm your defense if you do not mention when questioned something which you later rely on in court. Anything you do say may be given in evidence."

As PC Davies led him away, he didn't put up a fight. He just turned his head and looked back at Tessa.

"Once this is all over, you'll realize that we're meant to be. He can't bring you happiness like I can."

Davies put his hand on Fraser's head and helped him into the car. Once he was shut in, Davies turned back toward them.

"McCleary, will you be meeting us down at the station?"

"Yes."

"Bring the lot. We'll need to get everyone's statement on record."

"Will do."

Davies gave them a nod and got in the car and drove away. The other officers milled about, and Joe went to talk to them.

James turned around and looked at Tessa. Really looked at her. Well, as well as he could in the dark on the pavement.

She looked tired, and frazzled, but she mostly looked okay, which James thanked heaven for.

He smiled down at her.

She smiled up at him.

"Are you okay?" he asked.

"I'm okay. My head still feels fuzzy. But I think it's because he didn't know how to dose me when he knocked me out. I think it will clear up with some rest."

"I'm glad you're okay. When I watched you being carried—"

He cut off when he watched Tessa sort of sway on her feet.

"Tessa?"

"I'm fine." Her voice was weak, and as she said it like it was a question, he didn't quite believe her.

He reached out to steady her with a hand on her back and frowned when he felt something wet. He brought his hand back and held it so a streetlamp shone on it.

"Tessa, you're bleeding." He looked back up at her, meeting her eyes. "Why are you bleeding?"

She looked at him, confusion all over her face. "What?"

"Why are you bleeding?"

"I'm bleeding?" Her voice came out weaker than before.

"Medic!" James shouted. "We need a medic over here!"

Freddie came running from where he had been standing with Joe. "What's going on?"

"She's bleeding, and she's disoriented. Something's wrong."

Tessa narrowed her eyes at him. "I don't appreciate you talking about me as if I'm not here. I'm fine. I'm perfectly—"

She swayed as her eyes rolled back into her head. James wrapped his arms around her to stop her from hitting the ground.

"Help!" James shouted. "Someone, help us!"

"James?" Tessa whispered her eyes still closed. "I don't feel very good."

"You're going to be fine. Everything is going to be fine."

As Tessa went limp in his arms, James didn't believe his own words.

CHAPTER 32

TESSA

For the second time in twenty-four hours, Tessa woke without knowing where she was. Her head felt better than it did earlier, but not by much. Instead of feeling foggy, it ached.

She tried to open her eyes, but they felt heavy.

She was so tired.

She could hear machines beeping around her, and hushed conversations, but couldn't make out who was talking or what they were saying.

She tried to open her eyes again, but to no avail. They were not budging.

She gave up and relaxed, let the pull of sleep draw her under.

When she awoke again, her head didn't ache, and her eyes didn't feel as heavy.

She opened them and immediately shut them against the bright lights.

"Oh," a voice spoke up from next to her. "Let me fix that."

She heard James rustle around and footsteps walk across the room.

"There, try opening them again."

She opened her eyes, and the room was now dimly lit.

"Is that better?" James moved back to his chair next to her bed.

She nodded.

"How are you feeling?"

"My head hurts a little, and I'm tired."

"Yeah, you're going to be tired for a bit."

"What happened?"

"You lost a lot of blood."

"I lost a lot of blood? How—"

It suddenly hit her. Everything she couldn't remember. "Oh, my GTod, Mrs. Hudson stabbed me in the back! Literally and figuratively."

"Yeah, she did. At least someone stabbed you. Right near your shoulder blade area. Not deep, normally not a very serious wound. However, when you ran, your blood pressure rose, and caused your blood to pump faster. And it pumped out of your open wound at a much higher rate than if you'd been in a relaxed state."

Tessa closed her eyes. "So, I lost a lot of blood, and then I passed out in your arms."

"Pretty much. The doctors also think you still had some of that arsenic in your system, and that didn't help matters."

"I should have kicked Fraser in the bollocks rather than only giving him a good shove."

"Do you want to talk about it?"

Tessa sighed and opened her eyes. She looked over at James. His red hair was a right mess, and he had dark circles under his eyes. His five o'clock shadow stubble he typically sported was heavier, and he was still in the clothes he was wearing when he had broken up with her for her own good.

"It can wait until you go home and get some rest. How long have I been here?"

"Since about eight last night. It's now round five. Shit, it gets dark so early." He rubbed his eyes.

"Go home and sleep."

"I pushed the chairs together and had a kip sometime around one. I'll be fine until Freddie gets here in an hour."

Tessa smiled. "You have shifts?"

"Of course. We didn't want you to wake up alone."

"I appreciate it."

James leaned forward and took her hand in his. "Do you feel up to talking?"

Tessa turned her hand in his until she could lace her fingers with his. "About the Hudsons and their creepy plot, or about us?"

Her question hung in the room's silence, the only sound being the beeping of the hospital equipment.

She kept her gaze on James, watching him chew on his bottom lip.

"Either," James finally answered. "Both."

Tessa turned onto her side, keeping hold of James' hand.

"I was going to be held hostage in their flat, and they would deny knowing my whereabouts if asked. They were *so* confident no one would suspect them. They had these antiquated ideas that if I were to sign marriage papers, it would force me to stay with Fraser. Nothing they said made any sense. But that could have been because my head was feeling fuzzy."

"Wait, so you're saying Mrs. Hudson was in on the whole thing?" James leaned forward.

"Yeah, I'm pretty sure she might have been the mastermind? She's not as feeble as they led us to believe. And I'm pretty sure she's been manipulating Fraser his whole life. They have a very fucked up dynamic."

James shook his head. "The old biddy has Joe and Davies believing she's a completely innocent victim. That you ambushed her while she was in her chair knitting and stabbed her with the sedative."

"What a liar! I can't wait to give my statement to Joe."

"He'll be back in the morning for it, with PC Davies. Because of his relationship with Freddie, he's transferred the lead on the case to Davies. But Davies's a good egg, so we have nothing to worry about."

Tessa gave him a weak smile.

"I'm glad you could escape." James returned her smile.

"Me, too. I wasn't going to let them inject me with whatever I shoved into Mrs. Hudson. I could see you on the telly, with Fraser's cameras. When I saw you running out of my flat, I knew you knew where I was. But I didn't know how far we were from the shop, or how long it would take you to get there. When I noticed the keys on the table, I thought I would take a shot and get out."

"You did the right thing. You looked out for yourself, and you got away. Luckily, Fraser was a shit criminal."

Tessa laughed. "He was pretty terrible. He left the keys to my lock within reach. I didn't even have to try."

"He stored all the footage of the shop on his work account. Bruno had absolutely no trouble turning the evidence over to the police. Didn't have to hack anything. Simply typed in Fraser's work credentials."

Tessa's mouth dropped open. "No."

James nodded, his smile wide. "Yes. Ridiculously easy. Speaking of Bruno, he wants to come see you, but doesn't know if he will be welcome. He wants to apologize for everything, build bridges, that sort of thing."

"Of course he can stop by. He bloody well saved my life. What are the odds that Fraser would work for Bruno?"

"Let me get a good eight hours of sleep, and I'll be able to tell you."

Tessa laughed. "Go home and get some sleep. I'll be fine here alone."

"I don't want to leave you here alone. I have so many regrets in my life, but I think the biggest one would have to be breaking up with you yesterday."

"James—"

"No, I have to say it. It was arrogant of me, and chauvinistic. I shouldn't have swooped in and tried to protect you. It was everything you said you hated, and I did it, anyway. I know I probably don't deserve it, but I hope you will find it in yourself to take me back. I love you. And I'm so, so sorry."

Tessa squeezed James' hand. "I'm glad you could see the error of your ways, but I also need to apologize. I should have heard the meaning of what you were saying, but my heart was so broken by the words and not the intent."

"We were together for two weeks and I fucked it up completely."

"Two weeks. Has it only been two weeks? I feel like we've been together for a lifetime."

"To be fair, a lot has happened in the last two weeks. More than most couples have to deal with in a lifetime."

Tessa smirked. "You mean not every couple deals with a kidnapping in their first two weeks?"

"Well, I mean, Patrick and Evie did, so I am thinking it must be a pretty standard thing most couples deal with."

"We'd better warn Freddie and Joe."

They both laughed.

Tessa smiled at him. "I forgive you. In fact, I forgave you when I woke up on the couch in the Hudson's flat. Because you were right. Us being together was causing Fraser to escalate. But to be fair, you breaking up with me escalated him further instead of having him cool down."

"Well, that was a misjudgment but who's to say he wouldn't have escalated to that point, anyway? He was waiting for the opportunity to get you alone. Staying at mine and Freddie's didn't give him that opportunity. I think he was waiting for you to move home."

"I wish I had thought to look for cameras. We could have used them to our advantage."

James chuckled. "Yeah, I've thought about that while waiting for you to wake up. We could have used our acting skills to really put on a show and set a trap."

Tessa laughed so hard her head ached again. "I'm really glad you have the confidence in your acting skills, because I'm pretty sure I would have given it all up with my poor ones."

"I'm sure you're an excellent actress."

"I hope you don't rely on those delusions for any future cases, because if you do, you're doomed."

James smiled at her. "Don't worry. We'll stay in our lanes. You can do the baking and I'll do the sleuthing."

"I mean," she drawled. "If you want to come and help at the shop if you're having a slow day, especially over the holidays, I certainly wouldn't say no."

"Oh, so, *now* I'm allowed to spend my day in the shop, now that you're not being stalked by a madman?"

"Yes, because the only heroic thing you'll be doing is stopping grannies from caning each other over sticky toffee pudding."

"You want me to be your bouncer?"

Tessa shrugged. "Maybe through Christmas?"

"What sort of pay does a bakery bouncer get?"

Tessa smiled coyly. "Well, I can think of a few benefits a bakery bouncer would get." She waggled her eyebrows.

James' face colored a delightful pink before he recovered and shot her a devastating half smile. "Oh, could you now? I'm thinking this gig would be right up my alley. My first order of business as security is going to be to upgrade all the locks on your shop and turn all the spy cameras to our good PC Davies."

"Mmmm," Tessa hummed. "Tell me more."

"And then, if the grannies get out of hand?"

"Yeah?"

"I'll walk over to them and flatter them with some flirty attention, so they forget they were even annoyed that the one in front of them purchased the last of the shortbread."

"You're going to earn every bit of your benefits."

"That's my aim."

Tessa leaned forward and captured James' lips with hers. They had only been apart for a couple of hours, but in that time, she had come to the conclusion that she needed him in her life.

He was it for her.

And she knew she was it for him.

EPILOGUE

JAMES

"T-Minus one hour until the shop is closed, and we're finished for the weekend." James set up the ropes that managed the queue in the shop for the fifteenth time that day.

"Thank goodness." Freddie wiped down the counters. "Hopefully, things will be slow, so we can close up a bit early."

"I hope we don't have to close up early." Tessa carried out another tray of strawberry tarts. "If we don't get our typical Saturday evening rush, I've over baked."

Evelyn followed her through the door carrying a tray of mini pavlovas. "Yeah, I finally mastered these impossible desserts, and I want to watch them fly off the shelves."

James smiled at the girls as they set the trays in the window cases.

As predicted, Evelyn jumped at the chance to help Tessa in the shop over Christmas. And then, surprising everyone, she opted to stay on and help Tessa permanently. She still taught at the University, but three mornings a week, she would go into the shop and help bake.

Having a second baker lifted a lot of pressure off of Tessa, whose business kept growing, and it was a perk to be working with another of her close friends.

Patrick walked out of the back of the kitchen carrying a beautifully decorated carrot cake. "If we don't sell this, it's coming with us on holiday, yeah?"

James perked up. "Yes. Please tell me we can take it with us."

"You two are impossible." Tessa placed her hands on her hips. "I'm pretty sure you eat more than your fair share of my products. But, yes. The cake will come with us."

James and Patrick simultaneously fist pumped, and the girls laughed.

James and Tessa had been dating for almost eight months, and he couldn't be happier.

After the stalker incident, they took some time to adjust to what a normal paced relationship would look like. She moved back into her flat, and they would see each other a few times a week, really slowing things down.

The whole slow down lasted a month, and Tessa moved into James' flat, opting to commute to the shop rather than live above it, since her flat held too many traumatic memories after the whole Fraser thing.

James was more than happy to have her move in, since he was feeling like a third wheel in his own flat. Freddie and Joe did the opposite of slow down, and Freddie had moved into the flat within weeks of the Fraser incident.

The flat was crowded with four of them, but they were happy, and not looking to change the arrangement soon.

In fact, having been feeling left out of the group living a mere ten minutes away, Evelyn and Patrick had moved into a flat two doors down from them.

The six friends were closer than ever.

"Do you think the pavlovas will travel well, too?" Evelyn bent down to gaze at them through the window.

"Maybe? But honestly, the rush will be here in twenty, and there will be no pavlovas left," Tessa joined Evelyn bending down to look at them. "They are your best batch, though. You're really improving."

"Thanks. These dang meringues, they're going to be the reason I go bald before I'm thirty."

"I thought we were the reason you were going to go bald before you're thirty?" James gestured between him and Patrick.

"Yeah, love, isn't that what you tell us every time we recount one of our cases?"

Evelyn stood up and glared at them. "You *and* the meringues are going to make me bald before I'm thirty. Is that better?"

"Yes, because now we're not left out." James smirked.

"You are being very cheeky today." Tessa observed.

"It's been a long week," James answered. "Gotta let it all out before you're trapped on a train with me for hours."

"Hours? You're acting like we're not simply hopping over to Paris to spend a long weekend."

"An hour and a half is a long time for me to sit still these days."

After people found out about the Fraser incident in the papers and the fact that Patrick and James had been involved in another high-profile case, this time involving one of London's top bakery owners, their business saw an increase in traffic. This time they were being called in to consult on cases with the police. Joe and PC Davies had a huge hand in that, which meant James and Patrick were often off on cases slightly more dangerous than cheating spouses and cats who've run away from home.

"This holiday will be good for you," Tessa replied. "For all of us. We've been so busy with our jobs, we haven't had time to sit and relax. Three days away will do us all a world of good. Especially with the case starting up next week."

The wheels of justice turn very slowly. The Hudson's trial was starting soon. James woke up to Tessa's fitful sleep more than once in the last week. The approaching trial was dredging up many memories for her.

She'd been in therapy to talk through a lot of the trauma of the stalking and kidnapping, but being prepped by Patrick's dad as the trial approached was giving her a lot of anxiety of having to actually face Fraser again.

The door to the shop flew open and Joe came sauntering in, singing a song emphatically in French. Behind him, Bruno walked in, shaking his head.

"Why is he like this?" Bruno asked, pointing at Joe. "He's been doing this since he got on the fucking train."

Joe kept singing, while giving the two-finger salute. He walked over to Freddie and gave him a large kiss, blissfully stopping the singing.

"You're a fucking stick in the mud," Joe stated after he pulled away from Freddie. "This weekend, we're going to help you loosen up a bit. Get you laid."

Evelyn wrinkled her nose. "Promise you won't have the same goal with my sister?"

Elizabeth, Evelyn's sister, was currently living in Paris finishing up a study abroad program, which was one of the main reasons the group decided to go there for a quick holiday.

Joe held up his hand to his chin and pretended to think. "You know, I didn't have that goal before, but now that you mention it...I think I shall try to match make Bruno and Lizzy!"

Everyone groaned at once, and Evelyn and Bruno began talking over each other while Patrick and Freddie tried to keep the peace.

James looked over at Tessa, who met his gaze. They shared a smile. This life was crazy, but it was their life.

James put his hand in his pocket and touched the small box sitting there, ready for when he could get Tessa alone on their trip.

This was a life he looked forward to living for the rest of his.

Stephanie R. Caffrey is a romantic suspense author who lives with her family in the Midwest. When she's not working on her books, she's a substitute teacher, and loves to write fanfiction. She is a proud marginalized voice in the Mexican-American community. Besides writing, she enjoys sewing, knitting, and cross stitching.
www.srcaffrey.com

www.ingramcontent.com/pod-product-compliance
Lightning Source LLC
Chambersburg PA
CBHW011149310726
48973CB00010B/2834